Annie's World 2

Daniel Lance Wright

This is a work of fiction. Names, characters, places and events described herein are products of the author's imagination or are used fictitiously. Any resemblance to actual events, locations, organizations, or persons, living or dead, is entirely coincidental.

Annie's World 2

Copyright © 2016 Daniel Lance Wright
http://daniellancewright.blogspot.com/

Edited by Jake George www.sagewordservices.com

Printed by Sage Words Publishing
www.sagewordspublishing.com

Cover artwork by Greg Simanson
http://www.simansondesign.com

ISBN 10: 0-9970962-5-X

ISBN 13: 978-0-9970962-5-5

Contents

Chapter 1

Chance Encounter

Spring 2214 A.D.

"Don't move, Punkin," Annie Henderson whispered sideways to the youngster. "Remember what I taught you."

Six-year-old Eva quailed, whimpered, and held tight to the older girl's waist. Annie was more like her sister than simply a friend. The young girl looked to Annie, face tightening as if about to burst into fear-riddled sobs. "I can't help it. It's so big and mean looking."

"Shh." Annie stroked Eva's hair while allowing her bow to slide from her shoulder into her hand. Slowly, she sank to one knee, onto a soft clump of emerging spring grass, while repositioning the quiver of arrows at her back. In a slow fluid move, she reached for and felt the gnarled red mesquite wood handle of the knife sheathed on her hip, just in case. The knife had been made by her boyfriend, Ethan Turlock. Its presence was his presence, a small measure of comfort. With equal stealth, Annie took Eva's hand into hers and pulled the child down to match her non-threatening posture. "Always remember," she whispered to the youngster, "never stare directly into the eyes of a predator animal. They'll

1

sense it as a challenge. If they're hungry, the problem doubles."

Eva pulled her eyes away and dropped her head. "Okay." Her voice quivered.

Annie turned her head slowly to face Eva. She smiled. "You trust me, don't you, Punkin?"

"Uh-huh." Eva's voice remained strained and shaky.

Still smiling, Annie shifted her attention back to the rocky precipice a few paces up the trail. Vines and tree roots hung like unruly witch's hair up the trail a short distance. It was about eight feet above the surface where they knelt. Perched atop it, a large, black male wolf snarled, hackles raised, drool stringing from between its teeth. Annie frowned quizzically. There was something different in how the animal behaved. "I don't think that big fella is hungry."

Eva loosened her grip on Annie. "Why?"

"Shh. Keep your voice low and even. He doesn't appear hungry because he's not tensed and ready to pounce on us. And, it seems the big guy doesn't really know if it wants to be threatening or not." She pointed it out to Eva. "You see? It stopped snarling for a second. Did you see it?"

The younger girl glanced quickly, then turned her eyes down again. "Then why doesn't it just go away?" Her small nervous hand stroked the newly emerged grass beside her knee.

"I'm not sure. Maybe he's guarding a mate and a den of pups somewhere up the hill behind him. Wolves do mate for life, ya know. They're one of the few animals that do… and it is spring after all. There're lots of newly born animals this time of year."

"Oh." Eva released her grip on Annie entirely, but kept her arms tucked against her body.

Suddenly the wolf, standing four feet high at the shoulders, took an aggressive pose. This time the animal tensed, ready for action. It snarled. Drool slung from bared teeth as it jerked its head to the side abruptly.

"Annie!" Eva screamed.

Annie snatched up her bow.

As the wolf turned a quick circle where it stood, Annie nocked an arrow.

The wolf crouched, then leapt from his rocky perch, soaring over their heads.

Without drawing the arrow, Annie kept the point aimed at the giant wolf as it flew over them and landed some distance beyond. She instantly realized they were not the target. A pack of four gray wolves had eased to within attack distance while they were distracted.

The huge black wolf landed between the girls and the newcomers, the gray ones intent on challenging the black wolf for possession of Annie and Eva as a meal. The black one began pacing side-to-side, growling, snarling and partially lunging to keep the other canines at bay.

"Shoot him, Annie!" shouted Eva.

"Not yet."

"Why?"

"I think he's protecting us." She kept the arrow nocked and ready to draw, but relaxed the weapon down to her side and watched.

The black wolf grew impatient with the angry growls of the interlopers. He made a move toward the largest of the grays, also a male.

The smaller, but determined, gray held its ground and challenged the black.

The larger black wolf accepted and sprang at the gray, latching razor sharp teeth onto the scruff of the gray's neck.

The gray wolf attempted to wrench loose, shaking its head side to side, but the black wolf was too large and powerful. After only seconds of a loud, violent and wallowing battle in the grass, the gray yelped in pain. He wanted no more. The black wolf released its hold. Once free of the black's teeth, the gray male scampered away with its tail tucked between its legs, running after its pack that was already retreating.

Annie again sank to her knees and then sat back on her heels. "Well, as Dame Fortune would say, 'Ooh-wee, ain't dat a diddlin' shockin' turn of events'." She chuckled.

Eva sidled close to her seventeen-year-old friend and mentor. "How can you be sure he's not just saving us for dinner?"

Annie snickered. "I can't."

As Eva shuddered, Annie said, "Come on now, what did I just tell you about showing fear? Predators sense that."

"I can't help it," fretted Eva.

"We have a chance to find out how that lovely black monster views us. I'm going to take the high road and view *him* as a friend… until, of course, he does something stupid, like… chew my hand off."

"That's not funny," Eva whined.

Annie winked at her. "You might not think so, but I do."

Annie looked back at the wolf and tilted her head slightly as she considered what to do next. She set her bow on the ground, but close at hand. She bowed her head, extending both hands toward the wolf, palms up and relaxed, sitting on her heels.

Eva snapped a shocked look at Annie. "What're ya doin'?"

"Calm down. It's a show of submission and acceptance of his presence."

"Will it make him like us?"

"Don't know. Never tried it before." Annie glanced sideways to Eva. "Drop your head and hold your arms out like I'm doing. Let's see how he reacts." Annie kept an eye on the animal, but only in flicking glances.

All aggressiveness left the wolf. The hair on his neck dropped to a normal lay and he began to appear unsure, maybe a little nervous. He whimpered and took a couple steps toward them before turning a complete circle and backing away.

"It's okay, boy," Annie whispered. "I have no intention of hurting you. I sure hope you feel the same about us."

The animal stepped forward and then back again, ending up a few feet closer.

Annie noticed. "That's it, you lovely animal. I'm sure we're going to be the best of friends." Remaining on their knees, she and Eva continued quietly bowing with hands outstretched, almost as if in prayer.

The canine made another tentative exploratory move, taking one more step forward, but this time it didn't back up.

Annie glanced up. "That's it... "

The animal did a quick shuffle with its front paws, as if trying to decide whether it really wanted to close the gap. It whimpered, then took the plunge, stepping forward and licking Annie's upturned palm. He stood unmoving, and she felt his hot breath on her face.

In a low even tone, Annie said, "You took a big chance on us. Now it's my turn." She raised her head and gazed into the animal's beautiful, golden amber eyes that were set in its huge black face. "Are we friends now?" The beast remained near enough to rip her face off, should it choose to do so. Instead, the wolf turned away and trotted up the trail.

Eva finally looked up and watched. "Where's he going?"

Annie rose. "I don't know. Maybe he just wanted to know if we were dangerous, for future reference."

"What does that mean?"

"Next time we meet, maybe he *will* be hungry but won't look upon us as his next meal."

The animal only went about fifty feet and stopped. He looked back.

"What? Did I not say goodbye? Sorry. See ya later, my new friend," Annie called out.

The wolf trotted a few more feet before stopping and looking back again.

"I'll be darned. I think he wants us to follow him."

"Uh-uh, we can't, Annie. Mama said I needed to be back at Myrna's Glory before dark."

"You are a little worrier, aren't you? We will, Punkin. We'll be back with time to spare. Lana knows you're with me so she won't be too worried. Let's follow our new friend a little ways and see where he goes."

"Why?"

Annie shrugged her shoulders but kept her eyes locked on the huge black wolf for a few seconds longer as it hesitantly continued on. She looked down at Eva. "Aren't you curious?"

Although her brow furrowed, Eva smiled. "I guess so. Mama says I'm too curious for my own good sometimes."

"Me, too. Come on."

By the time they made the decision to follow, the wolf had disappeared around a bend in the trail where a dense cluster of staghorn sumac grew.

"Race ya to those bushes," challenged Annie.

"Well…" Eva said, as if deeply pondering the thought, but then took off in a blistering sprint, churning the ground beneath her feet into a trailing dust cloud. She ran so fast those gray wolves would've had trouble catching her.

By the time Annie began pursuit, the youngster was halfway to the sumac bushes where the trail turned, but Annie was older, stronger and faster. Her legs blurred as she caught Eva and passed the child just as the two arrived at the cluster of dense undergrowth.

"Doggone it. You beat me again."

"For a second, you had me fooled into believing you didn't want to race."

Eva giggled. "Yeah, well, it didn't help."

"There'll come a day I may not be able to beat you in a fair race."

"That'd be great."

Annie chuckled. "For you, maybe." She had grown to six feet tall with a powerful but lithe frame. She wore the pig hide boots and leather pants with a beaded waistline that Dame Fortune had made for her last year. Although fair of skin, a light tan on her face blended with long, straight honey blond hair.

Annie looked upon six-year-old Eva Louise McAdams as she would a younger sister. Eva was of Asian descent, a product of forced sexual servitude of her mother, Lana, to an evil man by the name of Fiam Lee Tam—a man Annie was forced to kill last year to free Eva and all the families from a compound called Stalwart.

"I hope I can keep up with you someday, Annie. There's no one else who's any fun to race. I can outrun everyone I know, except you."

"Yeah," she said, jostling the youngster's silken black hair that hung to the center of her back, "you and I are alike but different from everyone else… in a good way, right?"

"Right." Eva grinned.

Annie accepted how physically superior she and Eva were. Both were descendants of genetically manufactured prototypes two hundred years ago, when greedy governments sought to produce perfect soldiers, but the people Annie descended from had a flaw. Their physical and mental abilities were advanced, but so was compassion, to a dangerous degree. It made them illogical candidates as soldiers. Annie hadn't yet seen a weakness manifest in Eva but she sure hoped it wasn't the same as her father, Fiam Lee Tam. His was lust for sex and power—a weakness he yielded to, but lust can come in all forms and that worried Annie. Someday, Eva may have a weakness she'd have to struggle to control, like Annie's overly compassionate nature. Annie loved Eva. Shared abilities made that bond strong.

Annie glimpsed the wolf moving through the undergrowth off to the side of the trail about a hundred yards ahead. It stopped and sat on its haunches near a sprawling and artfully gnarled old oak tree, a magnificent sight worth remembering. The animal watched and waited for them to catch up. "Our friend up there seems interested in letting us know where he's going. I'm certain now that he has no desire to leave us behind."

The trail they walked paralleled the Brazos River. They were about three miles north of their home, a communal complex begun by a group of monk-like people calling themselves The Order of Theocratic Minds. The tenets of the organization were religious in appearance only. They were grounded in the philosophy that technology should be re-introduced to humankind and shared equally so that no person or group could use it to control others. All members of the Order were intelligent masters of various technological disciplines—mechanical, electrical, fuels and construction.

Annie noticed smooth round stones near a fallen, but still green, willow tree at the river's edge. "Hey, why don't you practice with your slingshot as we walk?"

The youngster reached into the pouch hanging to her side by a long leather strap around her neck. She retrieved a strip of well-oiled cowhide, anchored at its center by a formed hard leather cup, and trotted the few feet down the embankment to where the stones lay.

"Ya know, Punkin, that slingshot of yours is already getting too short for you. We'll get Ethan to make you a new and longer one, better suited to a growing girl like you."

Eva stopped. She stood straight and proud. "I am gettin' big for sure."

Annie chuckled. "You sure are."

Eva sorted through the small stones. As she pushed them around on the ground looking for the best, she glanced to Annie. "You like Ethan a lot, don't you?"

"Sure do."

"Ya love him?" Eva stopped fingering the stones when no reply came fast enough. She looked at Annie.

"Ethan Turlock," Annie said in exaggerated fashion with her eyes closed. She sighed. "I can't say yet, but one thing's for sure. I love the way his name feels in my mouth and how his face fits in my head."

"That sounded weird."

"To you, maybe. It'll make sense to you someday. I promise," replied Annie.

Eva went back to selecting stones of the right size, shape and weight. She found a dozen good ones and put eleven in the pouch.

Annie saw that the monstrous black wolf maintained about the same distance between them, regardless how fast she and Eva chose to walk, even if it had to sit on its haunches and wait. The afternoon sun had begun casting lengthening shadows. *I hope that big fella gets to where he's going soon. Maybe we need to walk faster to press him on.* It had been, and continued to be, a beautiful spring day in the former state of Texas.

Eva secured the flap over the stones in her pouch and hurried up the hill to join Annie.

"Come on, Punkin. Let's get a move on or we may not have time to see what our wolf friend wants to show us."

"First, watch this." Eva positioned the ends of the sling between her fingers and pressed the first stone into its center pocket. "Are ya watchin'?"

"Sure am."

The youngster swung it over her head once slowly, then one more time very fast. She released one end of the leather thong. The stone flew so fast it sang a high note, hitting a large nest of yellow jacket wasps suspended in a scruffy and sickly mesquite bush up the hill next to the trail. Countless yellow and black striped wasps came off the nest and appeared to form a small dark cloud.

"Uh, you're aim was perfect," Annie said as she began to walk and then to walk faster. I am, however, questioning your choice of targets."

The air filled with the hum of angry yellow jackets.

Eva's grin vanished. "Uh-oh."

"Uh-oh is right. Run!"

The girls sprinted up the trail.

The wolf took off when he saw the two running toward him. He had to run hard to maintain a buffer between them.

After running several hundred feet, Annie and Eva slowed. Eva looked back. "I think they gave up."

"Probably. Yellow jackets are territorial. They were only protecting that nest you just put a hole in." Annie dropped her gaze to Eva. "You toot. You did that on purpose, didn't you?"

Eva's cheeks flushed red. She grinned.

Annie waggled a finger at the end of Eva's nose. "I'll get you for this… you little…"

"Hey, look," Eva said.

The wolf made an abrupt turn off the trail and away from the river, up a boulder-filled crag that ended at a level, rocky ledge above the high-water mark. A weathered rock wall rose behind it in shades of black, gray and white. The flat stone shelf extending outward from it was overgrown with scruffy oaks. The wolf stood there looking down at them, as if inviting Annie and Eva to join him. Roots, limbs and vines grew horizontally behind where he stood, like giant fingers concealing something.

Annie took a moment to analyze the route the wolf took to get where he stood. The big canine had meandered and climbed toward that stone shelf. As her eyes again traveled up to see the wolf staring down at her, she noticed what appeared to be a cave entrance in the shadows behind all the overgrowth. "I just had a funny thought."

"What?" asked Eva.

"Well, it'll only be funny if it's not true. What if that wolf is so smart that it didn't want to kill us back where we met?"

"I don't understand."

"Think about it. He didn't have to drag our carcasses to his den. We followed him to his home. Now he has fresh meat and didn't have to carry it."

"That's not funny at all! It's scary," said Eva as she stepped around behind Annie.

"I was just kidding."

Eva pouted. "I don't like jokes like that."

"Let's climb up there and see what that gorgeous beast with the beautiful golden eyes has to show us."

The animal sat on its haunches at the entrance to what, indeed, turned out to be a cave. Once Annie and Eva committed to that direction and began climbing, the wolf casually turned and disappeared into the oblong entrance that was nothing more than a broad crack in the stone face.

"We're not going in there, are we?" Eva asked.

"Maybe, but I'll peek inside first. Don't want to barge in and startle the big black wolf or another wolf into attacking me."

Annie made it to the entrance, which was not quite head high but wide enough to walk through without having to turn sideways. It tilted left, giving it the appearance of a yawning mouth. She took Eva's hand and pulled her close. "Stay behind until I can figure out what's going on in there."

"Okay." Eva clutched a wadded handful of Annie's loose-fitting white linen top.

Annie glided laterally two steps and craned her head around into the opening. It was dark but thanks to genetically enhanced vision, she saw a black hairy figure lying on its side facing away from the entrance on a short, flat rock surface a couple of feet off the floor.

Eva leaned around to see what Annie saw. "It looks like another huge black wolf."

"I don't think so," Annie whispered.

"It's not?"

"Wolves don't make bedding out of animal hides and wear pants."

"But, it's so hairy."

The wolf eased over and nuzzled his snout between the arm and body of the figure. It apparently woke the person. An arm, totally covered in dark hair, reached back and stroked the wolf's snout with a hand that had an equal amount of hair on it. Then Annie heard, "Back already, Yowl?" The voice was decidedly human, male and deeply resonant. He coughed and rolled over to face the wolf. "I miss our hunting trips, too. I just haven't felt well. We'll go again soon. I promise." He sneezed, then sniffed. His head, face and neck included, were covered with the same thick dark hair. The hair on his head hung below his shoulders. His head resembled that of a maned lion.

Annie decided to make her presence known and took a giant sideways step to center her body at the cave opening.

The man sprang to his feet and snatched a long staff that had been whittled and fire-hardened to a sharp black point. He was at least six and a half feet tall and broad shouldered. "Stay back!" he bellowed. "You are not welcome here!" He looked to the wolf. "Yowl, how could you not know you were followed?" He raised the point of his staff and stepped toward Annie. "Leave this place and never come back."

"I mean you no harm," Annie said in a low even tone.

"I will do you harm aplenty, if you don't turn around and go back to wherever you came from," he said, his voice now louder and more intense. He looked to the wolf that just sat comfortably on its haunches. The man's head took a confused slant. "What's with you, Yowl?"

Annie pointed to the wolf. "You see. Your friend knows we are peaceful. I think it was his way of bringing you help." She stepped through the cave opening, leaving Eva outside.

"Oh no you don't." He lunged at her with the spear.

In a lightning fast maneuver, Annie sidestepped the business end of the weapon. She grabbed the staff near its thorn-sharp tip and shoved it upward. It jammed against the low rock ceiling and against the floor at the other end.

The hairy man could not stop and ran into the staff, now firmly wedged at top and bottom. It forced all the air from him in a rattling rush and he bounced backward onto his butt. "Damn, woman! That hurt!"

"Watch the language. I have a child with me."

Eva finally stepped into view. Her curious eyes ran all over the very large, very hairy man. "Are you and the wolf... family?" the youngster asked.

As the man rolled to hands and knees, he said, "Yes, but not in *that* way. It comes as no surprise that you'd think so

though. It's a curse I've been dealing with my entire life."
He coughed, sneezed, and then coughed again.

Annie reached for his arm and began pulling him up.
"You're not well, are you?"

He wrenched his arm from her grasp. "Don't touch me."
He coughed and wiped his nose with the back of a hairy
forearm.

"I'm just trying to help you up."

"Yeah, well, in my experience people look at me like
something tasty to eat or, maybe a source for a new winter
coat." He came to his feet and backed to the low flat rock
shelf where he had lain when she first saw him. He sat on it.
"Yowl is the only friend I need. So leave."

"You have the spring disease, don't you?"

"The what?"

"Spring disease. It's a seasonal thing with some people.
I know a very intelligent and beautiful blind woman who
sees things more clearly than anyone alive with good eyes
can. She says there are people who just can't tolerate
abundant new plant life at the beginning of each growing
season. I bet you're like this every spring. Aren't you?"

He sat straight. Even the hairy face couldn't hide his
surprise. "How could you know that?"

"Like I said, that old blind woman sees things no one else
can. For example, when Eva and I get back to Myrna's
Glory, where we live, she will tell me all about you before I
have a chance to speak. That, my new friend, is a guarantee.
She calls herself Dame Fortune. We just call her Dame. She
is a black woman with hair the color of cotton that looks like
a fluffy cloud. She cusses far too much and laughs at
everything. She's... well, she's wonderful, and I love her."

He sneezed. "So, the child's name is Eva."

"Oh, I'm sorry. I haven't introduced us." She gestured to
the youngster. "This is Eva Louise McAdams." She feigned

modesty. "And, I am your humble servant, Annie Henderson."

"I'm Bo Juster and this is my friend, Yowl. And, before you ask, which I'm sure you will, I'm not a talking animal. I'm not blood related to any animal," he said, shifting his gaze to Eva and pausing. "I'm just a man with a condition. It has run sporadically in my family as far back as memories and stories serve. My parents had normal hair, but my grandfather and my uncle on my father's side of the family were like me, totally covered in thick hair. They were killed by cannibal hunters in Old Dallas."

"Is that why you live isolated?"

"Yes. My parents were killed trying to protect me. I was only ten, and alone in a place where all people outside a family unit were considered fair game as a food source. I was viewed as a special prize for the stew pot. It wasn't paranoia because that's what happened to my grandfather and uncle."

"That's awful."

"More than you'll ever know. I managed to get out of Old Dallas and into the countryside. I would've starved if it hadn't been for Yowl and his mate. I owe them everything. I learned to enjoy the taste of bloody raw rabbit, squirrels, rats and whatever else Yowl and his mate brought back."

"Yowl has a mate?"

"Had. She disappeared almost two years ago. I fear hunters caught up to her, but I'll never know for sure. It's my guess that her hide has been stitched into clothing and is being worn by someone out there right now." He sneezed and coughed.

Annie pulled her knife from its hand-stitched, ornately tooled, leather scabbard and handed it to Eva. "Hey, Punkin, run back down to the river to that fallen willow tree where we found the stones, cut the bark away, strip some of the white fibrous stuff from beneath the bark and cut me a few pieces of it. Then, pluck some of those wild onions with the purple flowers on them and bring it all back here. Could you do that for me?"

Eva took the knife from Annie's hand with a self-assured swipe. "Sure I can. I'm a big girl now." She turned and ran for the entrance.

Annie smiled. "I know you are."

"What're you going to do?" Bo asked.

Annie pulled a chunk of flint and a short steel rasp from the pouch at her side. "I'm going to build a small fire and make you some tea."

"From that stuff the girl is going to bring back?"

"Yep."

"It sounds awful."

Annie chuckled. "I don't think it'll taste bad but it's not the kind of tea you enjoy. It's medicine. You're coughing and sneezing, and your head probably hurts, too. The tea will help. May I use that black iron pot?"

"I suppose. And… thanks… I guess. No one has done anything nice for me in a very long time."

"Get used to it," she said with a smile as she gathered sticks and dry grass. "How did you come to call your friend by the name Yowl?"

He gazed fondly at the giant black wolf for a moment. The canine sensed the lessening tension, turned a circle where it stood and lay on the cool stone floor. It huffed a contented breath and dropped its snout onto an extended paw. "The word 'yowl' I made up. It's the best way I can describe a sound his mate made when they were together. She only made it around him. She was a good mate and very kind to me, too. I always assumed that was her name for him… 'Yowl'. Didn't you say that you live with someone by the name of Myrna Glory?"

"Not exactly. It's the combined names of a mother and daughter, Myrna and Glory Jackson. Glory named the compound where I live Myrna's Glory. I guess Jake and Glory thought it was a clever play on names." Annie's head fell to a sad slant. "Myrna passed away a couple of years ago."

"Jake?"

"He's my adopted father. In fact, I was left without parents at the same age you were. So, I know about such things first hand. Although there has never been a ceremony, Jake and Glory are definitely married."

Annie made quick work of starting a fire and making the tea when Eva returned with the ingredients. Using his favorite wooden drinking bowl, she poured it full of the steaming pungent liquid. "Here ya go. If that doesn't make you feel better, then you're welcome to follow us back to Myrna's Glory. Dame will know what else can be done for you. She always does."

He tested the tea by sticking his tongue in it first. He smacked his lips, and then took a small sip. "Not too bad."

"Told ya."

He drank in gulps, as fast as the scalding liquid allowed.

As he did, Annie said, "Seriously, why don't you and Yowl follow us home? It's only about three miles downriver and then about a mile west. That way I can introduce you to my family and all my friends."

Bo abruptly stopped drinking. "I don't think I can do that." He wiped drops from the hair on his chin with the back of his forearm. "In fact, that's not a good idea at all."

"Why?"

"Yeah, why?" Eva added.

"I've spent nine years avoiding people, watching from a distance and trying not to be noticed. You're the first one

I've talked to in a friendly way in years. I'm usually shouting threats and warnings to stay away."

Annie smirked. "Yeah, I noticed. Then do it for Yowl."

"What are you talking about?"

"You just said you've spent nine years avoiding people. How old was Yowl when you first encountered him?"

"I—I don't know."

"I'm just trying to point out that, for a wolf, Yowl is very old. If there are others around to help care for him when he can't hunt any longer, he can live happily for a long time. Wouldn't you want that for him?"

"You are very persuasive. I've never considered how much faster he was aging than me." He stared for a moment at the wolf snoozing on the floor a few feet away. "Okay, I'll meet your people... for Yowl's sake."

Annie's face stretched into a big smile. "Yes, of course... for Yowl's sake." She winked at Eva and then looked beyond the cave entrance to lengthening shadows. "Then we'd better get going. It'll be getting dark in a couple of hours. I promised Lana, Eva's mother, I'd have her back by then."

Annie watched Bo stroke Yowl's head to wake the wolf. "Hey, old man, how about we take a nice walk before dark?" The wolf bounded up onto all four paws as if it knew exactly what Bo had said.

Somewhere between here and Myrna's Glory, I'd better tell him the truth about why I wanted him to come, she thought. *I can't keep something so dangerous a secret, and, I certainly need his help to get it done.*

Chapter 2

Walking Home With a New Friend

Annie walked the trail next to the Brazos River abreast of six-year-old Eva. She glanced back at Bo and Yowl. The large black wolf walked so near to Bo that it occasionally nudged the big hairy man off the trail. The affection the animal had for Bo Juster was clear, but Annie already knew that. What other mammal, human, or beast, would search out strangers to help a pal? It was certainly worth a smile. "You boys doin' okay back there?"

"Any reason you'd think otherwise?" Bo asked.

"I haven't heard you cough, or sneeze much in the past hour. What I have heard didn't sound at all like that barking hack you were making when we met."

"Humph," Bo said, "I haven't noticed. I guess you're right. That concoction you called tea may have helped after all."

Annie glanced back again at Bo's threadbare pants, held up by a rag belt, shredded up to mid-calf. He wore neither shirt nor shoes, and his appearance was, indeed, of a creature more animal than man. "You know, I bet Glory, Lana and some of the other women would be more than happy to collaborate on making a nice suit of clothes for you... in exchange for some kind of work, of course. The folks at Myrna's Glory are big on bartering goods and services so that everyone has an even chance of a good life within the fold." She stopped walking. "Come to think of it, would you have a problem with leather clothing made from various animal hides? I hope I'm not being insensitive for asking, but I remember the sadness in your voice when you spoke of Yowl's mate and her likely end."

"Not at all. It's the way of the wild." He nodded to Yowl. "Even he believes that. Otherwise he and I would be grazing in the meadows and never hunt meat to eat."

"Good." She turned and walked on. "Although the men of Myrna's Glory have rebuilt the looms, all we have available is spring wool and that might be a bit too warm for a person like you."

"Like me?"

"You know, natural coat and all."

"Ah… right."

"Later in the year, when the cotton is harvested, the ladies will have enough to weave a lighter cloth. I'm not sure what all they do have available but, for now, it might have to be animal skins. I'll ask them to create a hood as well, so you can talk to strangers without worry of scaring people into attacking."

Bo stopped walking. "I don't care what people think. I can take care of myself," he said in a raised voice.

Annie stopped, too, abruptly this time. She spun to face him. "I didn't mean to imply that you could not defend yourself. It's just that…"

"It's just that… what?"

Annie stared at him and thought for a second then said, "Bo, I have a favor to ask of you. It could be dangerous for us both, maybe more so for you. It's at the heart of my conversation on clothing and the need to conceal more of your appearance."

"Well, I won't know how to answer if you don't tell me what it is."

Annie glanced to a fallen log of substantial girth. "Let's sit for a moment and talk."

"Annie," Eva whined. "We've got to get home. Mama'll be angry if it's after dark."

"Hang on, Punkin." Annie looked to the setting sun, now only a squiggly orange lump on the western horizon. "There's still about an hour of daylight. We'll be fine." She guided the child to the long-dead fallen tree and made her sit. Annie sat, too. "Bo, would you sit next to me?"

"Why not?" He ambled over and sat on the log. "You have my attention. What's on your mind?" He leaned his sharpened staff next to him against the log. Yowl rested his snout on Bo's knee, as if he might be interested, too.

"See these scars on my face?"

"Yeah. So?"

"I almost died last year defeating an evil man who shared my advanced physical abilities. He got his licks in with a sword, and I nearly bled to death." Annie paused and stroked the top of Eva's head. "If it hadn't been for the courage of this little one, I might not have survived… but that's a story for another time."

"Was he that Tam fellow you spoke of?"

"Yeah. The point is, I was unconscious for a long time. Dame Fortune's abilities go far beyond knowing *things*; she also has the power to enter minds. She was in my head long enough to take me on a trip to Old Dallas. It wasn't a visit made as the result of delirium, or some kind of dream, or nightmare. She and I traveled, in real time, around the world ending in Old Dallas. But it was only our combined consciousness that made the trip. Our physical bodies went nowhere and had nothing to do with the journey."

"That has got to be the strangest story I've ever heard."

"Oh, that's not the story, only the means by which I know about it. You see, it was there in Old Dallas that I saw a family—father, mother and child—near a place the mother called the Brickyard District. The child was a girl, a young girl. She couldn't have been more than twelve years old."

"I know exactly where that is."

"I thought you might. As I understand it, people living in the heart of Old Dallas are cannibals and very comfortable with the lifestyle. They know no other way. I've been told the same thing exists in the ruins of other large cities here in the former state of Texas."

"As I've already said, I'm very well aware, but only about Old Dallas, no other place."

"That's why I need your help, to guide me through the ruins to find that family. Lizzy is the young girl's name. I vowed to Dame Fortune that I'd get her out of there, so she'll have a chance to grow up normally, sanity intact. Dame says a steady exclusive diet of human flesh drives people insane by the time they reach adulthood if not amended with plant-based foods. I may not be able to help the parents… don't know… but I can help Lizzy. I'll do what I can for the parents, too, if they'll let me. It will probably be necessary that you conceal your condition; that is, of course, if you choose to serve as my guide."

"That's a big favor to ask of someone you just met."

"I know. That's why I wanted to ask now, to give you plenty of time to say no. I won't make your help conditional on anything. It'll be your decision. Whatever you decide will not affect my feelings for you or Yowl. You both are now etched in my heart as friends forever."

Bo sat quietly and, with darting eyes, gazed upon Annie's face for a long moment. "How can you say that? You know very little about me."

"I know enough."

"What if I'm a cannibal and looking at your eyes for how tasty they might be and not how beautiful they are?"

She chuckled. "I'll take that as a compliment."

"You know what I mean."

"Dame always says, 'To have a friend, one must first be a friend.' Of course she says it with more flair and a few obscenities thrown in for emphasis. Obviously, it all begins with trust, and I do trust you."

"I think you're rushing to judgment, considering I've given you no clear reasons to trust me."

She smiled and placed a finger over her heart. "I sense it and feel it here."

Bo sat silent for a moment. "I need time to think about it."

"You have it; all the time you need."

Bo stood and stroked Yowl's head. "Well, old friend, it's looking a little like life may be changing for us both pretty soon." He snapped a glance to Annie and held a stern, hairy finger toward her. "That does not necessarily imply a yes."

Annie rose. "I understand." She wrapped her arms around him and hugged him tight.

"Hey! Stop that. I'm not comfortable with this stuff."

"You'd better get used to it, big guy. I'm a hugger."

Eva snickered and rolled her eyes. "She really is."

Annie grinned. "I suppose I could do like ol' Yowl over there and lick your face if you prefer."

"Now you're just being silly." Bo snatched his staff from its place against the log and then sprang to his feet. "Let's get on our way before we get your little friend in trouble with her mother."

A half-mile down river, the trail split. The main one continued southward, following the contours of the waterway, and the other turned west, disappearing at the top of a slope to the right, partially obscured by tree branches and brush reaching laterally into the walkway. Annie and Eva guided their new friends onto the smaller, less traveled path to the west. "Not much farther now," Eva announced.

Once they'd climbed above the high water mark onto level ground, Eva whispered and pointed excitedly. "Look, it's a covey of quail! They ran beneath that cedar bush over there. See?"

"I do see them," said Bo, "but we have no traps, so what difference does it make?"

Annie and Eva looked at one another and then Annie said, "Punkin, do you think it's about time we show Bo and Yowl what we can do?"

Eva nodded and retrieved her sling from the pouch hanging at her side. She found the perfect stone from those gathered earlier by the river.

"What is it you can do?" he asked.

"Watch and learn," Annie said.

Annie let her bow slide off her shoulder. She nocked an arrow on the string and put two more arrows between her teeth.

Bo scratched his head. "Are you going to try to shoot them on the ground?"

Annie shot him a frown as she pulled the two arrows from between her teeth. "Heck no, what fun would that be?" She looked to Eva. "Come on, let's flush 'em." She again clamped the spare arrows between her teeth and began to jog.

"I'll have to see this before I'll believe it," Bo called out as the girls ran toward the low dense cedar bush.

"Then don't blink," Eva said, laughing.

As the girls trotted, Eva placed the stone in the center pocket of the sling and began swinging it overhead. Annie raised her bow.

The birds flushed in a fast noisy airborne retreat.

Eva released first. The stone flew fast, hard and straight. It caught one of the birds no more than six feet off the ground, and its wings retracted and fell.

Before it hit the ground, Annie's first arrow hit one near Eva's. Both tumbled to the ground in rapid succession.

Another bird angled sharply away from the airborne covey, and in a flash Annie had another arrow strung. She sighted down the shaft ending at a razor sharp tip and swung the bow to lead the bird and released it. That bird hit the ground rolling. The time between the first and second arrows had to have been faster than a lightning flash.

Annie wasn't finished. She strung the third arrow and slid it to the perfect nock point. The remaining quail in flight had already begun descending to run on the ground, as quail will do. The lead bird some distance away had locked its wings and begun a glide to land. Annie drew the arrow, elevated it and let it fly. It arched high and came down in the middle of that bird's back and stuck it, pushing it to the ground.

Bo's jaw slackened, his lips parted and his mouth fell open in utter amazement. "What I just witnessed is not possible—three perfect strikes on targets that small in flight, and... and a girl as young as Eva downing a bird with a rock from a sling?"

Annie shouldered her bow. "You witnessed it with your own eyes, yet you still question it?"

Bo began shaking his head, slowly at first. "I did watch it happen and, yes, I still can't believe it."

"It's just a small sample of things Eva and I are capable of. All of our senses are extremely acute: hearing, sight, smell, and touch. Our ability to size up situations and react to them quickly comes to us as naturally as breathing does to you. We may not come out the winner in all situations, but we will employ the best available plan every time, and I'm reasonably certain I can outrun Yowl in a race. Eva might not be able to, but once she matures a little and her legs lengthen, she'll be just as fast, or faster, than me."

"I suppose attacking you back at the cave was a stupid thing to do."

"Yeah, but that's okay. You didn't know. How could you? That's why I never attempt to harm anyone unless I have no other choice. I could hurt someone rather easily… and it's not confined to men and women but most predator animals as well."

"I'll respect that fact," he said.

"Let's pick up the birds and get on home. We're starting to lose our light." Annie noticed Eva standing next to Yowl. The sight made the black wolf seem even larger. At the shoulders he was almost as tall as the youngster. Eva combed his coat with her fingers, clearly developing a fast fondness for the canine. "Come on, you two. Let's get moving."

Eva and Yowl ran out and retrieved three of the quail while Annie and Bo tromped through tall grass and around a cluster of Chinaberry saplings to fetch the last bird downed farther up the trail. After circling the thicket of brush, Annie encountered a man holding her arrow with the bird skewered at the end of it.

Annie stopped. "Well, I never thought I'd see another one of those," she said, pointing to the machete-like long knife in his other hand. The guy's appearance may have been unkempt, with a beard and long hair, but the signature long knife and style of clothing identified him as a supplier from the defunct compound called Stalwart. "Surely, you're not still an active supplier for Stalwart. Since Tam is gone, I thought thieving in the name of barter had ceased."

The man stood defiant and expressionless. "It has. I was asked to leave and never come back. I pressed for continuing the practice. They didn't like it."

"For goodness' sake, why would you *want* to continue it?"

"It's all I know how to do and, frankly, I enjoy it. It's better than scratching in the dirt, or slopping pigs."

Annie began to approach the man.

"Stay back! Or you'll feel this blade on your flesh."

Now, settle down," she said. "Look, mister, why don't you join us and come back to where I live? It's a place called Myrna's Glory. There is a marvelous group of men and women called the Order of Theocratic Minds who established it, and I'm sure they'd be more than happy to train you in a productive craft. There are many better paths to a livelihood. It's a foolish thing you have chosen to continue, and dangerous too."

"Careful, Annie, I don't think he's right in the head," Bo said as he moved in close behind her.

Annie held back a warning hand. "It's okay, Bo. Stay back." She squatted down and sat on her heels. "Let me make the first gesture of friendship," she told the stranger. "I'll gladly let you keep that quail in your hand, plus, I'll give you the other three. Cook those up and that'll keep you nourished for a couple of days. In the meantime, think about what I offered you. You'll be a welcome addition. I promise."

"I know the place you speak of. I didn't know it's called Myrna's Glory, but I'll not be taking you up on that offer. Like I said, tending animals, chopping wood and the like is not what I'm looking for." The stranger waved the quail still stuck on the arrow at her. "I will take the birds though, but I want your bow, arrows and that knife on your hip, too."

"Okay, you thieving pile of worm dung," Bo said in a booming deep voice, "the time for diplomacy is over." He glanced down at Annie, still squatting, as he walked by and announced, "I'll take care of him."

"Annie grabbed his leg as he passed. "I'm sure you can, but allow me, please." She rose. "You need to see how I handle such situations."

"You could get hurt," Bo hissed.

She snickered. "I was thinking the same thing about you," she whispered. "Just stand here. I'll be fine. He's only one man."

"Only one man? You're crazy. Look how big he is, and probably strong, too."

"Eh, doesn't matter." She again began to approach the guy.

"This is my last warning. Drop your weapons and turn and leave!" the man bellowed.

Annie smiled but kept walking toward him. "There are only two possible ways this can end; the best way is that you and I become friends. The other way, I introduce your face to the ground and then kick your ass." She stopped walking. "You've warned me and I sincerely thank you for that. As for me, I don't like tossing out warnings and ultimatums willy-nilly, so let me just call what I've told you an advisable alternative. What do you say?"

The guy tightened his grip on the long knife and held the skewered bird at the end of the arrow threateningly. His lip raised to a snarling slant. "You are an insolent brat. How old are you, kid?"

Annie recoiled. "Kid... you called me a kid." Her nose turned to an indignant upward angle. "I'll have you know I'm seventeen-and-a-half... almost."

The man advanced. "Well, kid, you're about to be taught a lesson that you might not survive."

Annie held her ground.

The man took a backward swipe at her with the knife.

She leaned away as it whooshed by her midsection, and then smiled.

As he reversed for a forehand pass with the blade, she caught his wrist above the knife and held it tight. Her grin grew wider.

He attempted to wrench free but couldn't. His eyes popped large, surprised by his inability to wrest his arm from her grasp. In that instant, the shock of her strength caused him to forget the arrow in his other hand.

Annie grabbed the wrist of that arm as well, twisted them outward and pushed both locked and stiffened arms up until his shoulders ground and popped.

He grimaced, clenched his teeth and groaned.

Using her thumbs, she pressed the fleshy parts of his wrists until he could no longer hold the knife or arrow. A squeal escaped from between his clenched teeth. His fingers sprang open, and the weapons dropped to the ground. She released one of the arms and twisted it.

A whine began in the man's throat behind closed lips, transforming into a pain-filled growl. He had no choice but to go with the pain and momentum, spinning around.

She wrapped a leg around his legs and shoved, tripping him onto his face, and planted a knee in the back of his neck.

He turned his face to the side and spit grass and dirt, but he continued to struggle.

Annie increased tension on the twisted arm until he howled.

"Enough!" he shouted.

"In that case, I'll forego the ass kicking part. That would have been sort of demeaning anyhow." Annie released him, rose and stepped back. "I still want you to have the birds, but you must leave us in peace. Know from here on that we are not your enemies, but we'll never give in to callous thievery either. We'll protect what is ours, but we'll share what we have just as quick. If you insist on continuing this lifestyle, someone will eventually take your life. Please, change your thinking. Let us help you."

Eva trotted up and handed the other three quail to Annie, who in turn handed them to the man. "Now go," she said. "Eat well tonight."

The man reached and grabbed the birds, but she didn't release them. "What's your name?"

"Barney."

She made no immediate response, but finally said. "I assume it's not Barney The Thief. What's your last name?"

"Tackitt... the name is Barney Tackitt."

"Nice to meet you, Barney," she said and released her hold on the birds.

He snatched them from her grasp and disappeared over the knoll.

"This has been a very interesting day, for sure," said Bo. "I'm assuming that the favor you asked of me did not include serving as your protector."

"We'll protect one another... always and ever after."

"Can we, *please*, go home now?" Eva asked.

Chapter 3

Back At Myrna's Glory

In fading daylight, as Annie, Eva and their new friends approached the place they called home, Annie saw Dame Fortune talking to Jake Henderson, her adopted father, and the big man, Henry, the self-avowed head protector of the Order of Theocratic Minds. They worked side by side about a hundred yards ahead. Each with an ax chopping alternately, the men were dressing a fallen cedar log for some construction purpose. Myrna's Glory, the name for the compound of dormitories, various workshops and storage buildings, stood as their backdrop. Annie poked her pinky fingers into each side of her mouth, rolled her tongue to the perfect angle, and whistled so loudly it echoed off trees hundreds of yards away.

Jake's head snapped up. A smile burst across his face, as he stood straight and responded with a hearty wave. The blonde hair on his head had lengthened in the past few months but Glory Jackson refused to allow his beard to return to the shaggy condition it was in when they first met last year.

Annie walked ahead of Eva, Bo and Yowl. They had not made the turn in the trail yet and were still out of sight.

Jake and Henry propped their axes on the log and casually leaned on the handles while mopping sweat from their faces onto long sleeved clothing. Henry, the big man with a smoothly shaved head and face, wore traditional garb of the Order of Theocratic Minds, the monk-like brown robe tied at the waist with a simple rope. They waited for Annie to come closer.

Once Bo and Yowl came into view, the smiles on both men's faces vanished. They lifted the axes and held tight.

Dame said something, using her long cedar walking stick as a means of gesture. Whatever she said started an argument. Dame Fortune was a large woman with skin the color of night and an explosion of solid white hair. Her blind eyes glowed milky white. She bore deep scars around her eyes—a victim of childhood cruelty that took her sight.

Annie walked on, continuing to close the gap. Her expression, a broad grin, didn't waver. Voices became audible. Dame waggled a finger at Henry and then at Jake. She said, "Ooh-wee! I be tellin' ya true, both you boys got heads harder'n dat damn log ya be choppin' at."

"But, Dame—"

She whacked Jake's ankle with her walking stick.

"Ow! That hurt."

"Dat not all I be hurtin' if'n ya don't hush it up, you fool. Doz' two be Annie's and Eva's new friends."

"How were we supposed to know?" Henry asked.

"You weren't. Dat's why I come out here; to keep y'all from gettin' into a ruckus for no good reason."

"Got some new friends I want ya to meet," Annie shouted, still some distance away.

"So I was told," Jake called out as he massaged his ankle with the other foot.

Eva began to run. Yowl trotted behind her.

As the giant black wolf came closer, Jake and Henry refused to alter defensive grips on the axes they wielded, gripping them tighter.

Dame shook her head. "Ya better be droppin' doz' wood choppin' tools. I guarantee ya right now, ya damn well don't wanna be provoking dat monster wolf."

Eva kept right on advancing but Yowl clearly sensed Jake and Henry's uneasiness with his presence and slowed, then came to a complete stop. He didn't snarl, or growl but hunkered into his own defensive posture, head swinging low, plainly sniffing hostility in the air.

"Yowl," Bo shouted. "Come on back. Stay with me until Annie and I explain things."

The wolf trotted back to Bo's side, as Eva ran straight into Dame's open arms.

"Oh, child, ya be actin' like days have passed, not just a few danged hours." Dame burst into a cackling laugh and then embraced the child.

Eva's tiny head almost disappeared into a knitted shawl between huge pendulous breasts. She turned her head to the side. "But I missed you."

"Dat be good, youngun. Dat be real good. Ya make an old blind woman feel wonderful wit' dem kind words." Dame kissed Eva on the forehead and then pushed her back. "Now, I don't be givin' a hoot in hell what comes next wit' da boys, 'cuz I already know, but let's let da story unfold naturally about Annie and her new friends."

Bo stroked the back of Yowl's neck as the wolf stood at his side. He leaned across the animal to Annie, standing on the other side and whispered, "You were sure right about Dame's appearance… somewhat disturbing at first glance."

"Humph, look who's talking," Annie told him.

He shrugged his shoulders and pulled a quick grin. "I deserved that, but that's the whitest hair over the blackest face I've ever seen, and those sightless eyes are striking, even somewhat shocking at first glance."

"I be beautiful. Dat be for dang sure."

Bo straightened and stammered, "I—I'm sorry. I didn't mean for you to hear that."

"I didn't. Not wit' dese ol' worn out ears." She pecked her temple with the tip of a gnarled finger. "I heard it here, in dis mind o' mine. I know whatcha be thinkin' all da blitherin' time. Don't ever be forgettin' dat."

Annie snickered. "You've just had your first lesson in Dame's most basic talent."

Henry, still holding his ax as if ready to use it, came around the log and did not stop until he was face to face with Bo. He maintained a stern expression.

Yowl began to emit a guttural growl.

Bo stroked the wolf's head. "Easy, friend."

Henry stood a head taller than both Jake and Annie, but he could look Bo in the eye. Both were big men. But, in every other way, their appearances were diametrically opposite. Whereas Bo's face and head were covered in thick dark hair, flowing like a mane down onto his back, Henry's head and face were shaved smooth. Even his eyebrows and lashes were light enough in color as to be nearly invisible. Henry stepped closer still. His eyes narrowed to slits. "You didn't try to hurt my Annie, did you?"

Bo gave no ground. "No, but I would have if I could've," he replied in monotone.

Henry didn't flinch—stern expression set, as in stone, upon his face. "Let me guess… you confronted her and ended up face down in the dirt with a knee on the back of your neck, spitting dirt."

"No, but that's only because the cave where we met was too small. Otherwise, she may have done that."

Bo took a step toward Henry. Henry reciprocated, and their noses were now only inches apart.

Annie became nervous. Her eyes darted back and forth between them, searching for signs of aggression, but then she saw Dame with a huge smile on her face. She settled back into a casual stance. *What on earth is going on between these two? It's as if they're playing some strange game of chicken.*

Annie's thought had scarcely finished when Dame's unspoken voice filled her head. *Jes' be another few seconds, Annie girl. Watch 'em. Dis gonna be good.*

Both of the big men stared deep into one another's eyes. Henry's lower lip began to quiver.

Bo's cheeks twitched.

Oh, no, Annie thought. *They're about to mix it up.*

Suddenly, Bo and Henry exploded in laughter.

Henry dropped the blade of his ax and extended a friendly hand. "Call me, Henry… just Henry."

Bo slapped his palm into Henry's. "The name's Bo Juster. Call me Bo." He patted the wolf. "And this is my friend and companion, Yowl."

The wolf licked the back of Henry's hand.

"I thought you fellas were about to come to blows," Jake said, coming around the log to join them.

"I'm pretty sure Annie wouldn't have allowed that," Henry said.

"Incidentally," Bo said, "your guess on what Annie did to me when we met wasn't far off the mark, but it didn't happen to me. She showed me how she chose to handle a thief we encountered on the trail, and what you thought she may have done to me is exactly what she did to that guy. She had him face down, spittin' grass with her knee on the back of his neck."

Henry let out a booming laugh. "That's what she did to me at our first meeting."

"As for me, she had me flying backwards to a hard landing on my butt," Bo said. He howled with laughter.

Annie's cheeks flushed rubicund. "Come on, guys, those aren't the kind of stories I want y'all sharing about me."

Jake put an arm around her shoulders and squeezed. "Don't worry, Annabelle. You know what we all think of you."

Annie pushed out a pouty lip. "A girl likes to hear it spoken aloud every once in a while."

Henry shook his head. "It's too easy to forget that you're only seventeen."

Annie's eyes narrowed, her lips pursed. "I'm going to start thumping people on the head if they don't stop calling me 'kid' or 'only seventeen' or anything else that implies I'm a child. I'm a grown woman." She lifted her nose to an indignant angle. "Besides, I'll be eighteen in a few months."

Henry guffawed. "Yeah. And, then you'll be *only* eighteen."

Henry, Bo, Jake and Dame shared a laugh. Even Annie could not prevent a grin that grew so large it disappeared into her dimples.

* * *

Bo leaned back in his chair. He lifted his gaze to the ceiling and moaned in deep satisfaction. In the light of the methane lamp overhead, his profile, the hair-covered head, long on top, resembled a lion at rest. "That meal was wonderful. I haven't eaten cooked meat in months. Thank you for inviting me into your home." He abruptly sat straight and looked to Glory. "Uh… sorry, but I don't know what to call you. Should I address you as Mrs. Henderson, Miss Jackson, or Glory?"

Glory reached sideways for Jake's arm and squeezed his forearm. "What do you think, Jake? What, exactly, do you suppose Mister Juster should call me?"

"The way I see it," said Jake, "ours is a union of soul, heart and mind. I am with this gorgeous creature as long as she'll have me, or until death, whichever comes first. How people address her is of little concern to me, but I'll defend to the death her right to be called whatever she wishes."

Glory kissed Jake on the cheek then addressed Bo. "Glory is fine, but I'll always answer to Mrs. Henderson, too." She laughed. "I think I might even be okay with the simple label of *Jake's woman*."

Jake pecked her on the lips, and they gazed into one another's eyes. Glory's skin, almost as dark as Dame's, glowed with health. Bright and exotic almond-shaped eyes remained fixed on Jake's face, evidence of love and respect.

"I'd say that's a marriage; even sounded a lot like a wedding vow," Annie said.

Bo pushed out his lower lip and nodded. "I'd have to agree."

Annie shifted attention to Ethan Turlock sitting next to her on the bench at the long cedar plank table. "You think we'll ever have what Jake and Glory have?" She bounced her eyebrows and kissed the air between them.

Ethan flushed red.

Seductively, Annie tilted her head. "Well, what do you think?"

"I don't know. I mean… maybe… someday." He glanced to Lana sitting across the table next to Eva. Lana remained focused on the plate of food before her.

Annie patted him on the shoulder. "Calm down, boy. I was just kidding. Did ya think I was going to knock you unconscious and drag you off to my lair?" She chuckled and then tickled his chin with her fingertips. "But, I have to admit, you are one fine looking guy since you chose to cut off that silly braided beard."

Ethan's long auburn hair covered his ears and touched the top of his shoulders. He picked up his spoon and hunkered low over his plate. "Yeah, well..." He loaded his spoon with beans before he could say another thing and continued to eat, refusing to connect with Annie or any other person at the table. Like every other member of the Order, Ethan wore a long hooded robe, the uniform of the Order of Theocratic Minds. Annie never saw him dressed any other way.

Annie chuckled again while rubbing a tiny loving circle on Ethan's back. As she did, her mind drifted. She stared out the window, through the open shutters, into a star-filled night sky beyond the cabin. A mild evening breeze brushed her cheeks. Her smile faded. The fresh nocturnal air wafting through the opening added to a beckoning call that serious things should be considered and flippancy ended.

"You be thinkin' about her again," Dame said.

Annie nodded. "I can't help it. That little girl crosses my mind so much these days it's almost continuous."

"Don'tcha ever be ignoring things like dat. Da universe be sendin' ya a message. Ya don't need ta be seein' da future like ol' Dame do, when ya got intuition like dat. You be one smart girl, Annie Henderson. Trust doze thoughts and, above all, trust in yaself."

"Are y'all talking about that little girl, Lizzy... the one in Old Dallas?" Bo asked.

"Yeah," Annie replied. "But the time for thinking and talking is at an end. It's time to do something about it."

Bo smacked the table with the flat of his hairy hand. "This is a crazy damn world we live in! Why should it be necessary to save a little girl from her own life?" He pounded the table again.

"It shouldn't be necessary at all," Annie said. "That's why I've made it my mission in life to change it." She thought for a moment and then refocused on Bo. "Don't misunderstand what it is I must do. I'm not giving up on her parents, unless I have no other choice. It's just that, if all else fails, I *will* get Lizzy out of there and into a safe environment."

"How did the world get this way? How is it that we've come to see such insane circumstances as normal?" Bo looked around the table hoping someone would engage him with an answer.

"Are you really unaware?" Jake asked.

"Uh-oh," Annie said, "you just opened the door very wide for a history lesson."

"Oh hush," Jake said. "I'll give him the abbreviated version."

Bo dropped his chin onto his palm. "Go ahead, Mr. Henderson, tell me. I spent countless nights in a cave, just Yowl and me, wondering about it. If you know, tell me."

"It began over two hundred years ago, at the beginning of the twenty-first century. Members of government in the former United States had developed insatiable appetites for power and wealth. Every player on the political stage sought personal gain by legislating favoritism to the largest of international companies until politicians and, eventually, the whole government machine became subordinate to them."

Bo sat straight. "I had no idea how it all started."

"Yeah. Kind of weird, isn't it?" Annie said.

"Anyhow," Jake continued, "That was just the key that started the machine. It got worse, a lot worse. Globally, it became contagious, like a disease. As it worsened, governments worldwide sought not to guide nations but to garner favor from individuals possessing wealth beyond counting. Every decision made led to the downfall of poor countries first, as the larger richer countries became nothing more than giant companies making laws for personal profit. Obscene amounts of money and wealth flowed into fewer and fewer hands. The country—our country—ceased to be a democracy, or a republic. Instead, it segued quietly into a corpocracy. Once the largest swallowed the rest, it turned into economic incest. There was no more wealth to be had, no more power to be gained and it collapsed under its own weight."

Clearly, Glory could see Jake was becoming agitated. He always did while telling this story. She covered his hand with hers and smiled. He knew immediately what that meant.

In a calmer voice, he continued, "The entire system fed on itself until there was nothing left but words and phrases of a bygone era. Things like 'independent consumers', 'chief executive officers', 'win-win situations', and many other terms that do not at all mean what they used to and really have no place in the world we inhabit. This place, this world you and I live in today, is held hostage by leftover greed two centuries old. The few people who still hold material wealth hoard it."

"I didn't know," Bo said.

"I could go on and on…" He looked at Glory and then laughed. "I'd better not though. I'll leave it with this barebones explanation. With more people like the Order of Theocratic Minds wanting to share knowledge and technology to better the human race with no profit motive, it doesn't have to remain this way."

Annie put a playful shoulder into Ethan and nudged him. "People like this guy and the rest of Theocratic Minds are the way out of this mess." Annie looked around the table, seeking confirmation. Her eyes landed on Lana, Eva's mother. Lana held a fixed gaze on Ethan. He refused to return it, choosing to keep his head down and eat. Annie thought Ethan's behavior had moved beyond embarrassment over her jovial remarks, to be rude and, frankly, odd. Something was on his mind. She turned attention to Lana. "You know what I'm saying; don't you?"

"I sure do. Ethan is not only the smartest guy I know but he has such a wonderfully creative mind as well." Lana's eyes never broke with Ethan even though she addressed Annie's question.

Annie noticed Ethan steal a glance at Lana while bouncing a quick nervous smile. Annie suddenly realized there was tension between Lana and Ethan, but born of what?

Lana broke her gaze on him. Her eyes quickly scanned faces around the table as if she were unaware of the attention she drew. Uneasiness splashed across her face. She stood. "The meal was great, Glory. Thank you. If you folks will excuse me, I need to help Eva get her bath and into bed."

"Aw, Mama," Eva whined. "It's early."

Lana suddenly became edgy, adding, "Eva Louise, don't give me any trouble. Come on." Lana seemed unduly eager to leave the room.

Dame scooted her chair back and rose. She held a stern, gnarled finger in Annie's direction. "All you need to be thinkin' 'bout right now, Annie, is Lizzy and her family. Take ol' Dame's word for it; things be happenin' like dey should."

Annie couldn't pull her analytical gaze away from Lana, but as her friend left the room, she looked to Ethan. "I—uh..."

"You trust ol' Dame; don'tcha, girl?"

"Of course I do."

"Den set your mind to Old Dallas and away from dis place, at least for a time. Okie dokie?"

Annie smiled. Her shoulders dropped as she relaxed. "As always, Dame, you're right." Whatever it was that she'd just witnessed still troubled her, though. Were there difficulties with friends and family that should be addressed before leaving for an undetermined length of time? She was denied information about something. Of that, she was certain. But why, and to what end? Her mind settled somewhat when Dame's calm admonition reverberated, 'things be happenin' like dey should'.

Chapter 4

Destination: Old Dallas

"I look like a monk that lost the bottom half of his robe," Bo told Annie. "A bit hairier, perhaps."

"I'm afraid you'll have to wait until we return from Old Dallas before our people can get that new suit of clothes I promised. We don't have time to wait for them."

"This'll do. I'm not complaining, just commenting."

Hands on hips, she examined the big hairy man. "Put the hood over your head. Let's take a look at how well that works for you."

Bo flipped the hood over his head and pulled it low in the front. "How's that?"

"That does create the appearance of an imposing and mysterious person. I like it."

It was a cloudless spring morning. Coolness that took all night to settle in had begun to abate. The early sun's rays beamed in from the east, radiating warmth, cutting through the light cool breeze.

Annie gazed across the grounds of Myrna's Glory. "Come on, let's walk." She took Bo's hand and guided him for his first lesson into what the compound was all about and to show him the purpose of everything.

Bo looked down at her hand clutching his. "You really don't need to drag me along. I may look like a dumb animal, but I think I can follow you without such direct encouragement."

Annie slowed her pace to walk abreast. Still holding his hand, she looked up into his eyes and grinned. "I like to hold hands with friends. It makes me feel safe."

"*I* make *you* feel safe? Humph."

"Okay, you win." She patted the back of his hand and then released it. "Although, I reserve the right to hold hands at a later date."

"Fair enough."

"I make you this guarantee..." She poked his arm with a stiff finger. "I will be exercising that right."

He stared down at her, clearly not knowing how to take the comment. "I don't mean any disrespect, but based on all standards of living that I've ever known about people, you're odd."

Annie chuckled. "Yeah, but in a fun way, right?"

Bo shook his head, sighed and then smiled. "I guess so."

Annie's whimsical expression metamorphosed into something more serious. "Henry's extra robe should be all you need for now. It has a hood to conceal your face when necessary and covers you down to the knees. And all Glory had to do was cut off the bottom few inches so it doesn't hinder your ability to move quickly, if necessary. I've never heard any members of the Order complain, and they wear them every day."

"My comment about the robe was simply an observation. I'm not concerned at all how I appear in it... really. I'll get used to it." His tone was dismissive. "It's seldom that I wear clothing up top this time of year, just pants." He pointed to the machine shop. "What do they do over there?"

"Well, it took me a while to figure it all out, but Ethan was patient with me while he explained all the functions." She pointed to a large, round, airtight tank connected by a tube to a similar but smaller tank. "This is called a digester. A gas called methane is made in it from human and animal waste. It burns easily. The gas powers that loud contraption over there just outside the building. It's called an internal combustion engine."

Ethan Turlock approached but said nothing. He stopped and listened to Annie's recitation of machine shop function.

Annie kept talking but smiled at Ethan. "That engine turns a shaft that extends through the front wall all the way to the back wall. At stations, along its length, are tools that are powered by the spinning shaft: saws, drills, presses, grinding stones, sanders... stuff like that. The brothers and sisters of Theocratic Minds can cut, shape and assemble various metals and woods for any desired construction need." Annie grabbed Ethan's arm and pulled him to her. "How'd I do? Did I explain it as good as you would have?"

"Good enough, I'd say." He smiled, but the pleasant facade melted away fast. "Annie, do you have a few minutes? We need to talk."

"Bo and I need to take care of a lot of business today. We don't have much time to get ready for our mission to Old Dallas tomorrow. I'm planning on only being gone for about a week. There could be as much as four days consumed just walking there and back. Can it wait that long?"

After a quiet second, Ethan nodded. "I suppose that'd be okay." His mouth seemed poised to verbalize a thought. He looked as though he might want to say something else.

"Are you sure it's okay?" Annie asked. "I mean... if it's important, I can make time."

Ethan drew a quick smile. "Nah, really, it's okay. It's nothing that can't wait till you get back."

Annie stepped closer and placed her head on Ethan's shoulder. "You're wonderful and more patient with me than I deserve."

Ethan pulled away, clearly unnerved by the gushing compliment. "Well, I have things that I must get done today, too. So, if you two will excuse me..." He left them and walked away toward another building—a place he spent hours each day drawing plans and designs for new machinery and other things needed to advance the work of Theocratic Minds. Ethan had evolved into the defacto manager of projects. His skill and innate dedication to planning and prioritizing were superior. People of the Order had come to depend on him for answers and guidance. His responsibilities were burdensome but, for a man in his twentieth year, he handled it well.

Annie couldn't stop the dreamy head-tilt and sigh as she watched Ethan walk away. "He's wonderful."

"I can tell you think so. If you're trying to hide it, you're not doing it very well," Bo said.

Annie grabbed his hand. "Come on, let's go inside the machine shop. My friend Corky will be working on something, I'm sure."

As they neared a large roaring engine, it radiated ample heat and smelled atrocious. Bo cupped his hands over his ears and then shouted, "That thing is noisy." The engine had no muffler, and it blew noxious fumes overhead as they walked beneath the roaring exhaust pipe.

"I know," Annie shouted back. She opened the door and they stepped inside, closing it behind them. It muffled the engine roar but the sound was replaced by the loud whine of the spinning shaft that the engine powered on the other side of the wall. "Hey, Corky," she yelled.

Corky remained focused on a piece of steel he was shaping on a grinding wheel for some purpose. Sparks flew in an arc away from his face.

"Corky," she shouted again.

He finally heard the call and pulled an idler arm, releasing the tension on a belt connecting the grinder to the spinning shaft. The noise subsided.

"Corky, I'd like you to meet a new friend of mine, Bo Juster." She looked up into the face of her hairy friend. "Bo, this is Corky McCann."

The shock of Bo's appearance was clear on Corky's face. His eyes moved from Bo's chest up to his hair-covered face and head. Bo was taller. Corky appeared ill at ease with the big man. Warily he extended a hand and then, equally cautious, said, "Nice to meet you, Bo."

Bo took his hand and shook it. "You, too." Bo grinned. "Annie, I have a feeling that if I'd walked into this compound unescorted, I'd have been beaten to death before getting the first word out."

"I apologize," Corky said. "I didn't mean to stare." Although shorter, Corky was square-built and muscular. He had been a guard in the Stalwart compound under the rule of the infamous Fiam Lee Tam at the time Annie liberated it. She had successfully changed his mind set on that place and helped him realize how manipulative and evil it was.

Bo shook his head. "It's okay. Nothing to concern yourself with. I've learned to live with shocked looks like that. I realize I look like my friend, Yowl, and that means less like you or anyone else around here."

"Yowl?" Corky asked.

"Yowl is the biggest, blackest wolf with the most gorgeous golden eyes you've ever seen. He's beautiful," Annie said. "Yowl may be imposing to look at all right, but once you get to know him, he's just a big ol' huggable teddy bear. Yowl and Eva are already the best of friends. They go everywhere together. I don't worry at all about Eva when she's with him beyond the compound."

"Interesting," Corky said as he looked over the shiny sculpted piece of metal in his hands, preparing to get back to work.

"How's your wife, Cynthia, and those two precious little girls of yours?"

Corky pulled his eyes from the piece in his hand and again made eye contact with Annie. He finally let a smile slip. "They're fine... and quite happy living here, but surely that's not the only reason you're here. Is there another?"

"Yeah, there is. Corky, would you and some of the brothers and sisters put together a small arsenal of weapons for Bo and me? We need arrows, throwing knives, sharp pointed throwing disks, and maybe a spear for Bo... sharp and barbed. You know, sort of like the one Henry prefers using? We have to take a trip tomorrow and I'm not sure how dangerous it's going to be. Would you help with that?"

"Of course."

"Would you also ask Ethan to make me a slingshot? Eva reminded me how handy those things can be, and all I need are stones I pick up along the way to arm it."

"You know how to use one of those, too?" Bo asked.

Annie backhanded his hairy arm. "Will you stop questioning what I can do?"

"Sorry."

A smile crept across her face. "I must say, though, I enjoy seeing that awestruck twinkle in your eyes when you do ask." She turned her attention back to Corky McCann. "Anyhow, I think it's to our advantage to be prepared. If you'll remember, Corky, I used every weapon Henry made for me last year fighting Tam and his men and wished I'd had more before it was over."

"How could I forget?" Corky said. He went silent, his facing taking a solemn turn.

"What're you thinking about?" she asked.

"You saved me and my family. Hell, you saved every resident of Stalwart that day and came close to losing your life in the process. I've thought about that every day since. What you accomplished—what you did that day—is still hard to wrap my mind around."

Bo waggled a finger toward Annie. "You see? Corky has known you longer than I have, and he still has trouble believing what you're capable of."

"Okay, point made."

A satisfied expression settled over Bo's face while his chin rose to a proud angle, as if he just won a major debate.

"Anyhow, it's ancient history. All is well. Let's leave it at that," she said.

"You've got that right," Corky said. "All *is* well, thanks to you. I'll round up some help and get busy making what you need."

* * *

At a particularly narrow place in the trail, Annie could no longer travel abreast of Bo and fell back to walk behind him. Yowl paced far ahead as if the big wolf knew where they wanted to go and led the way. Since she walked behind him, Annie took the opportunity to look at, and think about, this big hairy man she'd come to trust. Although appearing fierce, the addition of the shortened brown monk robe, tied at the waist with a length of rope, humanized him. Worry over the big man becoming a target due to his appearance eased. Still, the hood of the robe might be necessary to conceal his animal-like face over the next few days, possibly many times. No need taking unnecessary risks. She looked up the trail to Yowl and wondered if it was wise to allow the wolf to accompany them into Old Dallas. Hunters would desire him for his hide and, maybe as food, the same reason she figured Bo should conceal his appearance. There would be no way to hide Yowl's identity though. He would be targeted and hunted on sight.

Given his background, almost dying as a child while escaping the cannibalistic insanity of Old Dallas, Bo's desire, even eagerness, to help other children seemed ingrained from the moment she explained the mission to him. His slow acceptance to join the mission seemed staged from the beginning, as if he didn't want Annie to think he was an easy mark. Why should he have thought otherwise? He'd known her for only a matter of hours when she asked for his help. Annie was thankful he was willing.

Only fate and the mated pair of wolves that adopted him had assured his survival as a youngster. That happy accident was rare indeed. As problematic as his hair-covered body had been as a child in Old Dallas, it likely contributed to quick acceptance by Yowl and his female mate. Others could not depend on such happenstance. There had to be many children whose parents, or caretakers had been killed by ravenous rival gangs, or who happened to succumb to consumption insanity. Either way, children would be left to fend for themselves in a dangerous environment. Those children might escape the cannibals of Old Dallas, only to be attacked and eaten by wolves in the countryside.

Bo shared her desire to help others in the same, or similar, circumstances. In the brief span of two days, Annie had come to trust Bo Juster implicitly.

Annie shifted the heavily laden quiver of arrows at her back to a more comfortable position. She adjusted the two belts of basic throwing knives and disks slung across her body, all fitted neatly into slots in the leather for quick access. "Are you still sure of the way? It has been a long time since you escaped Old Dallas."

Bo offered a perfunctory nod. "Yes. We'll soon need to leave the river trail and head northeast. The Brazos River begins angling sharply away." He pointed through an opening between the trees where visibility was unimpeded for a mile or more. "You see that massive rock wall on both sides of the river?"

"Sure."

"That's the remnant of a dam that broke long ago. There is a dry lakebed behind it, once called Whitney. That's where we need to leave this trail."

"I'll stop worrying about getting lost. You seem to know where you're going."

"That I do." He looked back at her as she walked behind him. "I may have been young, but every moment of that ordeal, including the route I took away from that treacherous place, is burned into my memory... in terrifying detail, I might add."

The walk to the area below the crumbling dam took mere minutes. Although the dam had collapsed at its center and was breached decades ago, there remained a large pool of water below it. The river flowed through the center and created calmer eddies on the near and far sides. The water nearest them, among boulder size stones, was glassy calm. Yowl sat on his haunches at the water's edge, having already quenched his thirst. He waited.

"You think there are fish among those big rocks?" Annie asked.

"Yeah, I do... big ones. I was always pretty good at spearing fish in the shallows with a sharp staff." He proudly held his new spear with a fine barbed metal point. "I figure I could be even better with this."

"I'm certainly willing to let you try. I'm starving. I'll start a fire."

By the time Annie had a small fire licking the air with lazy flames reaching for rising smoke, Bo returned with three fish, one large and two smaller. She added limbs and twigs, forcing the fire to blaze higher.

"How about we let ol' Yowl have this big one?" He tossed it to his friend. Yowl attempted snatching it from the air but missed. It didn't seem to matter. The wolf tore into it and began devouring it.

Annie pulled her knife from its scabbard on her waist and gutted both fish, then scaled them. She skewered them with hefty, sharpened green mulberry sticks and wedged them in the ground angling over the fire. "It won't be long now."

The sun had set but it was still full daylight, the perfect time of day by Annie's reckoning. She drew a breath of the early evening air and scoped the pristine oak woods nearby. "Regardless of what people have done to it and whatever evil lurks, the world is still a beautiful place." She sat on the ground by the fire and leaned back, supporting her torso on her elbows.

"I guess you're right. It just needs a little work."

"Not the world, the people in it."

"Oh yeah, right, that's what I meant."

Suddenly, Yowl's head sprang up. Abandoning the fish on the ground, he sniffed the air.

"What's up, Yowl?" Bo asked.

"Shh," Annie hissed. "Listen."

"I don't hear anything."

"There's something moving behind those trees, and it's not an animal."

"I don't hear anything. Whatever it is you hear, how could you possibly know it's not an animal?"

Eyes remaining fixed beyond her hairy friend on the line of oak trees at the edge of the clearing where they camped, she whispered, "There you go again, questioning things I can do." She indicated with the flat of her palm for him to stay put as she rose to her feet. Again, she scanned the tree line and saw no one looking.

She sprinted to a big tree, nearer to where the sound came from. She squatted low and eased her head around its barky girth. She glimpsed a shoulder and part of an arm behind a large cottonwood tree not far away.

She silently sprinted on the tips of her toes to the opposite side of the same tree.

She heard the rustle of leaves as if whoever was on the other side was moving around for a look.

She stepped the opposite direction around the tree as she pulled the knife from its scabbard on her hip. There stood a man, his back to her, spying on their campsite.

With blurring speed she stepped behind the guy, wrapped an arm around his head and tilted it back to expose his neck to the blade in her other hand. "Tell me, mister, do you have mischief on your mind, or do you just wish to join us for supper?"

"Please don't hurt me," the man whined.

The voice sounded familiar. Annie spun him around and shoved him back against the tree so fast it forced air from his lungs in a rush. "Barney Tackitt?"

It was the man who had tried to rob them on their return trip to Myrna's Glory two days ago. His face was covered in dried blood with knots and bruises. A gash on his forehead was the source of all the blood, but it had clotted and stopped.

"What happened to you?" she asked.

"I—I was robbed and beaten."

She snickered, paused and then laughed. "I know you don't think it's funny, but it sure sounds like the universe meted out punishment designed just for you." Annie released her hold on him and stepped back. She clucked her tongue.

"Barney, Barney, Barney," she said as she sheathed her knife. "What are we going to do with you?"

"It was two of the dirtiest heathens I've ever seen that attacked me. One of them beat me with an oak stump until I was unconscious. I guess they thought I was dead and moved on. I haven't eaten in two days."

"The birds I gave you?"

"Taken."

"I'm tellin' ya, Barney, the life you've chosen is a recipe for disaster and will *always* be about who has the bigger stick... or stump." She made another quick examination of his face. "I see it wasn't you this time."

"The pain in my head is telling me I should agree."

"Come on. I'll get you something to eat."

They walked back to the campfire. Bo acted disinterested with Barney's presence, battered appearance and predicament. He continued tearing off bits of fish between his teeth and swallowing the mostly raw flesh. Without looking up, Bo picked up his spear lying next to him on the ground and held it out for Barney. "Catch your own."

Barney took the spear and walked to the water's edge.

"Bring me whatever you spear and I'll clean it and cook it while you get yourself cleaned up. You're a dirty mess," she said.

"Why are you being nice to me?"

"It's who I am," she said with a bright smile.

"Don't you be confusing her feelings with mine," Bo said. "I'll snap you like the twig you are if you disrespect her kindness. I don't trust you; not sure I ever will after that stunt you pulled on us a couple of days ago."

As Barney attempted to focus on fish swimming near his feet in the knee-deep water, Yowl sat on his haunches at the water's edge and watched with unflinching intensity. "That wolf of yours… should I be worried about him attacking me?"

Bo stared at Barney for a moment and then said, "That's entirely up to you. I will say this: Yowl will sense the meanness in you before you can act. Don't forget that." Bo took another big bite of the fish in his hand and swallowed it. "And Yowl is not my wolf. He's my friend, another thing you best not forget if you plan on hanging around."

At that moment, Annie knew beyond doubt that Bo had accepted Barney's presence, somewhat. It appeared as though they would have another traveling companion. She wondered if Barney had any useful talents. Something she would definitely have to explore.

Chapter 5

Once a Large City

Annie, Bo, and Yowl stood in the center of what once was a broad paved thoroughfare that gently fell away before them and seemed to lead directly into the heart of Old Dallas. Where they stood was high off the ground, suspended over another wide but deteriorating and crumbling roadbed crossing beneath it. In many places grasses, weeds, vines, and trees pushed through heaving concrete and asphalt, rendering it unrecognizable for what it had been in the distant past. Trees, some many decades old, had grown to considerable girth. It had to have been well over a century since the last motorized vehicles sped over its surface. Still, it provided ample flat area to walk on with a degree of comfort. Dilapidated buildings and debris littered the landscape. Some structures, many stories high, crumbled from the top down with the passage of time and neglect. This was the view to the horizon. "Does this lead to where we need to go?" Annie asked.

Bo nodded.

"Then we're almost there, right?"

Bo's hairy cheeks bunched into a grin. "Just because we made it to the outskirts means little. It's still at least a half day's walk."

"I wish Barney would've joined us," she said.

"I don't! That snake is trouble we don't need. He would've sold us to cannibals for lunch without a second thought. Are you losing your mind?"

"I didn't think I was." She looked up to her hairy friend. "But that does make me want to ask: Do you think so?"

"If you think we could've trusted him, then... yeah. You just might be out of your mind."

Annie sighed and then smiled sideways at him. "Aw, shoot, you might be right. We'll have to debate that someday. It's just that I have a feeling we'll need all the help we can get before this is over."

"I'd rather put faith in a friendly cannibal. At least I know where their allegiance lies. If he felt the slightest bit threatened, your new buddy, Barney Tackitt, would turn you and me over to them in a flash—no argument, no debate and certainly no effort on his part to prevent our death, or capture."

"You really believe that, don't you?"

"I do."

"In that case, maybe its best I shut up about good ol' Barney."

"Humph!" Bo glared at her. "I'm not perfect, but *good ol'* Barney is too flawed even for me."

"I will say one more thing about him. I think his pride, arrogance and bravado might have molded your opinion, but all that stuff you see is masking loneliness. Barney has no one in his life that he cares about, or that cares for him, that's all. That man is fixable. He's worth saving."

Bo's sudden silence on the issue made Annie think she may have gotten through to his softer side, but then he replied, "You're entitled to your opinion."

Annie shrugged and sighed. She again faced the direction they traveled, toward the heart of Old Dallas. She figured it might be best to set aside the subject of Barney. It seemed to be getting her nowhere. She fanned her arms wide. "Look at all this. Wow, this place is huge."

Bo scanned all that lay ahead and then nodded. "From the stories of my childhood, millions of people lived here at its peak population. But, like you and your family, most abandoned it to move into the countryside for survival. Only a few thousand still live here and they're the ones we have to watch out for because the only meat sources that remain are one another and maybe the occasional stray animal that gets lost in this maze of rubble. Be careful around people who treat you nice. It's likely they're hungry and sizing you up, and it's as clear as a babbling stream that you trust too much too fast."

"I know it's a problem. It's a weakness I struggle with."

"I'll try to watch out for you."

His concern touched her heart. She grabbed his arm and pulled him into a side-to-side embrace, arm circling his waist. "And I will certainly be watching out for you, big guy." She pressed the side of her head into his arm.

He attempted peeling her arm from his waist but wasn't strong enough to break her grip. "Come on, now. Stop that."

"Sorry, fella. I'm tellin' ya, you'd better get used to it. I may need to fight these feelings on occasion, but I won't even try around you." She acquiesced and released him. Yowl moved to her side and nudged her, sensing her affection. She stroked the heavy black hair on the back of the big canine's neck. Annie was becoming attached to him as well. "Bo?"

"Yeah?"

She kept her eyes trained on Yowl and continued petting the shiny black hair on the back of his neck. "If you told Yowl not to follow us, would he go back into the countryside and wait for us to finish our business? Or, would he follow us?"

"Why would I want to hurt his feelings like that? He and I go everywhere together, always have."

"To save his life."

"Oh." He stared at his canine friend. "I think I understand what you mean." Bo stepped around Annie and dropped to his knees to be at eye level with his friend. He set his spear on the ground and wrapped his arms around the wolf's neck. He whispered words of affection and then raised his voice. "You have to go back, my friend. You can't follow us." Bo stood and backed away. He made a guttural sound, something like a growl only softer—a very personal form of communication that only the two of them could understand. "Go on now," Bo said. "Go back the way we came and wait for us. It will be much more dangerous for you than for us in this place. I couldn't stand it if you were killed and became someone's winter blanket."

Yowl seemed to understand, but saddened. He whimpered. His tail went from high and proud to a doleful droop. His head eased downward, too. The wolf began walking away but then stopped and looked back.

"I'm sorry, friend. It has to be this way. Now go on."

Yowl turned away and again walked slowly, deeply forlorn.

Annie watched the wolf's retreat in silence for a time. She noticed tears glistening in Bo's eyes. "It won't be for long, and he'll be much safer this way."

"I know. It's just that he doesn't understand the rationale. He only comprehends that I sent him away, and he's doing it because we are friends. It hurts me that I can't make him understand why, that's all."

"Come on," she said, "let's not dwell on it or I'll start crying and change my mind and then we both might regret not standing strong. I don't want to do anything that would put that beautiful beast in harm's way."

Bo turned to face the direction of their travel. "You're right. Let's go." He drew a courage-building breath and then sighed. "I suppose even if I could've made him understand the purpose, he wouldn't have left us. He knows no fear and is very protective of me."

Annie scanned the northwestern skies. A spring thunderstorm towered in the near distance and appeared to be getting larger and darker as time passed. "It looks as though we'll need to find shelter soon."

About a mile straight ahead she saw smoke curling from several locations, all close together. They were easy to spot with the sun shining into the darkening storm, creating a dark blue backdrop for the rising smoke. "Those look like small cooking fires."

"That is very near where our destination is. It's probably in the same neighborhood as the girl you seek."

"Then let's go see just how hospitable cannibals can be."

It was late afternoon and the sun had sunk to the setting side of the sky. Annie and Bo walked in the direction of the smoke spires, until they got close enough that people milling about came into view. Other small fires dotted an area on the opposite side of the deteriorating highway they walked on. The sets of fires were several hundred yards apart.

Bo pointed to the other fires to the left. "That's what is referred to as the Brickyard District."

"Then we need to stay our course and go to the opposite side. That's where we'll find Lizzy. I hope she's still okay."

"If her parents haven't been consumed by the gang from the Brickyard District, I'm sure she's fine. No one goes after children with living parents. It's a code of ethics that may sound strange, but that's how it is."

"You mean there are rules to cannibalism?"

"When I was a kid in this place, there were. I suppose the law remains unchanged. Surprised?"

"I should say so. It's… well, there's no other way to say it; it's shocking and weird! The whole concept of eating one another is hard enough to wrap my head around, but to know there are actually *rules* that are followed is baffling."

"Even with my deviant appearance, I never had a problem living here as a child until my parents vanished. Then, all bets were off. I may have only been ten at the time, but I was old enough to know that I had become a target for someone's stew pot. I had no choice if I wished to survive, so I ran. Taking my chances outside Old Dallas was the only way."

Aside from the thunderstorm that still lay ahead, clouds also gathered in the direction they came from. The sun disappeared behind another anvil shaped thunderstorm. Ominous clouds surrounded them and closed in. Streamers of God's light sent brilliant fingers in a semi-circle from its hiding place.

"Look," Annie said, pointing to two adult couples standing and talking in what appeared to be a dirt path between living shelters. "Let's take the plunge and introduce ourselves."

"Might as well," Bo said. He pulled the hood of his short robe over his head. The front part of it hung to below his nose. Hairy cheeks, chin, and neck just looked normal, like a full beard, in a time when most men didn't shave.

The four people finally noticed their approach and stopped talking. They closed ranks, stepping nearer to one another. Body language indicated a collective pack mentality and lack of trust in people they didn't recognize.

"Hello," Annie called out to them.

Bo kept his head down and stayed at Annie's side.

One of the men finally responded. "If you folks are from the Brickyard District, you're taking a big chance by coming here."

"Oh, no sir," Annie said. She pointed back in the direction from which they had come. "We're from that direction, many miles from here out in the countryside."

"What is your business here?" the other man said. Two women stood on either side of him, but it was the one to his right that he put his arm around and pulled into bodily contact. She must've been his mate.

"A few years back, I met a very nice man, his wife, and their beautiful daughter near here. I thought since my friend and I were passing through I'd see if they were around and visit for a while before we move on."

"Got a name?"

"Well," Annie said, looking embarrassed, "the mother's name was Elizabeth and they called the little girl Lizzy. I'm sorry, but I just can't remember the father's name or their last name."

One of the woman blurted, "You're talking about Ragland and Elizabeth Longbow."

One of the men grabbed her arm before she finished, a clear indication that she should not have spoken. He frowned.

Annie had no choice but to gamble on establishing quick familiarity. "Oh, yeah, that's right. I called him Rag."

The man's serious look softened. "Yeah, everyone does."

Annie smiled and breathed relief. "Do they live around here?"

The man glanced to the other guy as if wanting confirmation. The other guy nodded approval. "Follow this path to the last shelter on the right. That's Rag's place."

Annie stepped closer to the man, grabbed his hand and shook it. "Thank you so much for your kindness."

Although hesitant at first, the man reached with his free hand and cupped Annie's arm above the elbow in what she thought would be a friendly gesture. But his fingers did more than squeeze. They probed the flesh of her arm. Annie tingled all over, realizing the reason for such an examination.

The woman, his mate, placed a hand on Annie's shoulder—again, a seemingly harmless and friendly touch. "You're very welcome." She did the same thing as her mate, walking fingers over the muscles between Annie's shoulder and neck. The other woman made a move toward Annie as though she, too, wanted to touch her. Still stroking Annie's shoulder, the first woman asked, "Are you and your friend planning on staying long?" As her hand continued moving over Annie's shoulder, her eyes swept Annie from head to toe and then back up. "I think it would be nice. We don't see too many visitors in our neighborhood."

Annie saw that the look in the woman's eyes could have been mistaken for one of sensuality, but Annie knew that the look was one of longing for a potentially prized commodity. Annie shuddered and snatched her hand from the man's grasp, stepping quickly back out of reach. That was enough of that brand of kindness. "Uh, we'll only be staying a day or two… maybe… not sure yet."

The man flipped a finger toward Bo. "Why does your friend not show his face? Does he have something to hide?"

"As a matter of fact, he does," she replied.

"Oh?"

"It's a skin condition that he suffers from and doesn't want to frighten people."

All four recoiled at the same time. "He's not a leper, is he?"

"Oh no, nothing like that. I'm speaking of a condition he was born with."

That seemed to satisfy their curiosity.

"Well, thanks again," Annie said. She took Bo by his very hairy hand and walked away. She shuddered and then leaned against Bo, whispering sideways. "That made my skin crawl." She glanced back and noticed one of the women gesturing to the man beside her. It was obvious she'd noticed Bo's hairy hand. Annie saw them begin to huddle and speak among themselves. With her advanced hearing it wasn't difficult to hear that they questioned who, or what, Bo was.

She and Bo followed the path as instructed. Although it was a dusty dirt path and all the shelters on both sides resembled chaos with small amounts of human arrangement, there seemed to be a semblance of method to it all. Each structure had been pieced together with salvaged materials but seemed sound and water tight, all similar in appearance.

One of the structures was an obvious deviation and looked nothing like the rest. It was the last one on the right, the one they had been told to go to. It was mortared stone. It may have been one of the original structures that still stood and had been repurposed as a home. There was no door, just a soiled and frayed canvas-like oiled cloth hanging over the entrance.

"This is the place. I remember that cloth partition from when Dame Fortune brought me here in the dream state."

Annie tried knocking on the stone but didn't make a loud enough sound to gain attention, so she said in raised voice, "Hello. Anyone home? Rag... Elizabeth... Lizzy... anyone?"

The filthy cloth covering the entryway swept aside and there stood Elizabeth, eyes red and puffy. She had been crying. "What? What is it you want?" she asked. She examined Annie's face and glanced to Bo, whose face remained covered by the hood over his head. "Who are you people?"

"I came here to talk about Lizzy," Annie said.

Terror swept the woman's face. "Has something happened to my Lizzy?"

"No," Annie blurted. "I mean... I can't be sure, but don't panic." She suddenly had a twinge of fear, too. "What is it that has you so upset?"

Bo stole glimpses from beneath the hood shrouding his upper face and head. He stepped closer to Annie's side, examining Elizabeth in flicking glances.

"Because of the way life is here in the Garden District, Rag and I have strict family rules. The three of us gather at home every day at the same time, so we know our family remains safe. It prevents worry." Her face tightened and tears streamed from between clenched eyelids. "Rag is late, very late."

"Where did Lizzy go," Annie asked.

She pointed toward the Brickyard District. "Lizzy ran to climb onto the roof of that big building over there to watch and see if her daddy has been captured. Rag goes on hunting expeditions very near the boundary separating the Garden District from the Brickyard District." Her face again scrunched. Fresh tears streamed. "I've told him over and over that the practice is dangerous, and he should not go alone or maybe even stop it altogether. Brickyard hooligans are ruthless. They don't respect the boundary separating neighborhoods. But he always insisted that it served two purposes; to guard the border against encroachment, and maybe to pick off one of those hooligans for supper."

The comment put a queasy knot in Annie's stomach— just the thought of people hunting people sickened her.

Lizzy suddenly appeared between two of the structures across the path. She was running toward them. "They've got him, Mama! They've got Daddy!"

Elizabeth wailed.

Lizzy ran past Annie and Bo as if they weren't there. She slammed her body into her mother. They held one another and cried.

Annie looked to Bo. "Let's get them back inside."

As Annie guided mother and daughter inside the dark cave-like dwelling, Elizabeth asked over her shoulder, "I still don't know who you are, how you know us, or why you came to our house. Are you from the Brickyard?"

"No," Annie said. "Your other questions are valid though, and I will answer them all. For now, though, I think I'll beg your trust that we are here to help. Every truthful answer I could give you would only lead to more questions, and we need to focus on getting your family back together."

Bo pulled a chair back from the rugged plank table and sat.

Elizabeth collapsed into a chair on the opposite side. She let her head fall onto stacked arms and wept. Her state of mind had deteriorated to a point that the presence of strangers in her home seemed less a concern than the absence of a mate and Lizzy's father.

Bo pulled the hood far enough back to uncover his eyes. Elizabeth did not look his way at all. She had been focused on Annie, and now grief swarmed her. She paid neither of them any mind. It was clear enough that Elizabeth assumed her husband was dead, or soon would be. Bo leaned across the table to get a clearer view of her facial profile. He tentatively spoke. "Elizabeth," he said in that deep resonant voice, "before you were married did your name happen to be Nolan... Elizabeth Nolan?"

Elizabeth finally straightened and looked at Bo. Dim light of the windowless room and the heavy shadow created by the protruding front portion of his hood made an examining gaze difficult. Elizabeth leaned forward for a better look. "Yes. How did you know that?"

He pulled the hood entirely off and let it fall onto his back. "It's me, Elly."

Elizabeth's watery eyes grew large. Once his face was exposed, recognition was quick. "Bo?"

She came out of her chair so fast it flipped backwards. She rushed around the table and embraced him. She did not give him a chance to stand. She did not stop crying, but the sound changed from despair to one of hope. "Oh, Bo, I thought you had been consumed long ago." She smoothed the hair on his face and head fast with shaky hands. "My friend, my best friend in the whole world is back. You are back," she babbled in shock and disbelief.

"I managed to get out of Old Dallas. It wasn't easy, but I survived."

Lizzy continued to shy away, fearful of the big overly hairy man with a booming voice. She stood with her back pressed into a far corner of the room.

Annie stepped to the child's side. "It's Okay, Lizzy. He's a good guy."

Elizabeth looked back to her daughter. "Yes, sweetie, he *is* a good guy... the best. He was my friend when I was about your age." She finger-combed the hair on his head and gazed at him. "He was my protector and never let me out of his sight."

Bo gestured to Annie. "This is my friend, Annie Henderson," he told Elizabeth. "I hope you know now that you can trust her... because I do."

Elizabeth rose and approached Annie, hand outstretched. "Oh yes, I most certainly do." She held Annie's hand sandwiched between hers. It was a truly affectionate gesture this time, not one that created a shuddering chill that she might end up as soup for supper in a big cast iron pot.

Annie pulled her into a full embrace and hugged her. She then pushed her back to arm's length. "Right now, Elizabeth, I need you to be calm and strong. Can you do that for me?"

Elizabeth nodded. "I—I'll try, but Rag is gone. There's no way to get him back. If he's not already dead, he soon will be, and then consumed." She looked to Bo. "And you should remember that a woman with no husband in this place is little better off than parentless children." She whimpered.

Annie held her and said in a calm voice, "Listen to me, Elizabeth, I not only ask you to trust me but not to underestimate what I can do for you. There are no guarantees, but all is not lost, not as long as I'm around."

Elizabeth offered an incredulous gaze at Annie. "But… you seem so young. What could you possibly do to help? How old are you?"

Annie could not prevent a faint but obvious look of indignation. "I may be young; I'm seventeen, but I promise you that I have what it takes to be of great help to you and your family."

"She is amazing," Bo said, "in ways you wouldn't believe if I told you and would still have trouble believing if you saw it for yourself."

"If you are as brave and talented as you are beautiful then you must truly be amazing."

Annie blushed. "Uh… well… thank you." Annie retrieved a strip of red cloth from the pouch at her side and tied it around her head to keep her long honey blond hair from falling across her eyes, impeding vision. Her soft blue eyes suddenly took on a glint of determination. If it were not for the taut and sinewy six-foot frame, she would have appeared even younger than her seventeen years. She knew it but tired of hearing it so often.

"Mama, listen to me!" Lizzy finally lost patience with how slowly things progressed. She tugged at her mother's threadbare and buttonless jacket. "I saw him," she said, urgency plain in her tone. "His hands were tied behind him. Two guys jerked him along at the end of a rope. He could barely stay on his feet. That was only a few minutes ago."

Annie spun to face Bo. "Then Lizzy's right. We are wasting time." She assessed available weapons. There were thirty arrows in her quiver, two dozen palm-sized, spiked throwing disks and two dozen six-inch throwing knives. Those and the disks stored in slits cut into leather belts that crossed over her chest. She patted the pouch that hung to the side at her waist where the slingshot was stored and realized she had not gathered stones. "Lizzy, is there a place nearby where I can gather stones for my slingshot?"

Lizzy frowned, sinking into thought. She finally brightened. "Come on. I have something better." The twelve-year-old youngster grabbed Annie's hand and guided her down a short and narrow hallway that exited through a draped door at the rear of the house into a large open area—a back yard—but it was so much more than a yard.

Annie stopped, enthralled with what lay before her. The area was huge, three or four acres large, about the size of the main complex of buildings at Myrna's Glory. It was one giant vegetable garden. The perimeter was a mishmash wall of stone and rubble all the way around the enclosure, probably thirty hands high, topped by giant shards of thick glass standing like sentries atop the wall. Woven around the glass was anything they could find that happened to be dangerously sharp: barbed wire, strips of metal and various other salvaged items. It was obvious that no one would be climbing over that wall without major bodily damage.

"Lizzy, this is beautiful! This is the finest garden I've ever seen. Even the gardens where I come from are not this nice… and they're great."

"Mama started it when I was a baby. It has been here since I can remember. She's always tellin' Daddy to stop eating so much meat and eat more of this stuff."

"Is it only your family who eats like this?"

"Oh no. All the neighbors in the Garden District share vegetables, and many of them also have their own gardens."

It struck Annie that the Longbows and their neighbors may not have the consumption disease common to cannibals that drives them insane. It seemed reasonable to assume that ingestion of fruits and vegetables may have tempered its progression, even into adulthood, but she remembered that during the dream-state visit, Dame Fortune told her that Rag and Elizabeth were not thinking normally. Annie also remembered Dame saying that future events did not have to occur as she saw them. It would only be as she envisioned if the course of events remained unchanged. That was the reason Dame would never share good outcomes she divined, but would always let bad outcomes be known, because then there would be effort put forth to change an undesirable future scenario. Could Dame have fudged the truth on that occasion? Maybe the old lady just wanted to plant a seed in Annie's mind that Elizabeth and Rag might be going in that direction but were not there yet. Annie smiled. *Dame, you clever old girl. You saw a bleak future for folks in the Garden District but knew I could change it.*

"Lizzy, do you know if people in the Brickyard District have gardens like this?" Annie asked.

"I don't think so. That's why Daddy and the other men have to really work at keeping them out of the Garden District. People around here disappear a lot."

Annie took a long admiring look at Lizzy. The girl had a smattering of freckles across her nose. Long brown hair hung to her waist in a single braid. She wore canvas pants that extended to below the knees and a dirty white shirt that laced up the front. "You are a very special girl, ya know that, Lizzy Longbow? You're very grownup for only twelve."

Lizzy beamed. "And you're very grownup for seventeen."

Annie's eyes narrowed at the comment. After a silent second, she said, "I think we'll be great friends... regardless of what I think about what you just said." Annie began looking around. "Okay, show me what we came out here to see."

"Over here," Lizzy said, trotting to a clear barrel-shaped jar near a small tool shed. She dropped to her knees and unscrewed the jar lid. "I bet these will be better than any ol' stones for your slingshot." She reached inside the jar and retrieved a handful of various colored glass marbles, all uniform in size and weight—perfectly round.

Annie held out her hand and Lizzy let the marbles roll off onto her palm. "Those are magnificent." She held one between her fingers and lifted it to better examine the colorful glass ball. Even in the fading light of late afternoon and a dark thunderstorm looming, the marble sparkled with a dazzling burst of purple set within the clear glass. All the others were various colors and equally beautiful. "Are you sure you want me to use these as weapons? You may never see them again."

"It's my daddy, Annie. The marbles don't matter."

Annie smiled. "Well said, Lizzy... well said." She put the handful of marbles in the pouch at her side.

"Take more," Lizzy said as she scooped out another handful and handed them to Annie.

When Annie dropped them into her pouch, it bulged. "That's enough. With the bow, arrows, knives, disks and now all these marbles, I'm afraid any more things to carry might jeopardize mobility and I may need to move quickly." Annie checked the sky. "Storms will converge over us soon, but I don't think that's a bad thing. It might be to our advantage. Can you take Bo and me to where you hid to watch the goings-on inside the Brickyard District?"

"Sure. Come on."

As they stepped back inside the house, Annie began speaking before entering the next room. "Elizabeth, I need you to stay here. As soon as Lizzy shows us where we need to go, I'll send her home." She spun and placed a firm hand on Lizzy's shoulder. "Girl, I want you to run back here as fast as you can when I tell you, with no argument. Agreed?"

"But I wanna help."

"Believe me, you will be helping if I don't have to worry about where you and your mother are."

Elizabeth stepped over and pulled Lizzy to her side. "Do what she says. You get back here right after you show them the way."

"Oh… all right."

Annie drew a breath. "Are you ready for this, Bo?"

"Of course, it's why we're here… sort of."

Elizabeth offered Bo a quizzical frown. "I don't think I want to question the blessing of your presence, but you two really need to explain what brought you here in the first place."

"All in good time," Annie said.

Lizzy pecked her mother on the cheek and trotted out of the house. Annie and Bo followed. As soon as Annie cleared the tattered drape over the front door, lightning flashed, spreading brilliant feathery fingers across the sky followed by a traveling crackle and then booming thunder. Annie hesitated. *Nature may have provided us with a diversion that might come in very handy*, she thought.

Chapter 6

Saving Rag Longbow

Annie, Bo and young Lizzy Longbow crouched on the roof of a dilapidated four-story building on the Garden District side of the boundary in Old Dallas. Annie and Bo peered around each end of a corroded and crumbling heap of metal and parts that must have once served some function for the building they were atop. They peered at a thin metal housing standing about three feet above the roof's surface that had virtually corroded away, exposing stacked thin and shiny metal fins with reddish tubing woven within it. Most of the reddish tubing had a green powder on it. Thanks to Ethan Turlock's excellent tutelage, Annie recognized the metals as copper and aluminum.

Lizzy hid behind a large pipe coming up through the roof. It appeared as though it might have been a smoke stack or a vent of some kind. The view from this vantage point revealed the deteriorating broad thoroughfare, once an asphalt and concrete highway, the dividing line separating Lizzy's home community with the Brickyard District—the same surface Annie and Bo used to walk here—into the heart of Old Dallas. From here, it was easy to see why the area in question was given its name. There were remnants of many piles of construction bricks, some still neatly and squarely stacked, but it was clear there had been no serious construction in many decades. The brick stacks that remained were encircled by choking weeds and intertwined with vines. Farther into the area, situated in the center of a cluster of buildings, stood the largest structure. It was still intact and appeared weatherproof. It had apparently become the central gathering point for residents. All the hovels and structures surrounding it must have been individual living quarters.

The thunderstorm moving in provided a light show that made visibility a bit easier, especially for Bo and Lizzy. The last vestiges of daylight had faded into night and without the flashes it would have been dark indeed. With Annie's advanced vision, it was of little importance. The night would have to be virtually black before her vision would become impaired. She had the natural ability to take whatever light the environment provided and concentrate it. So far, there had not been a night dark enough to blind her—just another of her genetically enhanced talents.

Large raindrops began splattering in random places across the rooftop.

Annie looked to where Lizzy sat on her heels behind the large rusty cast iron pipe. The girl was focused across the way. Annie snapped her fingers to get the youngster's attention, and then whispered as loud as she dare, "Lizzy, which building did they take your daddy into?"

Lizzy waited for the next lightning flash and then extended her arm to point it out. "That one... left of the taller building. See that door near the far corner?"

"Yeah, I do." Annie turned full attention to the youngster. "Thank you. You've made our job much easier. You have to go back now."

"But Annie—"

"No 'buts,' girl," Annie blurted. "This is not a negotiation. You promised your mother and me that you would. Now go! The next time I see you, you'd better be dry and warm in your house. Got it?"

Lizzy sat belligerently back on her heels and crossed her arms over her chest but did not pout. Her mouth hardened in a clear show of determination.

"Lizzy…" Annie drawled.

The youngster slapped her thighs in frustration. "Oh, all right." She sprang up and ran back in the direction from which they had come, disappearing through a rusted metal door to a staircase down to ground level.

Annie watched the girl and followed her as far as the door. She looked over the edge of the roof and down to the door that exited the building on the ground floor. She would not be able to concentrate on the dangerous task ahead until she was certain that Lizzy did as told. Annie remembered well what it was like to be twelve years old. There was an even chance Lizzy would hide somewhere in the building and then follow them into a treacherous situation. After a minute, Lizzy exited the building and took off running toward her home in the Garden District. Annie watched. Near continuous lightning flashes illuminated the girl's route. It was a relief to see that the youngster followed the order. Annie's mind eased. She rejoined Bo, still crouching on the Brickyard side of the roof. "Do you see any movement over there?" she asked.

"Nah. I'd have trouble seeing that far even if it weren't this stormy and dark. Besides, they've probably all gone inside for the night or, at the least, are staying in until the storm passes."

Annie kept her eyes on the area pointed out to them. It was at the far corner of the largest central structure, about two hundred yards from the building they crouched atop.

"Lizzy didn't know how many hunter types live in the brickyard. She just said, 'More than I can count, and I count good.' So, what do you think that means... fifty... a hundred, maybe?" she asked.

"I don't know, but if we're going to do this thing, let's say a hundred.,or more and act accordingly."

She looked at Bo with an affectionate sigh. "Ya know what?"

"Uh-uh," he muttered without looking at her.

"I'm so glad you're here with me."

"Well, I'll withhold judgment on how glad I am to be here until after this adventure into the pit of hell." He glanced her way. "And, of course, we walk away from it alive."

"Good point." Annie drew a deep breath. On the exhale, she said, "Let's go get Rag Longbow and take him home. Hopefully, we won't attract unnecessary attention in the process."

She and Bo made their way down the stairs, out of the building and then ran across the crumbling six-lane highway, frequently stopping to scan for movement from the brickyard. They finally made it undetected to one of the stacked piles of bricks and squatted in the tall weeds behind it. "See the window with the dim light coming from it, near that door Lizzy pointed out?" she asked.

Bo said nothing, and then lightning flashed. "I do now."

"Since there are few places to hide between here and there, I'm going to sprint the distance first because, frankly, you can't run very fast."

Bo stiffened. "Thanks a lot."

"Sorry, big guy. Didn't mean it the way it sounded; just an observation, not an accusation." She bounced a quick grin. "Wait for my signal and then run as fast as you can to join me."

"I'll see if I can get that done without tripping over my big ol' hairy feet."

"Hang on to that sense of humor. You're going to need it, I'm sure." She slapped his knee. "Yep, I'm sure glad you're here."

Annie sprang up and took off running. She covered the seventy yards in less than five seconds and stopped next to the window at the far left side of the building. She craned her neck to look around the corner of the building toward the rear. She saw no one. She then stepped away from the corroded structure and studied the entire area within view—up to the roof, right, left and the wide-open area back to the brick pile that Bo remained behind—still, no one in sight. It seemed obvious that residents of the Brickyard District did not fear attacks from the Garden District. There were no guards walking the area. As the amber glow of an oil lamp bathed her face through the small window, it occurred to her that if they left a light burning, brickyard residents would be coming back for some purpose. Otherwise, the light would likely have been snuffed for the night. Lamp oil had to be a precious commodity in a place like this. She shuddered at the likely source of that oil—rendered human body parts.

Annie waved to Bo. She saw recognition in his body language during a series of brilliant lightning flashes. Once his attention had been secured, she gestured for him to join her. As she waited, a disgusting but likely thought crossed her mind; if these people did not fear those from the other neighborhood, residents of the Garden District may have been viewed as livestock, a food source to be harvested at will. Guys like Ragland Longbow might be seen as an errant bull—an animal in need of pinning, or killing for easier access to the herd. Annie swallowed hard. She clenched her teeth and shook her head, trying to eradicate that visual image. It was difficult, indeed, to set aside such thinking, but she had to try. If allowed to fester, these small hitches in her ability to think and move quickly could become a dangerous distraction at a critical point in the plan to liberate Ragland Longbow.

Bo came to stand next to the window opposite Annie. He eased his head around to look inside. "Annie, there's five of them."

"What?" She finally took her first peek inside and saw one woman and four men bound and gagged, lying on a concrete floor. She recognized Rag as one of them. "We can't just rescue him and leave the others."

"Even if we tried, the other three would make such a ruckus at being left behind it would scuttle the effort."

"By now, you should know me well enough. I wouldn't consider leaving the others behind under *any* circumstances."

He nodded and sighed. "I know."

"But it does complicate things," she said. "Look at how they're bound. It was done without concern for their survival. When we get those ropes cut, it may take their arms and legs time to work well enough to be led out of there. There can't be circulation left in any of their appendages."

"I don't see anyone around. We'd better get it done." Bo stepped over in front of the door and pushed. It yielded with no effort. He had to duck down to clear the top of the door.

"I don't think anyone has ever attempted a rescue," she whispered. "There doesn't seem to be any safeguards."

Bo held the door open and Annie walked in first. The four people squirmed about on the dust-covered and severely cracked concrete floor, possibly scared they were about to be butchered by a large, beastly looking man. Annie put a finger to her lips. "Shh. We're friends. We're not from here." She knelt and pulled the wadded cloth from the bearded man's mouth. "Rag Longbow, right?"

From the bound and bent position on his side on the floor, he strained for a better look at her. "I've never seen you before. Who are you?"

Even before the question had cleared his lips, she had her knife unsheathed and was sawing through the heavy ropes encircling his entire body. Bo freed the others.

"There'll be plenty of time for answers to those questions once we get you back to Elizabeth and Lizzy." She flicked her chin toward the others. "And, of course, your friends back to their homes too."

"But…"

"Shh! I heard something. Do you know if there are people close by, and where they might be?" she whispered.

"I can't say. This is the first time I've ever been over here."

Annie raised an eyebrow. "Makes sense. I guess no one ever returns from this place to share information like that."

"All I can tell you is that we were thrown in here and tied up, then four men disappeared through that door over there, the one in the center."

Annie saw three doors, evenly spaced about ten feet apart. The center, draped entryway did indeed show obvious evidence of much foot traffic in the dust on the floor. She nodded and rose as Rag pushed himself off the floor to sit upright. "Okay." She looked back to check Bo's progress with the others and saw that one of the captured men could not sit upright under his own power once his bindings were cut and removed. His arms had been deprived of circulation too long. Bo pulled him upright. The others were not much better off. "How about you, Rag? Do your arms and legs work okay?"

"Not really. I'm numb, but I haven't been tied up as long as they have. I'll be okay."

Annie again heard something that no one else in the room could. "Everyone sit very still and make no noise," she said low and evenly.

She pulled two of the honed throwing knives from slits in one of the belts crossing her chest. She rose, intending to ease toward the doorless back entry, but before she took a step, a man appeared through the opening.

She prepared to throw one of the knives.

Bo sprang to his feet, but was off-balance. He blocked Annie's view of the man.

In a clumsy maneuver, Bo lunged at the man with his spear.

The man had knives in each hand and knocked the spear aside with the larger of the two. It was plain to see that he had butchering meat on his mind, and it was just as clear he came well-armed. "Intruders!" the man yelled.

It turned into a noisy melee, exactly what Annie wanted to avoid, leaving her no choice. Before the call for aid could be repeated, she sent one of the throwing knives whizzing right by Bo's ear, into the man's throat.

The man's second shout had begun, but completed in a muddled gurgle. She shuddered with revulsion over what she had just done, but had no time to dwell on it.

The big butchering knives fell from his hands and clanked upon the floor. He grabbed for the handle of the small knife embedded in his throat and fell, writhing on the floor.

"Get them out of here, Bo!"

"What about you?"

"Just run!"

Bo pulled the nearest captive to his feet, holding him long enough to make sure he could support his own weight. He then lifted the woman who had lain next to the male captive to her feet. She recoiled in horror at Bo's animal-like hairy appearance.

"It's not me you should be afraid of, lady. Can you stand?"

She nodded fast and spastically. Her wide eyes remained fixed on Bo's face, clearly confused and frightened by all that was going on.

He pulled her to her feet and then turned to help another, but she did not move.

He stepped back, grabbed her and yanked her arm. "Come on, come on!"

She continued staring at Bo's intimidating and very hairy face, but still did not make a move to follow him.

He slapped her hard enough to sting. "Get your wits about you, woman!" He released her, and she stumbled sideways. He righted her again. She took tentative steps. "Don't walk! Run!" Bo shouted as he left her and moved to pull a man to his feet. "Come on, come on. Let's get out of here before we all get killed!"

Rag made it to his feet under his own power and moved to the woman's side to assist her.

Bo began herding the four, stumbling toward the front door.

"Hurry, Bo. I hear others coming," Annie hissed.

"I'm trying," he said, keeping his eyes on the escapees while funneling them through the door.

Annie's attention became divided between the door at the rear of the room and Bo's efforts to get the four out the front. All the prisoners had problems with extended loss of circulation in their limbs; moving quickly was out of the question. It was cumbersome and slow while Bo went from one to the other, trying to keep them upright and moving. Just as Bo made his way out the door, the first attacker appeared at the back entrance.

With blurring speed, Annie flipped the second, six-inch throwing knife underhand with such velocity it disappeared into the center of the man's chest, hitting with so much force it stopped his forward progress upon impact. He fell onto the one with a knife in his throat. Now, two bodies partially blocked the doorway.

Another man appeared. His eyes darted around the room, and he raised a large butchering knife to attack position. He ran, hurdling over the dying men heaped upon the floor, in a full charge towards Annie.

She slipped a spiked throwing disk from the belt across her chest and sent it humming across the room into the man's forehead while he was in mid-air. It flipped him backwards. He fell on top of the downed men to partially block the doorway, but that only bought an extra second, maybe two.

Annie had to get out before becoming boxed in. Men would soon be streaming around to the front of the building. If she did not take this opportunity to join Bo and the prisoners in their getaway, defensive options would wither fast. She needed space to move about freely. Trapped inside, she would be swarmed and then overwhelmed. She ran out the front door into driving rain.

She scanned the area. Bo had made it as far as the brick pile that served as the final hiding place before approaching the building. Annie became encouraged they would make it, if she could control the situation brewing behind her.

Five men appeared from around the corner of the building as anticipated. That number swelled to ten in an instant and was growing. All carried various weapons—knives, pieces of pipe, wooden clubs and spear-like staffs. An unavoidable confrontation had begun.

Annie flashed back to the year before when Fiam Lee Tam's men from the Stalwart compound met her on the trail to kidnap young Eva. They, too, came at her this way, eventually clubbing her and taking her down, due only to an overwhelming number of attackers. This time was different. She had no one to protect but herself and could focus all her attention on self-preservation. Annie became a deadly tornadic whirl of flying weapons. She alternated between firing arrows and throwing knives and spiked disks, every one hitting intended targets.

Men fell. Others continued streaming around the building to replace the fallen.

She glanced in the other direction. Many men were running from the largest structure at the center of the brickyard behind her. Tactically, it might become deadly if she allowed them to surround her. The question became: Could she avoid it? The answer was obvious: no.

She had no choice but to fight on two fronts. She threw knives and disks in both directions, sometimes simultaneously. It slowed the attackers, but they kept coming.

Then out of the rain-drenched night, something huge flew over the top of her head and landed with a muddy splat, blocking the charging men. It was the wolf, Yowl.

All the men running at her froze. Even those in the other direction stopped, clearly disbelieving what they witnessed. Lightning flashes made Yowl's golden eyes blaze demonically.

The monstrous black canine did not slow, or even growl, immediately grabbing the leader by the neck. With a snapping bite, he crushed the bones in the man's neck. Yowl worked his way through the assailants. Once he felled the four who stupidly attempted attacking him, the others turned and ran.

In the meantime, Annie fended off others coming at her from around the corner of the building. When Yowl joined her, they also turned and ran. It was over.

Out of the night, she heard a raspy, angry male voice shout, "If it's war you want, then you'll certainly have it! Damn you all!"

Somewhat winded, Annie dropped to her knees.

Yowl turned and began licking her face.

"You beautiful, beautiful beast," she said between breaths. "I shouldn't be happy that you're here, but I am." She hugged his neck. She then thought about the man's declaration of war and pulled her head back to look directly into the wolf's golden eyes. "Oh my, Yowl, what have we done?"

The wolf nuzzled his snout to her cheek.

"I'm afraid we've started something we may not be able to control."

Chapter 7

Making Sense of a Senseless World

"Brickyard hooligans will not attempt anything tonight," Rag said, sitting at the rugged plank table in the Longbow house. His head dangled low from jacked shoulders, exhaustion nearing absolute. He continually massaged blood engorged bruises on his wrists and arms, left from the bindings.

The hovel they called home was dank; driving rain seeped from crumbling mortar between stones comprising the outside walls. A small, crude fireplace served as kitchen stove and living space heater. Rag sat in a chair with his back to the fire at the narrow table in front of it. It was clear that this table was the social center of the Longbow residence. Although unadorned and somewhat shabby, it exuded a feeling of a home that love built.

Rag straightened and groaned as he raised his head. He glanced to Bo and Yowl and flipped a finger their direction. "What assurance do we have that the big hairy one and the wolf over there won't kill us in our sleep tonight?" Although it was a serious concern, his tone lacked enthusiasm, as if he really didn't care what the answer might be.

"I'll answer that with my own question," Annie said. "What assurance do *we* have that you won't butcher us in our sleep and eat us in a breakfast stew tomorrow?"

Rag's head again came up, this time crisply. He sat straight. "What from Hades garbage heap are you talking about? We're not savages!"

"Oh really? I'd say that eating the flesh of a human could be described as exactly that, the ultimate definition of savagery," Annie replied with equal verve. "On top of that, to learn there are actually *rules* that are followed on who can and cannot be eaten, and times established that are more appropriate than others is…is ridiculous! It should *never* be okay to eat another human!"

Rag's eyes glowed with anger. In a deep even voice he said, "You are not so much older than Lizzy that a good spanking would be out of the question." He sprang up, scooting his chair noisily across the unlevel stone floor and aggressively stepped toward Annie.

Elizabeth hurried to his side and grabbed his arm. "Rag, don't." Still in her clutches, he continued toward Annie.

Annie did not show any outward sign of preparing to protect herself from attack. Instead, she stood with arms folded over her chest, as if waiting for a serious response that would make sense. "Do you really think a savage attack on me is the best way to make your point that you are not a savage?"

Bo gripped his spear with both hands and stepped in front of Rag, forcing him to stop the advance. "Hold on, Mister Longbow, I understand your anger. You don't know Annie Henderson. I barely do. I would be just as mad at such an attack on my lifestyle, but I need to warn you not to mix it up physically with her, if that is what you have on your mind. Regardless how young and delicate she appears, you won't win. That's a guarantee from a guy bigger and likely stronger than even you."

Annie went limp and nodded to Bo. "I'm sorry." She took a breath and turned back to Rag. She dropped limp-wristed hands on her hips and allowed her body to relax. She closed her eyes, took a breath and sighed. "Look, I apologize for the anger in my voice. I spoke too quickly and without realizing how disrespectful it must have sounded. But I cannot, and will not, deny my utter disdain for what is the main food source here in Old Dallas. It wasn't meant to be a display of contempt for you, personally, and certainly not Elizabeth and Lizzy. Honestly, I had no intention of goading you into a fight." She brought her voice down into an even calmer range. "It's just that I can't express strongly enough my dislike for your dietary choice and can't understand why you don't see cannibalism as intolerable too. That's all." She stepped toward Rag with a friendly hand extended. "Will you forgive me for my outburst?"

He stared at her extended hand.

"Please?"

After another second staring at her hand, he hesitantly took it into his. "I suppose. I can't deny that I'd be dead by now if you and your friend hadn't come to our rescue. Regardless of your feelings about our way of life, I shouldn't forget that."

Lizzy ran to him and wrapped her arms around his waist. "She saved you, Daddy."

"That she did," Elizabeth said, nodding while gazing at her husband, adoration obvious. She pressed the side of her head onto his shoulder for a moment.

Bo relaxed his stance and leaned the spear against the wall. "Can we all just rest now? For heaven's sake, I'm tired."

Yowl mimicked his release of tension. The wolf followed his own tail in a slow circle and lay upon the floor.

Rag lifted his chair from the floor and set it upright and dropped onto it again. Elizabeth sat next to him while Annie pulled a chair out and sat across from them. "Rag, I don't want to argue. I just want to understand. Do you crave human flesh?"

"Do I eat meat? Yes. Do I enjoy eating meat? Oh yes. Do I crave humans specifically? No. Neither does my family, nor anyone else in the Garden District for that matter."

"Are you confident speaking for everyone in your community like that?"

"Yes, very confident."

"But you and your neighbors will eat humans, right?"

"Sure. It's within the law and it's wasteful not to. Why do you ask?"

"A friend of mine, a very good friend, is a talented woman who knows things no one else can…things like the future, people in distant places, what they think and how they live, without having to physically stand before them. She can enter a person's dreams. Her name is Dame Fortune. That's what she calls herself anyhow. I call her Dame and I love her. She entered my unconscious mind last year and we traveled the world in a matter of minutes. She brought me here. I saw you, Elizabeth and Lizzy. Dame told me that an exclusive diet of human flesh drives people insane."

"Are you trying to tell me that I'm crazy?"

"Not at all. I'm trying to determine how many years of such a diet it takes to affect a person's ability to remain rational. I'm also thinking that since you folks in this neighborhood amend your diet with fruits and vegetables, whatever mental damage is done can be reversed, or at least be minimal if already permanent."

Rag looked sideways at Elizabeth. "It's something I haven't considered since this is the only way of life we've ever known. It also might explain why Brickyard hooligans seem bent on breaking laws that are supposed to be common to both sides of the boundary. It's becoming markedly worse over time."

"Am I right to assume that all those people on the other side of the boundary eat human flesh exclusively?"

Rag nodded. "I think so." He looked again to his wife as if Annie's thoughts on the situation were coming to him as credible. "That sure would explain the increasing brutality I've witnessed over the years that just isn't evident here in the Garden District." He again turned to Elizabeth, put a loving hand on her shoulder and said in a slow thoughtful way, "I've often wondered how we can live so close to them, yet be so different." He paused and looked back to Annie. "Your assessment, if true, would explain a lot."

Annie rose. "The simple fact that you're considering what I've said as possible tells me all I need to know about your state of mind. It's sound. Sleep on what we've discussed and we'll talk again tomorrow." Annie put a contemplative finger to her lips. "One last question: Elizabeth, were you aware that a woman and her three brothers went missing today?"

"No, I was not aware of it at all."

"Your family has rules to try and stay safe by having a set check-in time every day. How about your friends and neighbors? Do they all have such rules?"

"Every family handles it differently. Some simply assume the worst and never question. They might mourn for a time quietly, but, otherwise, never mention a disappearance in the family or speak of it at all, unless specifically asked the whereabouts of an individual. It shouldn't be that way. But, it is, I'm afraid."

Annie sighed and shook her head. "That is so bizarre to me. It bends the definition of love to the breaking point."

"Before we sleep," Rag said, "I need to tell you that there might not be time for discussions once dawn breaks. I'm sure they won't allow theft of food to go unanswered. By that, I mean the liberation of me and my neighbors. They will attack," Rag said. "I'm sure of it, but I'm just as certain they won't do anything tonight. They're no more familiar with the layout of our neighborhood than we are of theirs. Rain and darkness will keep them away long enough to rest."

"If we pitch in and work together, I think we can defend your turf." Annie reexamined the living space. "Your house is too small. Could Bo, Yowl and I sleep in that garden shed out back? That should keep the rain off."

"Sure," Elizabeth said as she came to her feet. "There's a spongy compost pile in there. I'll get a canvas to cover it with. You can sleep on that. It should provide a measure of comfort."

"Good enough," Bo said, already walking toward the rear of the house. "I'm so tired I might be able to sleep standing up."

Elizabeth led them through the rear of the house and outside into the yard. The rain had slowed to a gentle shower but remained steady and seemed as though it might linger through the night. Occasional lightning flashed and thunder became distant. The heaviest and worst was over. Washed clean, the air smelled fresh.

They entered the shed. Elizabeth shook out and then spread a tarpaulin over a framed area containing a pile of blackened composting vegetation. It had an earthy smell, nothing objectionable. "I hope this is good enough for a pleasant night's sleep," Elizabeth said.

Bo collapsed onto the makeshift bed. "Oh yes, better than I deserve." Yowl curled up beside him.

"I hope you and your family can relax and get some rest too," Annie said as she removed the belts holding the weapons that crossed her chest.

Elizabeth sighed. "Thanks to you and Bo, we will." She hesitated and offered Bo a very personal smile. "Good night and sleep well." She stepped out and closed the door behind her.

Annie leaned her bow against one of the shed's four debarked cedar corner posts and then slipped the strap of the arrow quiver over her head and hung it from a protruding peg on the same post. Rain plinked on the patchwork of corrugated roofing metal only inches above her head. She lowered her body onto the tarpaulin and lay on her back, resting her head on laced fingers of both hands. Although tired, eyelids heavy, Annie's mind spun out random thoughts, but then settled on one.

"Bo?"

"Yeah?" he said in a sleepy drawl.

"Do you believe there is a God?"

Bo rolled his head to face her. He suddenly seemed more alert. "Do you mean an all-knowing, all-seeing ghostly sort of guy?"

"Well, yeah...sort of." She pulled her eyebrows into a questioning frown. "Why couldn't it be a woman?"

He snickered. "Why does it have to be one or the other...or human appearing at all?" He rolled his head to face her and grinned. "I guess since we're fantasizing, it might as well be a woman. And, since we've gone that far, let's say she's very pretty."

She playfully backhanded him on the upper arm. "Fantasizing? So, you *don't* believe in God?"

"Not on this planet."

"How come?"

"Look at where we are and what we're doing. If there was a god, would we be spending our week trying to prevent people from eating one another?"

"Hmm…you might be right…don't know." She paused and then rolled onto her side to fully face him. "But think about the series of events that brought us here. I can't believe that it was all coincidence. It's almost as though a hand guided me in a particular direction for a specific purpose. Think about it. Yowl found us a couple of days ago, defended us and then led Eva and I to you…someone whose life began here in Old Dallas, a place I knew virtually nothing about but which weighed heavily on my conscience. Then I discovered that you knew exactly where this place was located. Most importantly, your abrupt appearance in my life provided the final motivation for me to do something I intended all along. Not only those things, but the timing of our arrival here proved crucial to saving the life of the most important and influential individual in the Garden District. There has to be more at work here than coincidence. I believe there is a guiding force in all this."

"A woman?"

"Sure. Why not?"

"Like Dame Fortune?"

She lifted her head. "Oh, wow. I've never thought about that." She paused. "But, no. Actually, I'm thinking about some-*one*, or some-*thing*, guiding her as well."

"You still prefer it to be a woman, right?"

"Of course."

"Good night, Annie."

"Good night, Bo…you, too, Yowl."

She heard a contented snort from the big wolf. Then she, too, drifted off to sleep.

* * *

"Annie girl, I must be tellin' ya somethin'. Come to me, child."

Annie looked around. She knew this place well. It was the hill overlooking home, the compound called Myrna's Glory. The countryside was beautiful, too beautiful. The sky was blue, too blue. Asleep and dreaming had to be the reason. "Dame, is that you?"

A beautiful young and sighted black woman materialized at some distance—the way Dame Fortune chose to appear when she visited Annie in dreams. In a blink, she came to stand before Annie. She was not the portly, blind black woman with scars around her milky eyes and cottony white hair that Annie had left behind at Myrna's Glory. This woman was beautiful, glowing with celestial radiance. "It be me for a fact, child." The voice coming from this magnificent creature was unmistakably Dame Fortune's.

"Why have you come?"

"You be underestimatin' da size of your problem in dat place."

"Are you saying I can't trust the Longbows?"

"Dat not at all be what I mean, child. I be sayin' dere are far too many of doze bad people in da Brickyard District ta be takin' on straightaway. You must take all doze dat will join you and get away from dere. Defendin' your getaway be all dat you can hope to do, cuz ya can't stand and fight dem all. No good be comin' from a head-on battle. Run, child, run…run…run…"

Annie sprang from sleep and leapt to her feet.

Bo woke, startled. "What's the matter?"

She opened the door to the garden shed and saw the first ribbon of light in the east. Dawn was breaking. "We've got to get out of here or we'll be trapped and die."

"How can you know this? You seemed confident when we went to bed last night that we could win a confrontation."

"Dame came to me in my sleep. She warned me that we can't win in a head-to-head battle."

Bo frowned. "You believe a warning that came to you in a dream? You can't be serious."

"Oh, yes, very serious. I know what Dame is capable of and she's never wrong. If she saw fit to warn me in a dream, then that can only mean she foresaw a bloody end to us all if we don't act and do it quickly." Annie put her head through the strap on her arrow quiver and tossed it onto her back. She placed the two belts of remaining spiked throwing disks and knives, one over each shoulder, crossing over her chest. She then shouldered her bow on top of that. "Come on."

Yowl came to his feet after Bo. They hurried outside. "Wake Rag and his family and get them out of here."

"What if they don't believe or listen to me?"

"I don't have time to discuss alternatives. Remember though, Rag himself realized an attack was coming. That should make it easier to convince them. If not, here's your chance to use your persuasive nature and imposing appearance. If need be, have Yowl snarl at them. Just don't give them a chance to argue about it. After you get the Longbows out, knock on every door you can, rouse the entire neighborhood and warn them. I'm going back to the roof on that old four-story building and see what's going on in the brickyard. With a little luck, maybe I can determine how much time we have and against what kind of odds."

Annie took off running without looking back and covered the distance in scant seconds, then went into the old building, up the stairs, and onto the roof. She raced across it, coming to an abrupt stop at the edge. She squatted, and sitting back on the heels of her boots, she watched and listened. The sight chilled her. At least a hundred men and women had gathered across the divide in the Brickyard District, massing for an attack on the Garden District. It seemed clear enough by the presence of sheer numbers that the Brickyard would, not only, be out for blood, but total annihilation of everyone—men, women and children—in the Garden District. More streamed in, swelling the ranks. All brandished some type of weapon, chanting up the planned attack. In just the few seconds since arriving on the rooftop, the crowd mushroomed into a formidable Brickyard army, and was still amassing. If that bunch was as insane as she believed them to be, they had annihilation on their perverted minds, with a gluttonous consumption orgy of human flesh to follow. The force could grow to three hundred or more at this rate. The only questions that remained doggedly fixed in her mind were: Will they attack in small waves before the force is fully assembled? Or will they wait and attempt one massive and decisive onslaught? She hoped for the latter because that would give them more time to get out of town, plus she would know where they would be when hell unleashed. But preparing for a piecemeal attack by smaller contingents would be the better way, attacking on several fronts. She had to assume that someone over there was smart enough to figure that out. This was no time to be second-guessing. She must plan for a worst-case scenario, wave after wave of smaller forces.

She hurried back to the Garden District neighborhood and saw that Bo had successfully recruited Rag and his family. The four hurried from house to house, rousing people. Rag shouted repeatedly for everyone to join him and his family in a specific area designated for emergency communal gatherings.

As people coming into the central meeting place outside slowed to a trickle, Rag climbed up and stood on a large concrete slab. "Listen everyone, Brickyard hooligans are gathering for an attack. This is not a hunting expedition to pick off a few of us. It's clear they plan on bringing an end to the Garden District altogether. Our lives…" He swept a finger across the crowd. "… All our lives…every one of us gathered here will become their feast before nightfall. I believe this to be fact." He paused to let that information sink in before adding, "They *will* have extermination of every man, woman and child in the Garden District as their goal."

The group became a buzz of whispers and grew louder until a male voice shouted, "Then we arm ourselves and fight! This is *our* home!"

"There are too many of them, many more than I ever thought to live in the Brickyard."

Annie hurried to his side, topping his comment with, "I just came from the top of that building over there and saw over a hundred gathered and more coming to join them. They were streaming in like ants to a mound."

"Even if only a hundred, that's more than the entire population of this neighborhood," said a panicked woman.

"Right," Rag said. "That's the point. If we attempt to stay and fight, they won't stop until all of us, children included, are killed and flayed for butchering. We have no choice but to leave our homes and not come back."

"That's not a plan!" a man shouted angrily. "It's just a fast way to end up homeless and hungry!"

"If we don't go, it's a fast way to be killed and you won't have to worry about shelter or hunger," Rag shot back. He took in a calming breath. "Look folks, here's the truth: If we stay, we die. There's nothing else that needs to be said."

Although Rag succinctly detailed the problem, Annie saw in Rag's eyes that he wanted to offer a choice, provide a measure of assurance, but demanding quick acceptance was all he had time for. They must leave the only life they had ever known and run. Annie read concern for these people in the way Rag spoke to them. He cared for them. That was clear enough.

He looked to Annie with questioning eyes. After a speechless couple of seconds, he looked back to the crowd. He connected visually with most of them. "You are all friends and families I've known my whole life. My first concern is the survival of us all. Beyond that, I—I don't know what to say." He looked to Annie. "The only thing I could possibly add is that this girl, this stranger, saved my life last night at great peril to her and her friend. I trust her vision of what's about to happen. I tell you now that you should too."

"She also saved the lives of my brothers and me last night," said a woman who came forward, followed by the three men who had been bound on the floor with her. They bore bloody bruises from the bindings on their arms and legs as proof. "We have all grown totally complacent with the disappearance of our friends and neighbors, always assuming those missing were killed and consumed by Brickyard hooligans." The woman swung a frustrated sweeping gesture across the crowd. "None of you even questioned the whereabouts of me and my three brothers. I don't care if that's the way it has always been. It's wrong—terribly wrong. Things *must* change or we are all doomed by our own dwindling numbers." The woman turned her attention and focused on Annie. "There is no way to describe what I saw this young woman do, other than to tell you not to be fooled by the way she looks. She's much more than a pretty teenager. She is a warrior like no other."

"She is for a fact. But that's not the point of my trust in her," Rag said. "She comes from somewhere beyond this dying city and she may have ideas for us. If so, let's leave this place and the Brickyard bastards behind to eat one another, not us." Rag looked to Annie and asked somewhat tentatively, "Do you have ideas for us, if we choose to leave Old Dallas and the Garden District behind forever?"

Annie stepped forward. "I sure do. Bo, Yowl…the black wolf there, and I came here from a place called Myrna's Glory. It's a two-day walk southwest of Old Dallas. We need to go now. You will be welcomed, houses will be built, and livelihoods will be created for all of you. This is my personal guarantee to each of you, but we have to leave now or I can't insure your safety. There is no time to gather personal items. We have to hurry so we might exit Old Dallas undetected and avoid a bloody confrontation."

"But, we have to at least take food," a man said.

"We can hunt and forage once we're safely in the countryside," Annie replied.

"You mean there are enough humans outside the city to keep us fed?" another man asked.

"No! If you follow me to Myrna's Glory, human flesh will *never* touch your lips again. Understood?"

"That's crazy!" a man shouted. "We must have meat."

"And you shall have it—as much as you want—just not human flesh," Annie said.

The crowd hummed with whispered questions and concerns. One stood out. "We don't understand."

"The only animals you ever see are strays that occasionally wander this deep into Old Dallas. Over the decades, you have come to believe that there is no more game, because those few strays are all you see. So you turned to a lifestyle that is abhorrent to anyone outside this dying city, yet has become commonplace, everyday life to you. Once we are in the country, beyond these decrepit crumbling piles of junk, wild game abounds. We can hunt for turkey, squirrels, deer, wild hogs, feral cattle, goats and sheep, plus many other meat sources."

"You say there's plenty?" a man asked, his voice steeped with skepticism.

"I do. You have my word and my guarantee," Annie said, and then turned an ear westward. "The time for debate is over. I hear rumblings of war getting louder."

"I don't hear anything," Rag said, "aside from our own discontent."

"Like I told you," Bo said with a half-grin, "Annie can do things. Hearing things you and I cannot is one of them. Now, let's stop talking and start walking. We have to put distance between us and this place quickly, and do it out of sight of an insane and very angry army."

Grumbling men, women and children fell in behind Rag, Elizabeth, Lizzy, Bo, Yowl and Annie. The exodus from Old Dallas had begun. About a dozen refused to believe that the situation was that serious or would change so drastically and stayed. Annie and Rag could not convince them otherwise, but time for debate had run out.

As they walked, Annie looked back and estimated that about seventy-five had joined the escape. "Everyone stay close together. Do not stray. If one must stop, we all stop. None of us will be safe until we make it into the countryside. I'm certain those from the Brickyard believe as you do, that they cannot survive outside Old Dallas. I feel safe in saying that to them, the edge of the city is the edge of the world. I know most of you are thinking the same thing. It's not true. Please trust me." She faced forward and picked up the pace.

Lizzy left her mother's side and sidled close to Annie. "This is exciting," she said, and then looked up to Annie. "I sure do like you."

Annie tingled, suddenly emotionally charged. "Oh, sweetheart, I like you too... very much."

They walked side by side. Annie stroked Lizzy's hair. Annie's nemesis, exaggerated compassion, swarmed her. Along with it came a rush of fear. Lizzy had pointed out that she, along with seventy-five other souls, placed full trust in her to get them safely away to begin a new life. The awesome responsibility she bore this group hit hard. If struck by lightning from the storm last night, it would have had no greater impact. None of the people following her knew any other way of living than what they were leaving behind. They carried few weapons, no food or water and no extra clothing. Accountability for one's own safety is one thing, but the responsibility of maintaining the safety of this number in a hostile environment was huge. Annie's fear threatened to reel out of control. It was greater than any she had yet known in her life. *Keep it together, girl,* she thought. *You can't let them see a shred of fear, regardless how bleak it seems.*

Chapter 8

The Exodus

Bo would rather have gone with Annie and Rag, but he had to agree with her that the nervous group needed a visual sign of leadership guiding them. Everyone would remain calmer and together, moving in the same direction at the same speed. He watched Annie and Rag move to the rear. All from the Garden District that chose to join the exodus meandered their way toward the southern limit of Old Dallas behind Bo and his friend, Yowl.

Bo also agreed that a guard had to defend the rear if Brickyard hooligans chose to give chase. She had told him in the gravest way, "Bo, I believe it's *when* not *if*. There will be an attack." Her assessment made sense. An assault seemed plausible. They simply could not move fast enough to stay ahead of an angry mob. Reticence was plain in their speed of retreat. People were scared to run, yet frightened to remain. The best Bo could hope for was to keep the retreat moving regardless of speed.

His over-the-shoulder view shifted from Annie and Rag's retreat to the rear of the crowd itself. He continually checked his pace to keep from opening up a lead that might leave them exposed to an attack, but made for a slower trek than he felt safe with. They had been on the move for over an hour and had not detected pursuers. It was no comfort and no guarantee of safety.

Annie appointed Bo as group leader because he was the only one who knew how to escape Old Dallas by navigating the side streets in the crumbling decay without being seen. He accepted the appointment without argument when Annie reminded him that he had done it seventeen years ago, even though these circumstances were drastically different. He now dealt with a large group moving at different speeds. The net result was that they walked no faster than the smallest, oldest and slowest. It worried him to jaw-clenching frustration. Heightened nervousness made him wary of any and all extraneous movement that caught his eye. Birds winging by, or leaves kicked up by the breeze kept darting eyes busy. If he was traveling alone, he could move faster up to his knees through a muddy bog, but he had to keep them together to offer that all-important sense of security.

After another half hour, his charges began stringing out behind him. It was a comfortably mild morning. The thunderstorm of the night before had cleansed the air. The beautiful morning, birds singing, and fresh clean air might have been contributing to an ill-timed general feeling of safety and well-being. It appeared as though most were becoming too comfortable. After an hour of walking, they had not encountered any of the Brickyard bunch. He heard calm conversations, even laughter—a sure sign of misplaced optimism. He had to remain alert for them. Lives depended on it. "Keep it tight, people," he called out. "We need to stay closer together. We're not out of trouble yet."

Elizabeth took Lizzy's hand and quickened her step to catch up to and then walk next to Bo. "We haven't had a chance to talk. I'm thankful and happy that you're alive and here with us."

Without facing her, he said, "I wouldn't have been here at all if Annie hadn't appeared in my life and spoke of Old Dallas. I came so close to dying of thirst and starvation getting out of here the first time, I tried hard to forget it." His eyes swept the horizon. "This place hadn't crossed my mind in years... until she showed up."

Elizabeth's shoulders drooped. Her head drifted down into a slump. "Oh."

Bo snapped a sideways glance. "Of course if I'd known you were here and in trouble, I'd have come on my own."

She lifted her head, face glowing with fresh enthusiasm. He now took a longer look at his childhood playmate. She had grown into a lovely woman with a child of her own. Elizabeth had matured beautifully, from that gangly ten-year-old with a dirty face and wildly disheveled brown hair. He smiled, remembering it so well. As children they'd spent every day together, playing from sunup to sundown. He became enamored, staring at her face until it occurred to him how self-conscious it must make her feel. He stammered, "As you can see, I'm much bigger now, but just as hairy and ugly as ever."

"Ugly?" she blurted, "You're a beautiful human being... you big lug." She backhanded him on the arm. "You were back then and you still are."

Bo's heart swelled. Memories filled his head from that time all those years ago when he and Elizabeth were inseparable. It now seemed like no time at all had passed and they were once again the best of trusted friends. "How has life been for you? I mean... married to Rag? Has he been good to you?"

"Yes, very good," she said and then looked over to Lizzy. "We have this beautiful child together." She smiled adoringly at the youngster. "Rag has been a model husband and father."

Bo looked over his shoulder again to check on the crowd following them. They appeared to be staying together and calm, considering the dire circumstances they shared. It still worried him that they were overconfident. To retain a slight edge of fear would be the safer choice, keeping them wary and observant a while longer.

So that Lizzy would not hear, he leaned sideways and whispered into Elizabeth's ear, "I know it's none of my business and you don't have to answer, but I'm compelled to ask a personal question."

"Go ahead. Ask anything."

"Do you love Ragland?"

Elizabeth's pleasant expression slowly faded. She stared straight ahead. "I would never betray Rag, or walk away. If it weren't for him, I'm not sure what might have happened to me by now." She took a step closer to Bo and looked up at him. There was an unmistakable twinkle in her eye that followed a smile.

Without verbal clarification, Bo had his answer. The childhood bond had been rekindled, but she'd made it quite clear there could be nothing beyond friendship, even though feelings for Ragland Longbow seemed to be limited to gratitude and the loyalty that came with it.

Still, it put his animal-like appearance back on his mind. He surreptitiously lifted his hand and looked at the back of it. Thick, dark brown hair covered it all the way down to long tough fingernails. To lend credibility to the move, should Elizabeth notice, he reached and stroked the back of Yowl's head, as the wolf walked contentedly next to him. Living with the canine for so many years, he'd lost self-consciousness about how he appeared to others. Now, how others viewed him had again become an issue—the presence of Elizabeth and knowing her feelings had everything to do with it.

Walking in silence, Bo flipped through a mental file of memories. All dealt with stories his parents had told him of people with the same affliction. People with his condition have been roaming the earth since time immemorial and like him, chose to remain isolated, at the fringes of society. It was easier than living among people with no hope of true assimilation. It was not easy being the center of attention as an oddity, a freak of nature. Centuries back, large overly hairy humans were given names like Bigfoot, Yeti, or Sasquatch, people who wanted nothing to do with the human race at large. They worked hard at staying out of sight, living in remote areas. He had heard that multiple generations sometime lived so isolated that they developed unique languages known only to them, and they sounded animal-like to people who might have stumbled upon them and heard it.

Bo glanced again at Elizabeth, this time with renewed hope that living as a human among humans was not as farfetched as he once believed. Thanks to her, a sliver of hope rekindled. To love and be loved might actually be possible.

"Tell me about Annie," Elizabeth asked.

"Huh?"

"Annie… tell me about her."

"Sorry, lost in thought."

Elizabeth smiled and nudged him with her shoulder. "I could tell."

"There's not much about Annie I can share. My own opinion of her is still developing. I do get a good feeling that she's quite sincere about helping people and willing to risk her life to accomplish it."

"She seems extraordinary."

"You don't know how true that is." He scratched his head. "As a cold fact, I have a strong feeling that I've only seen a tiny bit of what that girl is capable of. I'm fairly certain that the word 'extraordinary' may be woefully inadequate in defining Annie Henderson. There're many things about her we'll both be learning in time." He glanced and hinted a smile. "I think she's a keeper though."

She chuckled but then turned serious. "Where do you think Rag and Annie are right now?"

He looked over his shoulder to the rear and did not see them. "Probably farther back and hiding, watching our trail, keeping an eye out for those who would harm us."

"Should I be worried?"

After hesitating, he replied, "I don't think so. That said, if we don't see them by the time the sun hits its noon zenith, we'll stop. That'll give Yowl and I time to walk back and check on them."

Yowl abruptly halted, ceased panting, snapped his jaws shut and raised his head. He turned an ear to the direction Annie and Rag had gone. He stood frozen; only the pulse of his sniffing nostrils moved.

Bo stopped walking and gave the wolf full attention. "What is it, friend? What do you hear?"

Yowl's lip twitched. He snarled. Golden eyes set in hair black as midnight seemed to glow anger. He turned and ran in the opposite direction of their escape.

"Elizabeth, stay here. Yowl senses something. Annie and Rag may be in trouble. I have to go find them."

Just as he began to jog, a horn sounded about five hundred paces back. It must have been a mustering signal for attacking forces. Bo stopped and shouted, "Who has come armed?"

Six hands went up holding a variety of crude weapons—clubs, sharpened staffs, jagged shards of metal fashioned with handles as battle axes and the like.

"Follow me," Bo shouted. "The rest of you stay put. For safety's sake stay close together, very close. Huddle if you have to."

* * *

The shrill horn blast brought Annie out of hiding. She spun around to see a human form hundreds of paces away, standing atop the tall ruins of a grain storage silo. They had been spotted.

She scoped the area for a defensible location. Her eyes landed on a narrow alley between the remnants of two buildings. The walls were crumbling but it appeared as though it might provide a defensible long narrow corridor. As she sprinted toward Rag, she shouted, "Get between those walls!" She caught up to him and both ran for the narrow passageway strewn with rubble. The combination of narrowness and fallen bricks should slow and funnel attackers into a narrow column.

Before reaching the safer location, Annie heard the dull thunder of running feet coming their way. "Stay at my back. Our only chance is to make it so they can't surround us. We must force them to come at us in small numbers."

Rag was armed with a crude, heavy eighteen-inch knife and a hatchet created from an odd shaped piece of quarter-inch steel, tied to a wooden handle and sharpened. He stood ready, facing the rear of the alley, weapon in each hand. "I'll slide straight into hell before I'll let them take me this time," he growled.

Annie stepped backward until her back touched Rag's. She prepared for a frontal assault while he braced to cover the rear. She assessed weapons. She still had over twenty arrows in the quiver, a dozen spiked throwing disks and double that number of six-inch throwing knives. She also had the second knife Ethan Turlock had made for her, sheathed in its ornately tooled leather scabbard and strapped

to her waist. She took note of the pouch full of glass marbles
Lizzy had given her. In that moment, the slingshot seemed
the better weapon to begin with.

The first attackers appeared from around the corner of a
large pile of rubble about a hundred paces out. It was clear
on every face that negotiating a truce was out of the question.
All she saw were crazed empty eyes and rage on scores of
men and some women.

Annie snatched a handful of marbles from the pouch and
placed one in the pocket centered on the sling. She swung it
once, and then once more at blurring speed, before releasing
one end of the leather thong. The marble whizzed at
phenomenal velocity with a high-pitched hiss, hitting the
lead attacker between the eyes. It embedded in his skull,
flipping him backward.

The horde of thugs lost momentum, surprised and maybe
frightened that a shot could be made at that distance with
damaging speed and accuracy. Annie heard one of them
shout, "Luck! Nothin' but luck!"

Again they began to advance, then to run—screaming in
a primal bloodlust sort of way.

Annie swung and released the next marble—it, too, was
deadly accurate.

"How do you do that?" Rag asked.

"I hope I have the opportunity to explain it. For now,
keep your eyes trained on the alley behind us." She released
another marble. Like the first two, it hit a man in the forehead
with a loud crack. He collapsed.

No longer believing in luck, the assailants began
zigzagging as they charged. It did not help as they entered
the narrow alley. Another marble found its mark.

Annie accelerated the speed of release. Men racing
toward them reached formidable numbers, all psychopaths.
She now dropped men at the rate of one per second.

A number of the men split off and ran around the rubble of the still-standing walls Annie and Rag stood between.

"Get ready!" Annie shouted as she sent the last marble whizzing. "Some're coming around to attack from the rear!" The marble struck the nearest man in the head, flipping him, dead by the time he hit the ground.

She dropped the slingshot and pulled spiked throwing disks from the belt across her chest. Taking one in each hand, she flung them simultaneously. Keen marksmanship guided them to death-dealing strikes in both cases, but her aim began to suffer from the necessary speed of release to keep from being overrun.

Attackers kept coming in waves, but they had to funnel down to more manageable numbers to enter the alley where she and Rag made their stand. Annie heard Rag engage the first of those charging from the rear. She had no time to look as she sent two more disks toward targets, one embedding in the left side of a man's chest, the other a gut shot to the man next to him. Both fell and writhed in agony.

Bodies stacking up in the alley slowed the attack, leaving Annie time to check on Rag behind her.

Although valiant, he was not blessed with Annie's speed. He slashed with broad strokes at three men abreast, doing little more than keeping them at bay.

She pulled two of the six-inch throwing knives and hurled them, sending them sailing past Rag on each side of his head and dropping the two outside men. That only left the one in the center, and Rag slammed the hatchet into the side of his neck, dispatching him without trouble.

By the time Annie turned back to resume her own battle, she was about to be swarmed by raving armed men too close for bow and arrows; even throwing knives would be of little value at such close range.

Annie heard Rag groan and glanced to see a spear penetrating entirely through the lower right side of his abdomen. She whimpered, realizing how close he was to losing his life, and there was nothing she could do about it.

Annie pulled the knife from its scabbard on her hip and engaged men wielding knives, clubs and spears. She fought furiously, but there were too many. Suddenly, she heard agonized screams from beyond the alley ahead, and she hesitated long enough to look.

It was Yowl. Hackles raised high, snarling, growling and slobbering, the big wolf grabbed attackers by their throats one after the other. A remorseless and systematic killing machine, the animal worked his way to the alley entrance and blocked it, guarding against easy access to her and Rag.

Annie turned her attention to Rag. He was already blood soaked from the wound on his side, and the blood was spreading down one leg. He weakened, barely keeping attackers off, unable to inflict disabling wounds on anyone.

She shrugged the bow off her shoulder, nocked an arrow and let it fly. It took out Rag's nearest attacker, who was immediately replaced by another. With speed approaching impossible, Annie's arrows flew one after the other, dropping half a dozen men within scant seconds, when she heard Yowl yelp.

She spun around but could not see where the wolf was. Her attention suddenly split between Rag's predicament behind her and Yowl's ahead of her, she figured she might have an extra second or so as a result of the men she took out, before Rag would again be in jeopardy.

She sprinted to the end of the alley and saw Yowl fighting but he had a bloody gash on his shoulder. He limped, movement hampered. A man charged the wolf with a club.

Annie stuck him with an arrow before he could bring the weapon down on Yowl's head. Another was now charging with a long sharp staff while the animal was distracted by fighting another armed man.

Annie did not know which way to turn. Rag had fallen and was now fighting from a seated position.

Suddenly, Bo and a group of men entered the rear of the alley running and charging the attackers, weapons raised, forcing the thugs to abandon the attack on Rag and defend from behind. With a spear in one hand and a knife in the other, Bo slashed and stabbed his way through, giving Annie a vital extra second to send an arrow whizzing at Yowl's attacker—one the wolf had not noticed.

Apparently, the sudden appearance of Bo and the men with him were enough to force a retreat by the Brickyard gang. Bo made his way to the last man standing some distance away—the one still bent on taking out Rag, who had weakened to the point of sitting, legs splayed. Hatchet and knife remained in his hands but lay useless on the ground on each side of him. As the man lifted a spear high over his head, Rag only had strength remaining to look up at the guy and shout through clenched teeth, "Come on, you bastard of hell, get it over with!"

As the attacker began his downward thrust with the long sharpened staff to stab Rag, Bo ran as fast as he could, yelling, "Here! Behind you!" Still running, Bo threw his spear as hard as he could. It hit the man in the back, the barbed point exiting through the man's sternum.

The man's body seized but momentum had already been established. As he fell forward, the spear drove deep into Rag's gut.

Annie saw it happen and raced back to join Bo. They ran together over to Rag.

It was too late.

Blood covered and unmoving, he gasped one last time. Ragland Longbow was dead.

Tears exploded from Annie's eyes. She threw the bow to the ground and collapsed to her knees next to his lifeless body. He stared into eternity, mouth agape and frozen.

Bo used his spear like a walking stick and guided his huge hairy body down onto his knees next to her. "I tried. I came too late. I'm so sorry." He put a comforting arm around Annie's shoulders.

She sniffed and drew a ragged breath. "It's not your fault. It's not even the fault of those psychopathic killers. It's this crazy world. It's out of control, the whole damn world!"

Bo pulled her closer and pressed her cheek into his chest. He whispered, "It's probably of little comfort at the moment, but I don't believe we'll have any more trouble from the Brickyard gang."

"How can you be sure?"

"I can't entirely. Survival is deeply ingrained and they don't waste food under any circumstances. They'll gather the bodies but it won't be for funerals, or memorials. All of these dead men will keep them busy long enough for us to get out of town."

Bo's matter-of-fact comment frightened her. She rose and looked around. "We must get Rag's body out of here. I won't let that happen to him." Annie looked at the men behind Bo that came to fight with him. She saw how they looked at the dead. It was as if they stumbled into a meat market. "You men," she shouted, "whatever is on your minds, it better not be making a meal of what you see! Remember your promise. If I see so much as an odd pinch of a corpse, you will be banished and not allowed to continue on with us! You *will* be turned out to survive on your own. Understood?"

The six men grumbled, acting like children denied treats. Finally, one stepped forward. "Oh, all right," he said.

Annie looked down at Rag as she rose to her feet. "Now, you men will have your first lesson in how to honor the fallen, a hero that gave his life for you. Who will help me carry him back to his family?"

Bo remained on his knees, head bowed. He wept.

"I thought I was the only one afflicted with such depth of feeling," she said.

He looked up at her. Tears tracked over the dark brown hair below his eyes and over his hairy cheeks. "Oh, Annie, how am I going to tell Elizabeth and Lizzy that it was I who had a chance to save him and didn't?"

"There was no way you could've saved him. It wasn't meant to be." She sank back down to her knees. It was Annie's turn to comfort Bo.

Chapter 9

Struggle on the Road Home

Twelve-year-old Lizzy Longbow's lower lip quivered. She sniffed and drew an uneven breath as she sat on her heels next to the pile of large stones where her daddy, Ragland Longbow, had been laid to rest. Annie stood next to her, caressing the top of the girl's head with gentle strokes, allowing her young friend time to mourn. She then went down on her knees too. The massive oak tree that shaded the entire area around the grave seemed appropriate. It served to symbolize Rag's strength and unbreakable love for his family.

To Annie, this period of respect should have been a normal circumstance following a death, but that was by her standards. Putting dead relatives in the ground was a foreign concept to these people. The enigma of how any sentient being could love another, yet have no qualms about ingesting friends, neighbors—even family members—as food remained beyond rational grasp.

Lizzy wept softly. She placed her head on her new friend Annie's shoulder. As Annie saw the girl watching her mother carry on a whispered conversation with Bo, she realized Lizzy had not come to fully trust the big hairy man.

He and Elizabeth sat on the ground, leaning against the same large tree shading the gravesite and most of a larger area. They sat intimately close, bodies inches apart. The big guy was helping Lizzy's mother, just as Annie helped her. Annie noticed that even though only twelve, Lizzy realized something special was going on between her mother and Bo. Right now, even as her eyes remained locked on the two of them, it was clearly her father that occupied her mind. After a time, she turned her head just enough to look up at Annie. "Was he brave?"

"Your daddy?"

"Yeah. Was he a good fighter?"

"Oh yes, sweetie. He did everything in his power to make sure you and your mother would be safe."

She snuggled the side of her face onto Annie's shoulder and sighed. "That's the way I want to remember him." She sat silent for a moment, and then asked, "Annie?"

"Yeah?"

"Did you mean what you said? I mean, you know, about the way we lived. Was it really all that bad?"

"Yes, but that doesn't make you, or anyone you love, bad people."

"I don't understand."

Annie pushed dancing strands of hair from Lizzy's face as a fresh breeze rustled the leaves in the big oak tree overhead. "Many years ago, big cities like Old Dallas were populated with hundreds of thousands of people, all different kinds. In parts of town where people were poor, teens formed gangs. They roamed the streets and stole things. They threatened people and came to rule by intimidation in certain areas of the city. For them it was a feeling of control and power where they otherwise had none. When the world began losing its grip on civilized society and money no longer held value, the gangs had never been outside the city, so their idea of survival was to steal food and other necessities of life until they'd driven everyone else out. Food markets vanished. Food stopped coming in from the countryside and finally, one day, there was no more. The gangs and the children born to them had no basic knowledge of survival if there was nothing left to barter for, given to them, or to steal. They had no notion of where food came from, or how to produce it. In time, they had no choice but to eat dying people, or they would starve to death too. From that beginning, it evolved into hunting expeditions against rival gangs, and from what I saw, that lifestyle normalized and has been perpetuated to this day. Just because it's the only life you, your family and your neighbors have ever known, doesn't make it right."

"I've never heard that story before," Lizzy said.

Annie again put her arm around the girl and gave her a squeeze. "When we get back to where I live and the place that will be your new home, I'll introduce you to very special people who will tell you many stories about the world and how we all came to be where we are now. Jake Henderson is my father," she chuckled. "At least I think of him that way. And, I really want you to meet a wonderful old lady we call Dame. You'll meet other great folks that'll teach you plenty, but those two will teach you about history… where we all came from and how the world came to be what you see around you."

Lizzy sat silent for a time but finally said, "I think I like you."

Annie smiled. "Oh, sweetie, we're going to be great friends." She gave Lizzy another tight hug. "You just sit here as long as you like. I'm going to take a few of the men and go hunting for dinner."

Lizzy watched her new friend.

"I'll be back soon," Annie said as she stood.

Lizzy quietly said, "The first things I'm going to ask Mister Henderson when I meet him are: What is money, and what are food markets?"

Annie stopped so fast her step stuttered. She looked down at Lizzy. Her jaw slackened and her lips parted, surprised at Lizzy's level of naiveté but then she simply smiled and nodded acknowledgement. "Yeah, that's a great idea."

Lizzy wiped tears from her cheeks and returned the smile. Even in grief, Annie read on the youngster's face that everything would be okay—that she would be okay.

Just as Bo guessed, they had no more trouble with the Brickyard gang. The remainder of the trip to the outskirts of Old Dallas was uneventful. They did not have to stop once until a suitable place to bury Rag was located. They chose a site offering dual purpose. It happened to be on the edge of dense woods next to a small stream, where Annie figured she would find good hunting in such a thicket next to a water source.

Knowing this group's propensity for cannibalism when hunger struck, she knew any delay in finding food would kindle that kind of thinking. She had already noticed a nice patch of dandelion greens and wild onions not far away; also, dewberries hung from clustered vines on lower limbs of trees along the trail they walked. She only had two arrows left and none of the throwing disks or throwing knives, but Lizzy still had a leather pouch loaded with glass marbles. With more than a day's walk remaining, she thought it best not to use the arrows if avoidable, especially if they could not be retrieved.

"Bo," she called out.

"Yeah?"

"How about you take a couple of the men and head upstream to see if you can spear some meat. I'll take two of the guys and head downstream and see what I can find in that direction. Deal?"

"I'll do it," he replied, and then resumed a whispered conversation with Elizabeth. It only lasted a few more seconds before he hugged her and then retrieved his spear from where it leaned against the tree they sat next to. "Come on, Yowl," he said to the wolf as he rose and brushed dried leaves from the monk's robe he wore. "Let's do as the lady requests and see what kind of meat we can find."

Annie approached two of the armed men who had helped Bo during the attack by the Brickyard gang. She led them into the woods. They had only walked a couple hundred yards when Annie heard a rustling on the opposite creek bank, a few paces farther ahead. She turned to the men and put a finger to her lips. In low tones, she said with some excitement, "Stay here. I'll check it out."

Lifting high on her toes, she ran in stages, stopping and listening at each hiding place en route. Finally, the rustle of brush and soft grunts helped identify the exact location of the potential quarry. She came from behind a big pecan tree, ran a ways and then slowed. She crouched near a tangled thicket of thorny vines, hunkering down next to a creek with only a trickle of water in it. Just across the creek she spotted three wild hogs rooting around. From the pouch hugging her hip, she retrieved a green glass marble that flashed the sun's glint. She kissed it. "Fly true and hit your mark," she whispered. After rolling the marble between her fingers a moment longer, she placed it in the centered pocket of the slingshot and swung it overhead once and then again fast. It struck one of the pigs in the side of the head with a thudding crack. It dropped where it stood.

The other two pigs seemed confused and stood quite still, looking at their fallen companion.

Now that's what I call good fortune, she thought, sending another marble sailing to drop another one. When the third wild hog took the hint and began running, Annie shrugged the bow off her shoulder, nocked one of the two remaining arrows and let it fly. The third pig went down.

As she trotted across the creek bed to retrieve the arrow, Annie shouted, "Come on, guys. We need to get these animals field dressed and back to camp."

The two men came running and stood behind her as she knelt to pull the arrow carefully from the pig carcass so that it might be reused. As she worked it backward from the wound, she said, "If Bo and the other two guys come up with anything at all, I think we'll have plenty…"

Something solid struck Annie hard on the side of the head, knocking her over onto her side.

A searing pain at the base of her skull snatched away capacity to think.

Vision skewed through swimming eyes, she rolled over to see one of the men holding a club ready to do it again. *He's trying to kill me!*

She had an instant vision of the day her mother was murdered when she was ten years old. It was almost identical to this scenario, turning her back on a stranger that had not earned trustworthiness and should have been watched. The scenario had begun playing out all over again. It could end with her carcass rotating on a spit over an open fire if she did not react immediately.

Pulling the knife from the scabbard on her hip, Annie knew she had no choice but to fight her body's tendency to slip from consciousness. Her attempt at self-protection proved ineffectual as the guy swung the club again, this time hitting her arm with a bruising smash as she moved it to cover her head.

The attacker said to the other one, "Hit her with the ax! The club is not gettin' it done! Hurry up and kill her! You saw what she can do if she gets to her feet!"

Annie had no choice but to take her chances with the club as she threw the knife at the man wielding a large, but crude, axe before he got it up to attack position. Unable to see clearly, she hoped her aim was good enough. It was an awkward throw but stuck the man on the side of his abdomen and spun him sideways.

He righted his stance and came at her again, lifting the axe for a downward chopping blow. As it came down, she rolled onto her side just as the blade hit the ground behind her.

Thwack!

The fletching feathers of the arrow still stuck in the animal were very near her face. She had already worked it out far enough that it dangled near the surface of the pig's hide.

When the man began to make a move to pull the ax from the ground for another swing at her, she pulled the arrow in a smooth quick motion, rolled back and grabbed the axe just above the blade stuck in the ground. She pulled it up, jerking the man off his feet. As he fell toward her, she held the arrow aimed at his heart and let him fall on it. She yanked the axe from his dying grasp and hacked the foot of the man about to take his next shot with the club.

The man's agonized scream echoed through the woods. Enraged, he prepared to take a final lethal shot at Annie's head, but as he raised the club, his body seized and he collapsed into a heap on the ground, unconscious.

Standing over him was the thief, Barney Tackitt, holding a stumpy tree limb in both hands. After a moment of keeping the limb suspended high and ready to swing it again, he saw the man was not getting up. "I swear. Some people just don't have an ounce of loyalty in their whole damn body." He tossed the makeshift club onto the unconscious recipient and dusted his hands.

Annie fell back and lay motionless, her eyes squeezed tightly shut, holding her aching head. She moaned, opened one eye, and checked the bloody bruise on her forearm. Then she opened the other eye and looked up at her unlikely savior. "I never thought a guardian angel would come packaged looking quite like you."

"I just wanted something to eat and those guys didn't look like the type that would share." He turned and took a step but then stopped and looked back. "If you like, I can go ahead and kill him for you." He grinned, as if he really did not mind.

As she rolled onto hands and knees and began to rise, she said, "I realize you don't know me very well but killing another human is never a first choice. Instead, it's the last, when all other options have been exhausted." Now, fully standing, she swooned.

Barney rushed to her side and caught her. "Steady now."

"Thanks. You just might turn into a friend yet."

Barney smirked sideways at her. "I don't think so."

Annie massaged her neck and moaned. "Why not?"

"Let's see. How can I put this gently? Oh, wait, I can't. I don't like the way you think and I don't like your giant hairy friend at all."

"Oh, Barney, I'll make a convert of you eventually."

"Not unless you suddenly accept thievery as an acceptable lifestyle. I don't see that as likely."

Bo suddenly came crashing through the brush. "Annie, are you okay?"

Barney released Annie and stepped behind her.

"A woman from the group found me and said there was some kind of commotion that sounded like a fight over here."

Still massaging a growing knot on the back of her head, she said, "I'll be okay, just whacked on the back of the head with a club. Unfortunately,"—she pointed at the men lying on the ground—"I think those two thought I looked tastier than the three pigs I dropped over there."

Bo stepped toward Barney.

From behind Annie, Barney put his hands on her shoulders and moved her as he would a shield to keep Bo from grabbing him.

"Did this weasel have anything to do with it?"

Barney held a hand out defensively. "Hold on, Fuzzy. I didn't have anything to do with that lump on her head."

"He didn't, Bo," Annie said. "In fact, Barney saved me from getting beaten to death."

"Well... thanks for that," Bo said then paused. "But I still don't like you... or trust you."

Barney smirked. "I can live with that."

"That's enough, boys. Barney, we're on our way home to Myrna's Glory. I wish you'd join us."

"Nah, too many rules."

"You don't know that. How could you?" Annie asked.

"With that many people living in one place, how could there not be? Besides"—he flipped a thumb toward Bo— "Ol' fuzzy face would probably spear me in my sleep."

Bo glared at him. "I'll grant you that it does sound like a good idea, but if I spear you, you'll be awake and facing me."

"Be nice, Bo," Annie said, and then turned to Barney. "Well, do what you want, but remember, if you ever change your mind, I'll see to it you're made welcome. Right, Bo?"

Bo turned his back on both of them. "Humph."

Barney gestured obscenely to Bo's back, and then told Annie, "If you don't mind, I'll just cut a hindquarter off one of those pigs and be on my way."

Annie rotated her head and stretched her neck. "Go ahead. That's the least I can do."

As Barney pulled his knife, he said, "I sort of thought so too." He squatted and began working on the pig.

Bo grabbed Annie's arm and pulled her away. He whispered, "Someday, you'll have to kill that guy."

"Maybe, but that day is not this one. Today, Barney Tackitt is my hero." She looked down at the two men sprawled on the ground, one unconscious, one dead. She finally had time and presence of mind to think about what had happened. "Why did they have to do what they did?" Tears welled in her eyes.

"You said it yourself. Eating the flesh of humans drives men crazy."

"It's not their fault. They couldn't have been in their right minds."

"Probably not," Bo said, "and that concerns me. How many of the others would do the same thing, if given a chance?"

Annie only nodded, not wanting to address that possibility. "Did these two have families?"

"The dead one was a loner. The one ol' Barn whacked has a wife, but no children."

Barney stood and put the hindquarter over his shoulder. He offered Bo a cocky two-finger salute and disappeared into the woods.

"Okay," Annie said, "let's get that meat back to camp and get it cooked. We have to get those people thinking about something other than hunger." Annie drew an exaggerated breath and sighed. "Then I have to talk to a woman I don't know and apologize for cutting a couple of her husband's toes off, and beg her help in preventing him from killing me when he regains consciousness." She groaned. "I hadn't noticed how bad my head hurts until this instant."

Chapter 10

Things You Find in the Woods

After the harrowing experience and arriving back at the campsite, Annie's sense of her surroundings sharpened. A lump throbbed on the back of her head, a painful reminder that those senses should have never been ignored. Smoke curled from a dozen small fires scattered throughout the cluster of hungry people, all cooking portions of the three wild hogs she'd killed. The men with Bo had also brought in a small deer and several dozen pigeon eggs. The women had gathered and provided wild onions, dandelion greens and dewberries to supplement—adequate to feed the escapees from Old Dallas, for now.

Bo resumed the renewed association with Elizabeth. Lizzy grew comfortable in the presence of Bo's imposing stature and hair-covered animal-like appearance, since her mother showed no fear of a man who resembled a bipedal maned lion. Elizabeth's face could not hide the truth; her sparkling affection for Bo showed in everything she said and did. Annie did not want to intrude on what appeared to be the genesis of a family unit in the making. He and Elizabeth needed time to reconnect as friends and, eventually, maybe something more. Love must be offered and accepted whenever and wherever possible in this insane world. It was turning out to be a miraculous blessing that those two found one another after so many years apart—another sign that what she did was guided by unseen hands.

As she watched Bo Juster and Elizabeth Longbow, she thought about that and the late night conversation with Bo about the existence of a deity. In retrospect, things that had happened and were happening felt as if planned, and not by her. There might be more to it than simply reacting to circumstances, as she originally thought. There was no proof, just an odd feeling of purpose beyond her control. The existence of a god, or gods, might be worth further consideration. Maybe a long chat with Dame Fortune was called for. After all, it was Dame who had told her not to ignore intuitive flashes that seized her on occasion with sudden clarity of thought on people and situations.

Annie sat alone at her small fire, thinking, nibbling on a chunk of pork skewered at the end of a long stick and well cooked over an open flame. As she ate, thoughts shifted from philosophical back to present reality. Scanning faces among the clustered escapees, she searched for an odd set of eyes that looked at another in an unusual way, as if wondering what that person would taste like. Since the attack on her earlier, she now realized that she had come to trust these people too soon; she needed to rein it in and keep a closer eye on them. Dame Fortune had been right. People treated her like their personal savior, or a conquering hero and all but bowed in worship to her. Yet, through smiles and gratitude, as Dame warned, they were a peculiar sort with a dangerous mindset bent toward cannibalism. She'd learned a lesson. The attack that almost took her life would not happen again. That she vowed.

She watched, with particular interest, the surviving member of the duo that attacked her. His wife tended to his injured foot, whispering into his ear. All the while, he said nothing back, just sat and stared with angry intensity across the campsite to where she sat nibbling on her dinner. His wife looked her way in flicking glances. She appeared no less angry. It did not take Dame Fortune's psychic ability. or advanced hearing to know the woman's whispered words were about her.

Annie hoped the man's wife reprimanded him for pulling such a foolish stunt, but she had to be honest with herself; his wife might not be trustworthy either. She might be instructing him on how to get it done efficiently next time. True or not, it had to be considered.

Annie stared a while longer and then shook it off, disgusted that she allowed mental demons to sprout. Paranoia was not her style. The woman had done nothing, nor displayed reason for suspicion, aside from an annoyed expression. That look may have been directed at her husband.

She now knew his name as Alister Beane, a congenial sounding name for a man with what might turn out to be an insatiable appetite for human flesh. She feared more trouble from him and others if that repulsive mindset could not be altered. She looked across the clustered families. *I wonder who among you might also present such a threat.*

While Annie thought things through, the sun sank below the western horizon. Light mellowed as shadows faded—the air calm, temperature mild. It was a pleasant spring early evening and everyone seemed at peace. Sleep should come easy tonight. She heard many murmured conversations, and regardless how far away they sat, she could tune her ears to any one of them and listen, if she chose to do so; however, an innate sense of right and wrong prevented it, unless danger seemed imminent. Instead, she reclined back onto her elbows and crossed her extended legs at the ankles and relaxed, ready to put this day behind her. Calmness permeated the air and she became drowsy. All those conversations blended into a gentle hum that lulled her. She flipped the leather loop restraint from the sheathed knife strapped to her hip, just in case, and then allowed sleep to take her.

After a time Annie woke, startled. An odd sound woke her, one that did not blend with the rest. Why? She listened. There it was again, a cracking limb and the rustle of forest litter in a direction away from where she knew everyone to be. It was not fully dark. She could not have napped more than a few minutes.

It crossed her mind that one from the group may have been persuaded by urges to make another attempt on her life. Maybe Alister Beane had been angered to the point that he did not want to wait for a better opportunity. She looked his way, but Beane and his wife remained at their campsite and had not moved.

The sound in the woods should be investigated, but which direction had it come from? She listened again to get a clearer sense.

Slowly, she slipped the large hunting knife from its scabbard and held it down to her side. She separated sounds categorically, those normal from any she could not identify. After a few moments of lying perfectly still and listening, she finally heard it.

It confused her, sounding much like a child in the woods whispering. What would a young child be doing in the woods alone at dark?

It was no longer a guess. She distinctly, but faintly, heard a child whisper, "Please hurry. I am so hungry."

It was followed by a hissing hush from an older voice.

Annie tensed, believing the earlier fear to be valid. Someone with a child planned on taking her life for food.

She went into extreme stealth mode and crawled on her belly away from the light of the dying fire she lay next to.

Once she had snaked her way to the blacker shadows of trees and brush, she sprang to her feet and moved quickly and quietly from one deep shadow to the next, coming to a stop next to a large dying hackberry tree. Again, she heard the whispered voice of a child. "How much longer do we have to wait?"

Using it for reference, Annie circled behind where she believed the voice was coming from.

Nearing the spot, she slowed, watching where she stepped, coming to a full stop and kneeling behind a clustered tangle of thorny vines. She tuned her ears to the spot just ahead beyond the vines. After a moment, the child's voice whispered, "Please, Cal, let's…"

"Shh," another voice hushed. That sound was, indeed, more adult-like.

Annie slowly and fluidly rose to stand and then on up to the tips of her toes. She peeked over the top of the thicket before her. Although daylight waned, it remained light enough for a good visual on the source. Annie saw an older girl, likely in her teens, crouching behind a bush, holding a long cedar staff sharpened to a fine point. Two younger children, much younger, squatted on each side of her. The children could not have been any older than her friend and sibling by circumstance, Eva—six, maybe seven years old. She did not recognize them as part of the Old Dallas escapees.

Annie came around the tall thicket of tangled vines. She moved to within scant feet behind the three, and then finally spoke. "If your plan is to make a meal of me or anyone with me, you are sorely mistaken."

Still on her haunches, the girl spun so fast she lost balance and fell over, but sprang back to a sitting position, legs stiff and splayed. She pulled the children behind her like a mother hen protecting her chicks and scooted backwards on her butt. From that position, she held the makeshift spear in a threatening manner and blurted, "Stay away from us! I'll stick you! I swear I will!"

Annie tipped her head sideways, thoughtfully. She returned the hunting knife to its scabbard on her hip. "Stabbing me with that spear will be very difficult from where you're sitting." She then crossed her arms over her chest. "I do admire the effort to protect your... children, if that's who they are."

"Stay away from us. We don't want any trouble."

"If you didn't want trouble, why are you skulking about behind bushes in the woods watching us?"

"We don't trust anyone, and that includes you and everyone with you, but the smell of food cooking drew us in."

In a thoughtful pose, Annie pushed out her lower lip. "That makes sense, but you don't have to behave like thieves in the night. I'll be happy to get you something to eat."

The girl allowed the tip of her spear to drop between her spread legs. "You will... I mean, you would?"

Annie took a step toward her. "Of course."

"Why?"

Annie chuckled. "You *are* hungry, right?" She extended her hand to help the girl to her feet.

The girl denied the hand and snapped the spear back up. "Yes. We're very hungry, but I don't trust your quick agreeable nature. It's not natural."

"Okay, you don't trust me. I heard you the first time. If it makes it more *natural* for you, I'm not so sure that I trust you either." Annie smiled. "The way I see it we'll just have to work on that together until our trust of one another is mutual. Now, won't we?"

"You sure seem calm, considering someone is threatening your life with a very long, very sharp stick." She jabbed the air between them with the pointed staff.

Annie bounced a shoulder shrug. "Well, it seems I find myself in these situations more frequently than I'd like. I suppose I'm becoming accustomed to it. After what happened earlier, I think I will take your implied advice and keep an eye on that sharp pointed stick of yours." Annie offered her a hand again. "Please, let me help you up. I'll take the first step in our journey toward mutual trust."

The girl stared at Annie's outstretched hand and said nothing for a moment. "We haven't been given a reason to believe in anyone or anything in many months. We escaped human-eaters in Old Dallas, only to make it into the countryside to be kidnapped and turned into slaves by a very cruel man, Barclay Weems. He, too, wanted us to trust him. We did, and it was a huge mistake. I have to believe that you want something or you wouldn't be in such a hurry to gain our trust. It's safer to believe you want us calm and then fatten us for slaughter… or make us serve you somehow, like Weems did."

"Oh, I want something all right."

"I knew it." The girl extended the sharpened staff toward Annie. Her eyes narrowed to squinted slits. She squeezed her lips together in an angry straight line, clearly determined to do damage. "Get away from us and leave us be!"

"Not until I tell you what I want. I want y'all to eat, sleep well tonight, and then live a long, happy life. If you care to travel with us, you're certainly welcome to do so, or you can be on your way with the two little ones. Either way, you'll be rested and fed and know that not everyone in this crazy upside down world wants to harm or use you. Plus, you'll have a new friend… me. Now, you know what I want."

The girl reared her head back, frowned, and wrenched a tighter grip on the spear. "Are you out of your mind?"

"I suppose that's a possibility. It has been said, or so I've heard, that crazy people think they're the only sane ones left and everyone else is nuts. Occasionally, I do think that." Annie again extended her hand but this time snatched the spear away from the girl before she had a chance to react. "By the way, nutty people like me don't appreciate having sharp objects pointed at them." She tossed the spear to the ground. Once again, she extended a hand. Now, almost pleading, she said, "Please, take my hand."

The girl hesitatingly did.

Annie pulled her to her feet. The girl was a bit shorter but could be near the same age. She had dark brown skin with long, full-bodied black hair. Even beneath raggedy clothes, Annie saw that she suffered from malnutrition. So did the two younger children. "You and the children haven't eaten much lately, have you?"

The girl brushed dried leaves from her backside. "We haven't eaten anything but a few wild onions and a handful of berries in the past two days." She abruptly straightened and blurted, "But that doesn't mean I can't give you a good fight if I have to."

"Drop the attitude. Come on, I can solve the hunger problem right now." Annie took off walking. After a short distance, she didn't hear them following. She stopped and looked back.

The girl didn't attempt to follow, just gathered the young boy and girl in close to each side and held them. "Are you sure we can trust you?"

"In case you didn't notice, *I'm* the one that just turned my back on *you*, which I learned the hard way a few hours ago, is not a smart thing to do around strangers. I have this knot on my head and still have a headache from that experience, but I've decided to trust you. I suggest you do the same. Now, come on."

Annie waited for the girl's courage to kick in.

A roll of the eyes was a clear sign from the teen to, at least for a time, suspend trust issues. She hurried forward to walk even with Annie.

"What's your name?" Annie asked.

"Calamity Bloom."

"Calamity? That's unusual. Even your name suggests you'll give me trouble."

"Well, Cassidy was my birth name. My parents thought of me as a little troublemaker when I was very young, so as a joke they started calling me Calamity. It stuck."

"Calamity it is."

"Just call me Cal."

"And the kids?"

Cal placed a hand on top of the girl's head. "This is Pammy." She tilted the staff toward the boy. "This little guy, who can't seem to keep his mouth shut, is Peter. They're twins."

Annie noticed the grimy faces on both. Beneath that, she saw fair skin and lighter colored hair than Cal. "Your children? Or siblings, perhaps?"

"Nah, but we are family. Each other is all we have. My mother was Native American… Choctaw, and my father was Hispanic. My mother had almost talked my father into getting out of Old Dallas and heading north back into Indian Territory, her ancestral roots… but not soon enough."

"Indian Territory?"

"Yeah, the former state of Oklahoma, but it's much larger than when it was a state."

"Wow, I'm impressed," Annie said. "It seems you know a lot about it."

"It's mandatory within Native American cultures to preserve a spoken history of the people. My mother made sure I knew it. Being Choctaw, one of the Five Civilized Tribes in the south, my mother made sure that I claimed the heritage fully regardless of mixed blood; therefore, I am Choctaw. The other tribes—Cherokee, Chickasaw, Muscogee Creek and Seminole—joined together when the Union crumbled, and took back the land. It's under their joint control. Someday, I want to go there and make that my home. I have family there. Besides, I'm of the opinion it might be the last place on earth where sanity and common sense can still be found."

"Really? I think I can prove you wrong on that point. If you truly want to get back, though, I'll help you but not for a while. I have other things to take care of first," Annie said.

"Why would you do that?"

"Do what?"

"Help me. You don't know me."

"If you're around me long enough, you'll come to realize that it's exactly the kind of thing I do. I'd call that common sense and sanity. Wouldn't you?" She grinned and then looked to the twins. "How about the children; what's their story?"

"Pammy and Peter's family were white. Our families were neighbors. I still remember the day these two were born. Eventually, both sets of parents were captured by a rival gang in Old Dallas and taken away. I'm sure all four are dead and consumed by now. It has been over a year since we last saw them. I took the twins and escaped into the countryside. I sure regret not heading north then, but I took the path of least resistance and that happened to be south."

"You see, right there… that makes me like you a lot."

"What, that I headed south and not north?"

"No, not that; the fact that you'd take those kids out of harm's way, adopt them and then protect them is wonderful."

"It was the right thing to do."

"That's what I mean, Cal. It was the right thing to do, so… so sane and loaded with common sense. I love it."

Cal stared at Annie for a moment as they walked and then, for the first time, something akin to a smile appeared. The girl had not smiled once and clearly had not been offered many reasons to. Her face seemed natural with that solemn expression. Annie figured Calamity Bloom did not smile much, if ever. Annie made a mental note that, if she had the pleasure of knowing this Native American girl long enough, it would be something worth changing if she could. Cal was a beautiful girl. Annie wanted to see that attractiveness decorated with a smile.

* * *

The final day of travel back to Myrna's Glory had been uneventful, pleasant even. It was early afternoon as they neared the final bend in the trail, after which the compound would come into view. As they approached, Annie became interested in what Cal's reaction would be when her new friend took her first glimpse of the place Annie called home. She glanced sideways at Cal, not wanting to miss the moment as they came to the bend in the trail that circled around dense undergrowth.

Annie relished that Cal chose to travel with them but the girl made no commitment beyond that. She walked near to Annie's side all day, at times bumping shoulders, the twins always next to her or very close behind. Trust issues seemed to dwindle as the day progressed. Cal's need to remain near Annie's side seemed to indicate that the same desire did not extend to anyone else. Each time Annie looked Cal's way, she needed no heightened perception to see that the new girl felt each of her stolen glances. Annie thought it interesting that Cal's expression softened each time she glanced the girl's way, but Cal still did not smile. Annie grew confident that Calamity Bloom just might become a friend after all.

As they made that final turn in the trail, Annie fanned her arms and announced, "There it is, my home, Myrna's Glory." She turned to Cal. "It can be your home, too, if you like."

Cal stared at Annie, as if searching for the lie in the offer. "I think I prefer Indian Territory, but we'll see," she said. She stroked the top of Pammy's head, then Peter's. "What do y'all think?"

The twins looked at each other then up to Calamity. "I don't know," said Peter. "Whatever you say, Cal," said Pammy. The kids crowded to each side of the girl and put their arms around her. Pammy pressed the side of her head into Calamity's ribs and looked up at her. The youngster then added, "Anywhere is fine, as long as we're together."

Annie swallowed hard. "That's beautiful."

"What?" Cal asked.

"Family."

Calamity nodded. "Yeah, it is." She suddenly looked more serious. "I still won't make any promises, if that's what you're after."

"Ah, must be that ol' trust bugaboo."

"It's a little that, but also a longing to return to the home of my ancestors."

"Well," Annie said, "commit to a few days here, see what Myrna's Glory is all about, and meet my family and all my friends. I wager once you do, you'll not want to leave."

Cal looked straight ahead toward the compound. "Let's see how it goes."

Annie waved at the crowd trailing her, motioning for them to come forward. They had all begun bunching tighter, angling for a better look at their destination.

Cal stopped walking as they neared Myrna's Glory. "It's so big. It's twice the size of Barclay's Outpost... maybe three times the size."

"I assume Barclay's Outpost is that compound you and the twins were taken to and held as slaves," Annie said.

"Sort of. It's the town surrounding Barclay's School and Home for Children. The town is named after Barclay Weems and he runs the children's home." She dropped her voice to a breathy whisper. "The bastard."

They again walked. "How many children were held there?" Annie asked.

"I'm not sure... never counted. I don't know if the other buildings on campus housed children too. There were about thirty in our building."

"How many adults were there?"

"Not sure about that either. Ten or so is all I ever saw. It seemed that several times a week, I'd see a new face and then never see them again. I don't know if they were in from the outside, or had jobs that seldom required interaction with the children. The ones I saw most were supervisors of one sort or another. To the outside world, the place was viewed as an orphanage and school. Those supervisors were called teachers, or board members, but the only things taught were how to skin animals, tan hides, weave cloth, sew, work fields to raise vegetables and any other tasks they deemed profitable. Otherwise, the children are never allowed outside to play."

"I'm not sure I understand," Annie said. "It sounds like they simply tried making the place self-sufficient so they wouldn't have to depend on the kindness of outsiders for support."

"Yeah, and that's exactly the way they wanted it to appear."

Annie couldn't prevent a confused frown from pulling her brows together as she contemplated why Calamity thought it was such a bad way of life.

Calamity noticed. "Look, kids at that place were forced to work twelve to fifteen hours a day, every day. The only clothing we had were scraps of hides and the occasional piece of cloth we could scrounge and stitch together ourselves. Even then we had to finish our day's work first before we could take care of things that benefited us personally. Our food was leftovers the School Board didn't want, mostly slop and bones. We had to cook it ourselves. By the time all of that was taken care of, we collapsed exhausted, repeating that cycle every day. There were no days off, no personal time whatsoever. That's not even the worst of it. When a resident hit eighteen years old, those boys and girls are given a so-called graduation party. Strangers are invited, not locals. In reality, it is an auction. Teenagers are sold to the highest bidders. Girls fetch the higher prices. I don't think I need to tell you why."

"Oh, Cal..."

"I'm approaching my eighteenth birthday. I wasn't going to let that happen to me and be taken away from Pammy and Peter. All the while, Weems and the School Board live regally in large, well-furnished homes with plenty of fresh food and nice clothes donated by the community. They have become powerful and influential. No one dares cross them. Those that try to help the kids disappear, never to be seen, or heard from again. Annie, we were nothing more than livestock, raised to service every need of Weems and his cronies. We were slaves!"

They stopped at the entrance to Myrna's Glory. Annie turned and grabbed Calamity by the shoulders, forcing her to face her, eye to eye. "Last year, I found myself in a situation in a compound called Stalwart. They wanted to use me for breeding stock. I'll tiptoe through hell before I allow that, or anything similar, to happen to anyone else!"

Calamity's eyes darted around Annie's face, plainly looking for signs of deceit. "Do you realize what it is you're saying?"

"Oh, yes. I do. When a sordid operation such as Barclay's School for Children is legitimized in the community, it's very difficult to take it down. They have supporters that will not understand its true nature and may come to its aid if attacked."

"Exactly! I can't believe you have grasped its true intent so quickly. That's why the kids are powerless there."

Annie nodded. "It's something that must be done from the inside." She pondered the situation, but then re-animated after a few seconds. "Let's get everyone settled. We can plan something later… something that will take care of Mister Barclay Weems and that so-called orphanage and school for children."

Annie turned to face her followers as a whole… Calamity and the twins, Bo, Elizabeth, Lizzy and Yowl behind them and then the seventy-five others trailing them. She announced in a loud voice, "Welcome to Myrna's Glory, your new home, if you wish to make it so."

Chapter 11

Situations at Home

Annie relaxed. Explaining cannibalistic tendencies of the group, especially among the adult male members accompanying her back to Myrna's Glory, proved cathartic. She welcomed sharing responsibility with those she trusted most: Jake Henderson, her surrogate father; and Henry, the self-avowed protector of the compound. Even if only for a short time, letting her guard down felt nice. Now, some of the burden had shifted. Others could maintain wary eyes on the group from Old Dallas. Protection of the Order of Theocratic Minds was in the most capable hands. Of that, she was certain.

As a result of the ill-fated encounter on the trail, she stated emphatically that no matter how well they behaved, some had uncontrollable urges when it came to consumption of human flesh. She did not know how many, or if the compulsion would be, or could be, reversed. There were variables she could not predict. She could not be sure if the impulse was mostly among the men or not. Two of them proved untrustworthy, so the genesis of an opinion had been formed on that question. Still, Annie realized she must keep an open mind or risk turning her back to the wrong person.

Jake and Henry vowed to watch the refugees closely for signs of aberrant behavior, Alister Beane topping the fledgling list. To end her report to Jake and Henry, Annie said, "I hope that horrible state of mind can be changed. Many of those men have wives and children. Children need their fathers, but only if they're right minded and not eating the neighbors."

Jake had naturally assumed the role of CEO of Myrna's Glory. His common law wife, Glory Jackson, was always at his side and Henry, the big bald man with a big heart, committed his life to protecting the sanctity of the Order of Theocratic Minds and all people coming into the fold at Myrna's Glory. The common goal remained—all who sought refuge and were willing to contribute expertise and work would be welcomed and that Theocratic Minds would press forward to restore technology to a world still devolving and stuck in the muck of generalized anarchy.

Annie hung her bow and quiver of arrows on a wooden peg protruding from the wall in her cozy bedroom. She lived in the same cabin as Jake and Glory. She removed the ornate hunting knife from her hip and tossed it onto the bed. To no longer need weapons, even for a short time, was reason enough to draw a sweet breath of fresh air. Responsibility now shifting to others left her mellow. Now breathing easier, she became tired, very tired.

She stepped outside the cabin and stood beneath the overhang on the front porch of the cedar log structure she called home. The late afternoon in this part of the former state of Texas was warm, but pleasantly so. Shadows lengthened. The rosemary bush and jasmine vines that had consumed the sun's rays all day released the accumulated warmth in the form of seasonal fragrance. It smelled of peace and serenity. She leaned against one of the porch support posts, crossed her arms and drew in the perfumed air as she looked across the large, open and grassless central yard of the compound. Home. It was nice to stand and take it all in.

Young Eva played with the new arrivals—Lizzy and the twins, Pammy and Peter—thrilled to have children near her own age to play with. They squealed, engaging in a rowdy game of tag.

Yowl lay next to the nearest cabin watching the children. Residents walked a wide circle around the canine, but Annie was not concerned. They would be comfortable with his presence soon enough. Regardless of their uneasy feelings toward him, he would protect them from outsiders bent on doing harm. Bo and Yowl were welcome additions as protectors of Myrna's Glory, alongside Jake and Henry. As gentle as he was, Bo had the heart and courage of a warrior.

Eva grinned and waved wildly. Annie returned the greeting, the bond between them tight and becoming stronger by the day. Although of different mothers, and far apart in age, they were indeed sisters blessed with common genetic superiority physically and intellectually, a deviation not shared with most other humans on earth. Their ancestors could likely be traced to the same laboratory over two hundred years ago. As Annie watched the children, she wondered: *How many people in the world do you suppose are like you and me, Punkin?* She blew Eva a kiss.

Beyond the children, Ethan Turlock, the only guy who could make her heart flutter, walked across the compound with Eva's mother, Lana—another favorite person. Lana had endured much until Annie liberated her from sexual servitude, controlled by that evil man Fiam Lee Tam last year at the corporation called Stalwart. She endured hell but from that hell was born an angel, a genetically blessed child by the name of Eva. Lana richly deserved that beautiful youngster and a chance for a measure of happiness. Myrna's Glory happened to be the best place for that life.

"*See* what ya be lookin' at, not just starin'."

Dame Fortune walked up behind her while her mind, heart and eyes were otherwise occupied. Annie whirled around. "Oh, Dame…" She opened her arms and let Dame walk in to them. "I missed you so much."

"Ya don't need to be sayin' it, but it does dis ol' blind woman a world o' good when ya do." She laughed, sounding much like a hen's cackle.

Annie pulled back. "What is it that you mean by 'see' what I'm looking at? Are you talking about the children?"

She tapped Annie's booted foot with the long cedar walking stick. "You know what I be referrin' to. It's what ya be lookin' at beyond dem younguns. I jes be sayin' look at doze two with your heart, not your eyes."

Annie glanced back to her two dear friends walking side by side. "You mean Ethan and Lana?"

"Damn, girl, do I need ta be spellin' it out for ya?"

Annie abruptly backed away and drew a sharp breath. "You mean *together*… as a couple? Are you serious?"

"I can't be lyin' to ya child. Both dem fell in love from a real high place. Dey still be fallin'. Dat be a fact."

Annie's lips parted, her jaw slackened, shocked beyond words, unaware of something that had been right in front of her all along.

"Dey both be lovin' ya so much, dey didn't want to be hurtin' your feelings and have been puttin' off talkin' to ya 'bout it for months, tryin' to find a way to tell ya, girl."

Tears spilled from her eyes. She shot intermittent glances at the pair through watery eyes. "I—I didn't know."

"Das why I be tellin' ya now. You need to be knowin' it. You be havin' a big ol' blind spot for dat Ethan feller."

Annie's face screwed down tight as she began to cry. Her heart squeezed between desiring happiness for her two friends and wanting to keep Ethan Turlock's romantic affection for herself.

"Oh, baby, I not jes be makin' you aware…" She groped for Annie's face and stroked her cheek. "Ya need ta be understandin' da good comin' from all dis."

"Good?" Annie's voice shifted into a higher range. "How could news as devastating as this be good?" She stepped away from Dame's touch, bursting into shuddering sobs.

Dame felt for Annie's arm, grabbed it, and pulled her back in to an embrace. The old lady forced her to accept a shoulder, gently pushing Annie's head down onto it. "Oh, baby, I know ya be hurtin' and no amount of good words gonna be changin' dat right now. Lana be a good mama to dat special child, Eva Louise, but dat youngun be needin' a daddy and dat Ethan feller be makin' a damn good one. And, child, all three o' dem be needin' you to keep on bein' deir friend."

Annie sobbed. "But Dame, I feel so alone."

"Baby, who ya are and what ya be is a blessin' for sure, but it comes with a cursed price."

Annie pulled her head back and wiped tears from her cheek. "I don't understand."

"Look around, youngun. Tell me what ya be seein'."

Annie didn't feel the need to stanch the tears. She was having tremendous difficulty with Dame's philosophical approach to losing the love of her young life. Ethan was slipping through her fingers. What could be good about that? With a pulsating lip, she lashed out, "I don't know, Dame! What is it you think I should be seeing… buildings, people, dirt, sky… what?"

"Keep dat frustration under control, child."

Annie breathed deep, trying to retrieve reeling anger. "I'm sorry. I'm mad at myself for letting it happen."

"Oh, baby, ya didn't *let* it happen. It be *destiny*."

Annie clenched her jaws, working the muscles. She did not comment for fear of losing her temper again. Bruised sensibilities needed time to heal. How could Dame say that this heartbreaking situation might somehow be right? What did she mean by *destiny*? That didn't sound fair. It certainly didn't feel fair. In fact it was absurd. There was no way to respond to such a statement. She held her pain and said nothing.

Jake Henderson considered Annie to be his little Annabelle, but Dame was the one who saw the tightrope she balanced upon. The old lady dealt daily with the huge chasm that represented Annie's life. Annie was a child of seventeen with thoughts and feelings of any other teen, but also a bigger than life deviant—a fighter, a killer, a person capable of waging wars and winning them. All of Myrna's Glory placed hopes and dreams of a better future squarely on her shoulders. By birthright, she had been set apart, far apart, from everyone else. Loneliness now filled the chasm between those two extremes.

Annie realized the old lady, who was as much mother as friend, happened to be the only one who understood the burden of those expectations. No matter how blessed, if it were not for Dame, Annie might not be able to cope with all that was expected of her. At the moment, she was not a battle hardened general, just a little girl in need of hugs and solace.

Dame again searched the air for Annie's face, sliding gnarled black fingers beneath her chin. The old lady lifted Annie's head away from its somber tilt. "Now, look around like I told ya. What is it ya be seein'? I be blind as a damned ol' bat, but I be seein' it plain as day, child."

Suddenly, Dame's mental image of Myrna's Glory became clear through Annie's eyes. Annie realized the blind seer had entered her head for the purpose of opening her mind to realities taken for granted. It was then she saw what her eyes beheld. "I think I understand now what you meant for me to see." She sniffed and whisked a streaming tear from her cheek. "The children are playing and laughing. People are coming and going at peace. Some of the wives are pregnant and starting families, feeling secure and confident that things are better and life is worth living. Myrna's Glory is growing into a beacon of hope. Oh, Dame, I see it now!"

Dame's smile bunched her black cheeks into shiny lumps. "Dat's right, child. And, dis whole damn place wouldn't even be existin' today if not for you. Das what I meant by *see* what ya be lookin' at. Ethan and Lana only be part of a tapestry of life dat *you*, girl... *you* are buildin' here. I don't be meanin' cabins, dormitories, machines and all dat damn stuff. I be meanin' hope ta hundreds, and you, child, be da one layin' da rock-solid foundation."

The instant Dame's fingers left Annie's chin, the vision of Myrna's Glory reverted back to what it was before Dame touched her. The view she witnessed with such clarity suddenly lost depth, even colors of trees, grass and sky dulled a little. Dame was no longer in her mind. Regardless, the old lady's insight was now etched into her memory. She understood what the old woman with the lopsided wad of white hair meant. Annie patted Dame's hair into a slightly better shape. "I love you."

The old lady blew a satisfied sigh. "I be knowin' dat ya do."

"Should I approach Ethan and Lana and... I don't know... offer my blessing or something?"

"Not yet. You be too distraught. 'Sides, I be knowin' Ethan will be comin' to ya soon enough. He be holdin' deep feelin's for ya. Dey jes be changin', das all. He be real tired of hidin' da truth and feelin' bad 'bout it. His heart be heavy wit' da news he must be tellin' ya'."

"You're right. I need to be alone tonight. I don't want my sadness to become theirs."

"Dat be a better way for sure."

"Dame?"

"Don't need to be askin', I be knowin' your heart. You be scared dat love will never be part o' ya life. And ya know very well dat I can't be challengin' the cosmos by tellin' ya what I see in da future. Don't wanna take da chance to be changin' anythin' I be seein'."

Annie took comfort in Dame's words. The old lady refused to share good outcomes she envisioned, for fear of jinxing a future already divined.

Annie kissed Dame on the cheek. "I'm going to my bedroom. Would you ask people not to disturb me? Just tell them I'm tired from the ordeal in Old Dallas and the trip back."

"Rest easy, child. I be sittin' my big ol' behind right here on da porch and keep 'em away."

Annie shuffled into the cabin and trudged with a lead-footed slide to her bedroom. She slipped off the pig-hide boots Dame had made for her and fell backward onto the bed. She rested her head on laced fingers of both hands and stared at the ceiling. Images of Ethan Turlock marched through her mind's eye, beginning with the night she first saw him. He'd fallen, unconscious, into their cabin last year after having been nearly beaten to death by Stalwart suppliers bent on destroying the Order of Theocratic Minds. Memories spun out until her heart broke under the unbearable weight of a love that would not, could not, be.

It angered Annie to an explosive extreme that she could be so intelligent and sharp minded, yet, when it came to matters of the heart, she remained an immature dolt, even retarded, stumbling through life without a clue—trusting too much and loving too much. She hated it. The defect had almost gotten her killed yesterday after turning her back on two men she did not know and should not have trusted. Frustrated, she clenched a fist and hammered her pillow.

She rolled onto her side and drew her knees up until she resembled a fetus in the womb. Alone and now lonely, she wept. There was no need to hold anything back, not tonight.

* * *

Annie felt the sun on her face. Light penetrated closed eyelids. A veil of sleep thinned. Before opening her eyes to greet the day, the heart-wrenching session with Dame Fortune came flooding back, but it did not seem as crushing as it had the night before.

She opened her eyes to see the rising sun, yawned, drew her first big breath of the day, and then sat up on the edge of the bed. The shutters of the nearest window were open. A gentle spring breeze caressed her cheeks while her eyes were fixed on the view beyond the window. It was certainly worth an appreciative moment.

People were coming and going. She heard the sounds of conversations and children laughing as Myrna's Glory came to life for another day. She picked up her boots from the floor and rose, then ambled to the front door of the cabin Jake had built for her and Glory, and out onto the front porch. Dame was no longer on the bench—no surprise. Dame would have known when she drifted off to sleep and probably went to her own home at that moment, the small cabin known as The Think Tank. Jake and Glory had already left to begin their day as well. For now, Annie was alone and she preferred it that way.

She recalled her dreams of last night and smiled. Dame had entered them with a mission. The whole night, she experienced one beautiful dream after another of all the people she loved and all the times they'd laughed together. The old lady wanted her to have a restful night. She did.

Annie thought for a moment, attempting to frame her day and how she wanted to fill it. She began building a mental schedule that did not include the one thing that should be on it, a talk with Ethan.

She kicked her boots closer and slipped a foot into one of them. Reaching for the second, she hesitated and thought, *Maybe I can have a talk with that Alister Beane guy and see where his head is at on this whole cannibalism thing... or, maybe I can talk Bo and Yowl into a day in the woods, hunting. I should spend time with Glory, though. We could forage for roots and wild vegetables. She and I haven't had quality one-on-one time in quite a while.*

As she poked her toes in the second boot, she glimpsed Lana approaching, Ethan a step behind. Annie's body tightened, realizing that the dreaded and unavoidable conversation was about to take place.

"It's a beautiful morning," Lana called out, still some distance away.

From her seat on the cabin's porch, Annie scanned the skies over Lana's head, not wanting to make eye contact as she approached. "It sure is."

Ethan came around Lana to walk abreast. "Annie?"

Before Annie could answer, Lana added, "Ethan and I need to talk to you. Can you make time?"

Annie's head whirled with innumerable reasons why talking right now was not a good idea. "Well, I do have many things to…"

"Please," Ethan said, "it's very important that we not wait a day longer… even another hour would be too long."

Annie heard a quaver in Ethan's voice—uneasiness palpable. She suddenly felt bad for mortaring a few emotionally resistant bricks into a defensive wall. She sighed. "Okay. Sure." She patted the open bench seat next to her. "Sit. Let's talk."

Suddenly, it was they who hesitated. Lana glanced at Ethan. He had stopped walking and seemed frozen to the ground. Twice he appeared about to take a step but his feet never left the spot. Lana wrung her hands as she stepped up onto the low wooden planked porch and lowered her body to sit next to Annie. She remained on the edge of the bench, as if prepared to jump and run.

"Look, y'all, I know why you're here together and what it is you're about to say," Annie said.

Ethan straightened. "You do?"

"Don't look so surprised. You should've known that Dame is playing a part in this. She's known for some time."

Lana's eyes had already begun to glaze with tears. "Oh, Annie…"

Annie placed a hand on Lana's knee. "Dame thought it was time I opened my eyes to the situation, and I'll not lie. It hurt, terribly."

"It's not something we planned," Ethan said. "Lana and I worked together in finishing out her new cabin and I… *we*… just happened." He looked to Lana.

It would have taken a blind, deaf and dumb person to not notice the all-consuming love in his eyes for Lana. How could she not have noticed it before now? Annie suddenly felt foolish.

"It was during that time she and I started…"

"Please stop right there." Annie covered her ears. "I don't want to hear anymore." She saw that Ethan had stopped talking and uncovered her ears. "I had time to think about it and it's clear you make the perfect couple, and you, Ethan, will make Eva a wonderful father, but you both need to remember how poorly I handle emotional things and I don't want to start crying." She tried to smile, but offered only a nervous lip twitch. "It might leave the wrong impression because I wish you two nothing but my blessings and my love. I look at both of you as family. How could I possibly see this any other way than with deepest respect for the wishes and happiness of you both?"

Lana leaned in to Annie and embraced her firmly. "Never in my life have I had a friend as true as you."

"You are my sister, not just a friend."

Ethan stepped up onto the porch and stood next to Annie. "I wish we hadn't taken so long to tell you. The longer we put it off, the harder it became to get it said. The last thing we ever wanted to do was hurt you."

"I'll be sensitive about it, maybe cry some more, since one of my talents seems to be losing control that way." Her head bobbed and she chuckled as fresh tears glossed her eyes. "In my heart, I know it's the greatest thing that could happen for you, Lana, and certainly for sweet little Eva... you too Ethan. After considerable thought, I've come to the conclusion that it's the right thing for me as well, considering the tasks that will keep me away for weeks, maybe months at a time."

Ethan took Lana's hand as she rose from the bench. They stepped off the porch together. Ethan stopped and looked back. He smiled softly, sentimentally. "Thank you for understanding."

Annie nodded and bounced a quick smile. Her lip shook as she fought an urge to openly weep. A lump swelled in her throat. Hands lying limp in her lap curled into clenched fists as she began losing the battle against bursting into sobs. She wanted desperately to wait until Ethan and Lana walked away.

Ethan put an arm around Lana's waist, and Lana reciprocated. A gaze between them lingered as they turned to leave. It was a small thing, but too much to bear. Annie lost control.

She sprang to her feet, raced back inside the cabin, closed the door and burst into bellowing sobs. She fell back against the door and let it out. Attempting to force her mind into a different frame, she turned thoughts back to scheduling the day, but it proved impossible. At the moment, her heart had total control.

She meandered, ending up in her bedroom sitting on the edge of her bed. She then lay on her side facing the window, pulling her knees up, poking hands between her legs, and staring through the open portal to the outside world. As frustrated as she usually was by people taking issue with her age, she did not even feel as old as seventeen right now— simply a child in need of loving hands to soothe her. Annie was trapped between childhood and adulthood. She squeezed her eyes shut and wept.

"Annie?"

She looked. Calamity Bloom stood peering at her through the window. She whisked tears away. "I'm sorry. I didn't mean for anyone to see me like this."

"I wasn't eavesdropping, really, but I overheard your conversation with that guy and girl on your front porch. I'm a little shocked. I didn't know you had that kind of emotion in you."

Annie sat up and faced Calamity as her new friend leaned against the windowsill. "It's a terrible weakness."

"Terrible? No, it's not. There's nothing terrible, or odd about loving. or wanting love. I yearn for it. We have that in common."

"Ya know, you've come into my life at the right time. I need you... someone who understands me, someone to confide in."

Calamity shrugged. "I don't have many talents, but I can listen without judging and be your friend. I need one too."

"That's huge, Cal." Annie stared for a quiet second at her new friend and then said, "How about we go have a late breakfast and then I'll introduce you to several hundred of my closest friends here at Myrna's Glory? I'll spend this day showing you what my life is like. How about that?"

Calamity's freshly scrubbed dark-skinned face glowed with youthful freshness. "That sounds wonderful." Her words were joyful but her expression remained neutral. Annie looked upon Calamity's inability or unwillingness to smile as odd, but she now thought that it might be the way the Native American girl was, a cultural thing. If so, that was fine. It certainly wasn't any worse than crying over every little sad thing. Calamity's glistening coal-black hair caught the morning rays as a gentle breeze pushed it into a sideways sweep. She was radiant, and Annie saw that the girl had a heart to match—a friend-becoming lifted her spirit.

Annie wiped away one final tear and then went outside to join Calamity. The rest of her day seemed to offer promise after all.

Chapter 12

A Plan Comes Together

"Eva? Eva Louise?"

Eva hesitated upon hearing the sound of her name, but then continued evading capture by Lizzy Longbow in their rowdy game of tag. The youngster checked her speed, allowing Lizzy to get near enough to touch her on occasion, to keep the game interesting and at least offer the appearance of fairness for her new friends.

Annie appreciated and admired Eva's innate sense of kindness to all in all things—a trait that went beyond childish innocence. Annie had begun developing the opinion that Eva might be yielding to a genetic predisposition. If so, it could develop into a dangerous weakness that the girl would spend a lifetime trying to control. Like Annie, the child's talents, both physical and mental, were advanced but there would be a price to pay. Annie did not yet know what it would be. Only a few more years and maturity would reveal what Eva's weakness would be.

It was a problem Annie knew too well. Over-the-top trust was her nemesis. She struggled to keep it within manageable limits. It was a daily battle to walk that thin line. She never wanted to stop believing the best about people but vigilance had to be maintained. Too many people in this crazy world had selfish interests to serve, regardless how they smiled or how nice they seemed.

Eva finally stopped running from her new friend, Lizzy. She looked to the source of her called name and ceased raucous laughter. Her eyes landed on Annie, and she waved.

"Come talk to me for a minute," Annie shouted across the well-trodden barren ground of the central yard of Myrna's Glory.

The youngster put on a burst of speed not demonstrated for Lizzy or the young twins, Pammy and Peter. She churned a cloud of dust off her swift feet as she ran to Annie. "Whatcha doin'?"

"I see you've introduced yourself to Lizzy and the twins but I wanted you to meet and get to know my new friend Calamity Bloom. Pammy and Peter were with her when they agreed to come to Myrna's Glory and stay… for a while, anyhow."

Eva bounced high on her toes holding an excited grin. "Hi, Calamity."

"Call me Cal."

"Okay, Cal, are ya gonna be stayin' with us… I mean live with us here at Myrna's Glory? I sure do like Pammy and Peter. Would y'all think about stayin' a long long time, even forever? Please."

"I'll think about it, no promises. Thank you, though, for making them welcome. They are my family but, like me, they need friends closer to their age." Calamity appeared relaxed and appreciative, but again, grateful words came without a smile.

Annie focused on Calamity. "I have a special reason for introducing you to Eva, Cal. She's like me. We both are descended from genetically altered humans developed over two hundred years ago. All of our senses are heightened far beyond normal human capacities; plus, physical strength and speed are enhanced as well."

"Is that how you were able to sneak up on us outside your campsite yesterday?"

"Yes. Although I couldn't quite understand what was said at first, I heard Peter whispering to you from over seventy-five paces away. Once I determined the direction the whispers were coming from, I focused my hearing in that direction and understood every word. After that, finding you quickly and quietly was easy."

"So, you and Eva can do things no one else can. How strong are you? Can you... oh I don't know... pull up trees by the roots?"

Annie laughed. "Heavens no, but if guys like Henry," she pointed across the yard, "that big bald guy standing by the machine shop over there, and Bo tried to pin me in a wrestling match, they couldn't... even combining their formidable strengths they still couldn't. If four, maybe even five guys the size and strength of those two should try it, given the right circumstances, I might be able to take them all down."

"Wow, I'm impressed."

"Really?"

"Of course," Calamity said. Her response sounded sincere, but the face remained bland.

"I do have a reason for telling you all this. I'm not just bragging. I've been thinking about that so-called orphanage and school you and the twins escaped from."

"Why?"

"Simple. I trust your opinion that it's an awful place. I can see where outsiders, maybe the entire surrounding community, could be fooled into believing that everything that happens is in the best interest of the children. I'd like to take the children out of there and bring them here, to Myrna's Glory if, of course, I find that to be true."

"Oh, it's true all right. Barclay Weems and the teachers live a fat life off the backs of those kids. I'm sure he and the staff would explain it differently, but I was in the middle of it and know what they're doing and getting away with. I've overheard Weems tell the other teachers about the 'sweet arrangement' they enjoy. They get support and donations from area residents. They have a strong hold over hearts and minds around that area, and you're right, locals believe they provide a legal and much needed community service. It's a distortion of the truth. The goodness of their mission is for show to insure continued support. It could have been a wonderful place for young people like the twins and me, but greed by Weems and his followers ruined it."

"That only strengthens my resolve to act, and do it soon," Annie said.

Calamity's head drooped. "I believe that you are a talented person, but I don't think you can get the children out of there. Even if the school board can't stop you, they'd enlist help from the community. You'd be overwhelmed."

"That's why I told you about mine and Eva's abilities. You see, you're looking at such an operation as an armed assault on the place. That's not what it would be. I'd allow myself and Eva to be taken in. We'd walk into that place unarmed, except for slingshots, and act appreciative of a place to stay. The organization needs to be taken down from the inside. I cannot guarantee non-violence, but we'll do everything possible to prevent it and still accomplish our goal."

Jake approached, Henry at his side, both wielding axes and saws for a day of harvesting cedar logs for the latest construction project. Building cabins had become an endless endeavor to provide housing for the growing numbers within

Myrna's Glory. A dozen men and two women trailed behind, all carrying assorted tools. "Annabelle," Jake said, and then clucked his tongue, "I see it in your eyes, kiddo. You're plotting something."

She smiled. "As a matter of fact, I am." She gestured to Calamity. "Jake, Henry, this is Calamity Bloom." She looked to her friend but pointed back to Jake. "Cal, although Jake and I are not blood related, he is definitely my father."

Jake blushed. "Well, Annabelle has done a better job of raising me than the other way around." He glanced to the men and women behind him. All grinned in a knowing way. "Henry, why don't you take the crew and go on ahead? I'll join you in a few minutes."

Henry, also grinning, said as he passed by, "So, Annie raised *you*, did she?" He let out a thunderous laugh. "And a fine adult she made of you."

Jake's blush escalated into bright red embarrassment. He put a hand on Henry's arm and pushed. "Go on, get out of here."

Henry walked on laughing.

Annie threw her arms around Jake and hugged him. "Henry was kidding. I wouldn't be alive today if you hadn't come into my life when you did." She kissed his cheek.

"The family a baby is born into is often not the people a child ends up with," Calamity said and then sighed. "This insane world throws people together as created families too often."

"Yeah," Annie said, giving Jake an extra tight hug. "And sometimes it works out. Right, Jake?"

Jake pushed her to arm's length. "Come on now, enough of this. If you keep it up, I'll be crying. Now, what is it that you're planning?"

"A rescue mission."

"Another one so soon?"

"It's a child sweat shop disguised as an orphanage and school for parentless children. Cal and the twins escaped from there."

"You had better not be planning a mission without including me," came a deep voice from behind.

Annie backed away from Jake and turned to see Bo Juster nearing where they stood. "Well, my big hairy friend, this is not a job for burly strong guys. It's better suited for young sweet things... like Eva and me."

Bo's eyebrow went up. "I thought you didn't want anyone calling you young. And, what do you mean by sweet?"

"I don't want you calling me young, or youngster or kid or anything like that, but..." she sighed, "as long as I look the part, I might as well use it to my advantage."

"Hold on," Jake said. "You're planning on taking Eva with you into a dangerous situation? I bet Lana will have a strong opinion on that."

"This is not to be a physical battle, like with Tam at Stalwart, or the cannibals of the Brickyard District in Old Dallas. The end game is to turn the school board on one another and the entire community against that Barclay Weems guy. Greed is a powerful motivator and according to what Cal has told me, there's plenty of arrogance, ego and greed among the leaders there. I might be able to feed those traits until distrust causes the entire infrastructure to crumble."

"Now I see where you're going with this," Calamity said.

Annie nodded. "I need Eva because of her age and abilities. Her age lends legitimacy to my presence. If they believed Cal and the twins escaped from Old Dallas after their parents were killed, I see no reason why they wouldn't believe the same about the two of us. I can't foresee a scenario that would put Eva in serious danger, but her abilities may prove helpful should the plan take a dangerous turn. Either way, I have to go in with my eyes wide open and be prepared."

"Yowl and I could be useful. Let us tag along," Bo said.

"You're right," Annie replied.

Bo's head recoiled in surprise. "I am?"

"Well, except for the 'tag along' part. Since you and Elizabeth Longbow seem to be rekindling an old friendship—"

"I'm hoping it turns into something more than friendship."

Her head took a mischievous slant. "I'm sure you are and that's exactly the reason I need you to stay here. The group from Old Dallas had great respect for Ragland Longbow. I'm thinking they may respect the wishes of his widow as well. That means I need your influence here to work with Elizabeth to quell *urges* that might arise. You know what I mean."

"You are smart," Bo said.

Annie frowned. "You say that as though you had doubts."

"Not anymore. Okay, we'll do it your way. Yowl and I will stay and see if we can pacify the Old Dallas crowd. Hopefully we can do it without being eaten in the meantime."

"Good. Just keep their stomachs full of meat from animal sources and maybe, given time, that crazy lust for human flesh will fade. Pay special attention to Alister Beane. He's very angry that I hacked his foot as he tried to kill me. Watch him closely." She faced Jake. "As for you, dear father of mine, I'll need you. Cal will guide us there, but once we've arrived, I'll need you to protect her and keep her a safe distance away until Eva and I can get the children out."

Jake nodded. "Sounds simple enough."

Annie placed a hand on Jake's arm. "I may need you for another reason that might not be so simple."

"Oh?"

"It's that auction for the older kids turning eighteen, disguised as a festive graduation party. I need Glory to find clothing that makes you appear wealthy. I want you to attend one of those events as a bidder. I have to know how it works and if departing teens are destined for something other than good lives and jobs, like sexual servitude, or some other form of forced labor. I may need to round up as many of them as I can and get them to safety as well."

"You said you've thought a *little* about this," Calamity said. "This sounds like a full plan that took days of intense thought."

Annie shrugged her shoulders. "It's what I do."

"I'm beginning to think you do it well."

"You and Jake may have a lot of idle time on your hands while Eva and I do our thing inside that place. I'll leave you my bow and plenty of arrows. You can practice."

"Sure. I may not be able to take the eye of a deer at two hundred paces, but I can take the animal down. Maybe I can improve on that."

"Great," Annie replied. She looked to Calamity, then Jake, and then Bo. "I'd say the plan is set."

* * *

Annie walked alongside Jake. He gripped the halter rope of a gentle horse that Ethan Turlock had bartered for. The animal put Ethan back on Annie's mind. She stared at the old horse, his head slung low, plodding along behind Jake. She struggled to keep romantic feelings to herself, while attempting to put them in historical perspective. It was tough. Lana needed him. Whereas she merely wanted him. The answer was simple, in theory... keep it suppressed until romantic leanings transformed into friendship only, and all these swirling romantic feelings could be compartmentalized and become little more than a sweet memory. It would take time, maybe a long time, but right now, she had more important things to consider.

If expected to impersonate a man of means, it would be advantageous for Jake to approach Barclay's Outpost on auction day riding a horse rather than on foot. The animal was loaded with supplies to set up a campsite for an indefinite length of time… a safe place at a safe distance for her Native American friend, and father by circumstance. Annie and Jake trailed behind Calamity and Eva as they walked the trail.

Calamity remained stoic, an expression Annie came to accept and admire. The girl hardly ever smiled, but she hardly ever frowned either. Calamity wore an emotional mask. Annie was a bit jealous of that, considering that every tiny mood change splashed across her face. She was helpless to prevent, or stop it. That bland expression somehow looked right on Calamity. It had nothing to do with mood. She did not wear her feelings on her face as readily as Annie. The girl could be the opposite side of the same emotional coin. Calamity might help her remain grounded.

Eva chatted up Calamity with a string of unrelated topics, going from one to the next without pause, to which the girl nodded occasionally. Eva might as well have been a gobbling turkey. Calamity did not appear to hear any of it. Annie smiled.

The smile vanished as she felt a rush of responsibility for six-year-old Eva. Her mother, Lana, began to object last evening to the notion of Eva becoming involved in a potentially dangerous rescue mission, but Ethan changed Lana's mind. Annie thought his quick defense may have been sensitivity for choosing Lana over her. Whatever his reason, Lana allowed it. Now, Annie was completely responsible for the child's safety and responsible for proving Ethan's judgment correct as well. She knew beyond doubt that Lana would hold her personally accountable, and should.

Annie glanced to a leather luggage pouch. It swayed to and fro, dangling from the side of the horse. "What sort of clothing did Glory come up with for you?"

Jake patted the pouch draped over the horse's flank. "It's something she had been working on anyhow. She was tired of seeing me in the same two pairs of pants and same two shirts all the time. Over the past few weeks, Glory has been cooking up the notion of staging regular parties at Myrna's Glory. She is growing weary of the endless cycle of work and no play, and she wanted me to have a suit of party clothes reserved for such occasions." He nudged Annie's shoulder with his own. "I suppose ratty clothes didn't fit into her ideal of how people should dress for a party." He chuckled. "I'll leave that for her to figure out. How in the world should I know? I've never been to a party."

"Never?"

"Never."

"That's just… sad. If Glory doesn't do something about it, I will."

He smiled sideways. "Okay."

"A reason to dress up and shave occasionally, you need that."

"Regardless what I think, Glory will have something planned within the month. Wait and see." He again patted the leather pouch. "She was almost finished making this suit of clothes anyhow. She hurried the project along last night to put finishing touches on them. It's a brown wool jacket, red-stained cotton shirt and cotton canvas pants dyed a color between those two." He glanced to Annie and nodded approval. "It really does look nice... maybe too nice for someone like me."

"Don't say that."

"Glory even had a short strip of black cloth and showed me how to tie it in a bow around my neck."

"Ooh, nice."

"I won't wear it."

"Why not?"

"Too girly."

"I hope you realize that if you refuse to wear it, I'll know it and use it against you someday."

"You wouldn't..."

"Oh, yes I would, if I need a favor."

"Humph. All right, I'll think about it. I'll just have to keep on wearing these beat up old boots though. We didn't have time to do anything about them."

"Maybe no one will notice if you clean them a little."

"Maybe."

"Once we get a campsite set up for you and Calamity, you'll have plenty of time to put a shine on them."

They began the journey to Barclay's Outpost at daybreak. It was now mid-afternoon. Annie, Calamity and Eva were young and hadn't realized how long they'd been walking without a break. She noticed Jake slowing, favoring his right leg. "Are you okay?" she asked.

"The old knees aren't what they used to be. The right one is giving me pain."

"Can you walk another hour, or do we need to stop for the day?"

"I'll be okay for a while longer."

"I may have to put you on that horse sooner than I anticipated." She reached for and held his hand, swinging his arm in a childish way as they walked. "I remember a time when I had to take three steps to your one."

The look on Jake's face indicated he knew the image she painted and began describing the scenario. "It was a trek northward along the Brazos River looking for a place to build a cabin, a time before Glory and Dame Fortune had come into our lives." The memory was clearly sentimental. "Yes, I remember." He put an arm around Annie's waist and pulled her into a side-to-side hug. "You were ten and needed a bath in the worst way."

"Me! What about you?"

He bobbled his head. "Okay, me too."

"I have wondered how long we would've gone without a bath had Glory and her mother, Myrna, not come along, handed us a lump of soap and insisted on it."

He laughed and then abruptly stopped walking. "Interesting question... I've never thought about it."

"You didn't give it any thought at the time either," she laughed. "That is, until Glory pointed out how awful you smelled."

They walked on for another hour. Eva never stopped talking, and Annie figured it was time to give Calamity relief from the youngster's chatter. "Hey, Eva, I've noticed a number of squirrels around these pecan trees along the trail. Why don't you take your sling and show Cal how good you are with it? It's about time to stop and cook something to eat anyhow. We'll set up a camp for the night and get a fire started. You go and take down a couple of squirrels."

"You kill 'em, I'll skin 'em," Jake said.

Calamity looked over her shoulder to Annie and then focused on Eva walking next to her. "You can knock squirrels out of a tree with a slingshot?"

Eva giggled. "Gosh, yes."

"Come to think of it, Eva, see if you can take three or even four of them," Annie said.

"Isn't that wasteful? We won't eat that much," Calamity said.

Annie gazed with a smile into the thick undergrowth next to the trail. "I have a feeling we might need extra food."

They walked a short distance farther. A squirrel ran down the trunk of a pecan tree about twenty paces away and then up a much taller tree, scampering to the backside of the trunk out of sight.

Annie trotted past Calamity toward the bigger tree where the squirrel took refuge. "Watch this, Cal."

Annie ran to the huge pecan tree and clapped her hands once. The squirrel ran up the thirty-foot behemoth into the smaller branches, fully visible to Eva on the opposite side. "Now, Eva!"

The youngster placed a pebble into the center of the sling, spun it once overhead and then once again very fast. She released the end of the leather thong, and the stone flew with such velocity, it hummed. It was on the mark. The squirrel flew from the branch on impact and fell bouncing from one limb to the next all the way to the ground.

Calamity jogged over and examined the animal. "A perfect shot! How did you do that?"

Eva giggled.

"Eva and Annie have hundreds of ways to amaze you," Jake said.

Calamity looked to Annie. "Since I already know how acute your hearing is, I assume you hear something in the woods, something that might want to eat a squirrel perhaps. Am I right?"

Annie nodded. "Yes, but it's not some-*thing*, it's some-*one*." She rolled her tongue between her lips, whistled loudly and then shouted, "Come on out, Barney. You're not fooling anyone and you're bound to be hungry by now."

Shuffling forest litter and cracking twigs became audible to everyone. Jake unsheathed the knife on his hip.

Annie pumped an open palm at him. "Settle down, Jake. It's okay."

"I don't understand," he replied.

A man appeared, walking toward them. He maneuvered around a thicket of vines and a large tree. "I suppose I was a little naïve to believe I could shadow you and not be noticed."

Annie made one deep affirmative nod. "Yep."

"I'm not putting this knife away until I get an explanation," Jake said.

"Jake, Calamity, I'd like to introduce Barney Tackitt. He's a thief that tried to rob and kill me and then saved my life."

"Huh?" Jake's head snapped back on hearing the strange comment.

Annie smiled. "Never mind, I'll explain all that another time."

"Where's the big hairy guy?" Barney asked.

"It was agreed that he and the wolf would stay behind at Myrna's Glory. Bo has an important job and is uniquely qualified for it."

"Ah, good. In that case, I'd be happy to stay for supper," Barney said and then smirked. He strutted a few steps closer to where Annie stood surrounded by Jake, Calamity and Eva.

"Be serious," Annie said, "you would've stayed even if Bo had been here."

"Oh, sure, but I'll feel safer without the hairy mutt pointing a long sharp stick at me the whole time."

"You two really should learn to get along. Bo's a great guy and you *could* be..." She frowned and added, "I think."

Barney shook his head. "Nah, I like thievin' too much and y'all seem to have a problem with that."

Annie sighed. "I'm not giving up on you."

"Whatever." He clapped his hands, vigorously rubbed them together, and then looked to Eva. "Get that sling to swingin', kid, and knock down a few more squirrels. I'm hungry."

"Do we need to worry about waking up in the morning with all our stuff missing?" Annie asked.

Barney dropped chin to chest, appearing dismayed. "Aw, come on, you know me well enough by now to know that question is unnecessary."

"That's just the thing, Barney, I don't."

Barney's lip rose on one side into another smirk. "Trust me." He turned and briskly walked away looking up into the trees. "Now, moving on to truly important things." He twirled his hand at Eva. "Come on, kid, let's find some more squirrels." Eva trotted past him.

Somehow, Barney's attempt at a smile didn't inspire the requested trust. After a moment watching him follow Eva up the trail, Annie shrugged and sighed. *Okay, Barn, I'm going to try this trust thing with you. But, I'm sure dealing with a heavy load of doubt at the moment.*

Chapter 13

How Many Chances Are Enough?

"Annie girl be havin' trouble enough without worryin' 'bout you, foolish boy." Dame swept the ground in front of her with her walking staff, a well-worn stick of cedar as long as she was tall. It stopped at Bo's foot. She whacked his shin.

"Ow! That hurt!"

Yowl bristled at his side, lip twitching. A low guttural growl came from deep inside the canine.

Dame turned her head toward the wolf and said nothing. She projected a simple thought to remain calm.

The hair on the black wolf's neck went down. Yowl whimpered and sat on his haunches.

"That be better, you beautiful beast."

Bo bent at the waist and massaged the growing knot on his hairy leg.

"I be havin' no intention of hurtin' your man-pet," she said to Yowl, then addressed Bo. "Although, it sure be a quick way to make my point so dere be no debatin'," she said, amused.

"Man-pet! If you…"

"Oh hush up."

He pursed his lips and huffed displeasure at Dame's indirect reference to his appearance.

Dame grinned. "You be a big strong boy wit' a big heart. So, you be gettin' used to dese love pats from ol' Dame. I be likin' you a bunch, bigun."

"You're a hard one to read; ya know that?"

"I be knowin' dat for sure, but, you need to be knowin' dis... nobody here at Myrna's Glory be difficult for ol' Dame to be readin'. Ya hear?"

He sighed. "Look, I just thought Annie might need my help, that's all."

"And what if you get dere and upset a delicate plan? I don't be needin' eyes to see plain as day dat you jes be gettin' in da way if you be dere wit' her." Dame's voice rose into a higher range. "Plus, fool, it be puttin' her in danger if she be distracted lookin' after you. She be havin' enough on her mind wit' dat youngun, Eva. Is dat whatcha be wantin'?"

Bo's head slumped. "No," he mumbled.

"Dats all ya need to be sayin'. It be settled then. Don't ya be runnin' off to dat Barclay's Outpost place."

"I just wanted to help."

"Dat need burnin' inside ya be good, real good, but you be helpin' right here at Myrna's Glory, not off down da damn road."

"How so?"

"I see a dark storm brewin' dat has nothin' to do wit' da weather," she said, her voice sinking to a deep drawl. "Right now, it be small, barely worth a notice, but it be out dere on da horizon o' my mind, and it be growin' bit by bit, day by day."

Bo stepped up onto the porch of Dame's cabin, the building dubbed the Think Tank. He sat on a bench. "I don't know what you're referring to, but I..."

"Keep dat big hairy mouth shut for a minute longer and ya be knowin' what it is I be sayin'."

"Uh..."

"If dose fellers, Jake and Henry, not be so damn busy buildin' cabins, and Corky not be so damn occupied in dat shop buildin' machines and even Ethan be spendin' all his time designin', dey'd have noticed da grumblin' 'mongst dem cannibal people."

"Are you saying that we're headed toward a showdown with them?"

"Yep. But, it not *have* ta be dat way. Lean on dat fine lady, Elizabeth Longbow. She be more important dan you know. She not be sharin' da cravin' to eat people dat some of dem idiot men do."

"I will." Bo relaxed. His demeanor softened at the mention of Elizabeth's name.

"'Sides, dat Elizabeth be sweeter'n cane syrup and she be likin' you bunches."

Bo sat straight. "She does?"

Dame lifted her walking staff. "You want me to be whackin' your other shin?"

"Of course not."

"Den you jes take what I say to mean dat she be ready and able to help, dat's all. Keep dat head outa dem stars and take care o' bidness first. Be watchin' Elizabeth. She be our friend but she also be da trigger for what's comin'."

"I don't understand."

"Jes keep her in your sights. She be needin' you real soon."

"Yes, ma'am."

Dame smiled. "Dat's better." Her smile widened. "After dat, you can be makin' all da whoopee wit' Miss Longbow dat ya like." She laughed but cut it short, adding, in a dreamy lilt, "Or as much as Miss Longbow be wantin'." She covered her mouth with gnarled fingers and stifled a snicker. She then turned and walked away, probing the ground with the cedar staff as she went.

* * *

Elizabeth sat on a low stone retaining wall watching her daughter Lizzy play with Pammy and Peter.

Bo walked over to join her. "May I?" He pointed to the spot next to her on the level row of mortared stones.

She glanced up with a broad smile. "You should realize by now that you never need to ask permission to sit beside me."

Bo sat and stared at the ground a moment, and then asked, "Elizabeth, do you think we have a problem with the cannibal urges of your Old Dallas neighbors that are here at Myrna's Glory?"

The affectionate smile metamorphosed to something more serious. "It's possible. I haven't said anything. It may just be a figment of my overactive imagination, but, yes, I worry about it." She lifted her eyes to meet his gaze. "If true, I have no idea how widespread it might be. I'm confident, though, that it would not be all of them. I believe it's only a few of the men that refuse to give up the old ways. With them it's as much a symbol of power as an addictive craving. I believe that some of them see giving it up by decree a form of emasculation. I witness too many whispered conversations that end suddenly when I approach. They know very well that you and I are close. Without Ragland at my side, they may not trust me to keep their secrets anymore."

He nodded. "I see. Are you mainly referring to that Alister Beane fella?"

"Yes, him and a few of the others, mostly men; I believe the only women we need to be concerned with are the wives of those men. I'm not so sure if Rag were still alive that I wouldn't support the urge in him, if it should have gone that way. After all, it's the only way of life our family and friends have ever known. Wives will follow the husband's lead, whichever way it goes. Everyone else is just happy to be here and safe from the ravages of the Brickyard gang."

"How many do you think?"

"Four that I have reservations about. I've overheard Alister talking it up with three men and their wives on numerous occasions."

"That seems manageable."

"Maybe, but don't forget that, although appreciative of having been saved from the Brickyard gang, you might not be able to trust some of the others either. Don't ever turn your back on *any* of them if you confront them alone. Remember what happened to Annie when she trusted too much. If she had been a lesser person, Alister and that other guy would have killed her." She scooped his hairy hand into hers and squeezed. "I like… no, that's not accurate; I *love* having you in my life again. Be careful."

Bo patted the back of her hand and then kissed it. "I'm not going anywhere, not this time."

"Don't get yourself killed trying to be the good guy."

He smiled. "I won't… especially now. I have a really good reason to be careful."

Bo and Elizabeth shared a moment, gazing into one another's eyes.

* * *

The sunset was beautiful, leaving an arc of brilliant colors on the western horizon. A short time later, light began to fade. Elizabeth sat alone, looking beyond licking flames of her small cooking fire to the shell of what would become her new home, a cabin to share with her daughter, Lizzy. It was only one of many under construction, and Jake, Henry and the construction crew worked long hours to complete it as quickly as possible. She sat with an unchanging lazy grin, visualizing Bo as a partner, a husband, living with her and Lizzy in their new home. Bo had gone with Yowl into the woods to keep him company while his canine friend hunted for his supper.

She began rolling over the earlier conversation with Bo in her mind, analyzing the depth of her own conviction as to the truth. How big was the problem with those few men from her previous neighborhood in Old Dallas? How tightly were they holding on to the old ways? After a few moments of contemplation, attention shifted to a huddled group of the Old Dallas transplants some distance away next to another campfire. At the center of a quiet conversation was Alister Beane. He sat on a tree stump with his injured leg swaddled, protecting the foot with a deep gash on top of it that Annie put there with an ax. He had it propped on an adjacent stump. Hand gestures indicated he worked at making a point to the group, and it appeared to be a rather emphatic point. He was clearly in pain and angry, likely due to having been bested by a mere teenage girl.

Curiosity brought her to her feet. She wanted to know the specific subject of that conversation. For a moment she stood, stared, and wondered. Although she preferred being proven wrong, suspicion hardened about Beane, his followers and their intentions. She had to be sure. She had to know.

She turned and strolled in the opposite direction for a short distance and then slipped behind a cabin. She worked her way in a wide circle back toward the group, still sitting in a tight circle around Beane. She moved from building to building and tree to tree in a broadening arc, taking her time, knowing that if she were noticed the subject and tone of their conversation would change, or end abruptly as it normally did. Overhearing without being spotted was the only way to know the truth.

Shadows began blending into the coming darkness as the light of day continued abating. Elizabeth stepped behind a low growing oak tree to within twenty paces of Beane and his followers. She watched her every footfall, placing each step carefully. Even the snap of a twig would be too much. The bent and knotty branches and dense foliage near the ground made this place ideal. In the slowest of motion, she lowered her body onto her knees and listened. Most of what Beane was saying she heard well.

"Think of it this way," he told the two men and three women near him. "How is my foot going to heal properly without a steady intake of good meat? And I'm not talking about wild pigs and rabbits, either."

He's trying to convince them, but, it's a lie, just a load of crap, she thought. *And, for God's sake, the others are listening.*

The people around Beane nodded and mumbled agreement. Elizabeth had always known Alister Beane as charismatic and persuasive. While still living in Old Dallas, she herself tended to believe him when he spoke, but that was then. He now sowed seeds of sedition that could get people killed, even her own people—his own people.

"There are many people in this place they call Myrna's Glory," he continued. "I think it'd be easy to catch one occasionally away from this compound and harvest them for our purpose."

"But they'd be missed," one of the women said, clearly disturbed by the bold notion.

Beane grinned. "Haven't you noticed how many mountain lions, wolves and coyotes there are around here?"

"I guess I have," she replied.

"I bet Juster's pet wolf could become ravenous and turn on people if the pangs of hunger were strong enough."

She shrugged. "That's true I suppose."

"You see? It'd be easy to make it appear as though the ones that go missing just fall prey to wild animal attacks."

The others listening to Beane voiced agreement.

Elizabeth pressed her teeth together, clenching them tight, angered by the weak wills she witnessed. The last shred of doubt about this small but dangerous group had just been blown away by Beane's suggestion. *I have to tell Bo right away.*

She rose and turned.

Her breath hitched after a quick draw of air.

There stood Ace Hammond, the spouse not present with the others around Beane. "Ace! You startled me."

Holding a two-foot wooden club, he crossed his arms over his chest. "I bet."

"I—I was just about to walk over and see if anyone wanted the rest of my roast pork. I couldn't eat it all."

"If that's the case, why are you skulking about behind trees?"

"You misunderstand. I was just out for a walk and circling back when it crossed my mind to make the offer."

He grabbed her shoulders and spun her around to face the gathering. "You're a terrible liar."

"Ace, please!" she whispered. "We've known one another my whole life. Don't you trust me?"

"I trusted you and Rag, but not you and that giant ape you call a friend."

She whispered one last time, "Come on, Ace. You can trust me to put your safety first. You all can."

He shoved her, stumbling into the light of the fire.

All eyes turned. "What do we have here?" Beane asked.

"A problem, I'd say," replied Hammond. He nodded in the direction they had walked from. "She was crouched behind that tree listening to your conversation."

"Well now, isn't that an interesting turn of events?" Beane said. "I think we may have discovered our first poor soul to succumb to a wild animal attack."

Elizabeth glanced to Hammond.

He licked his lips and swallowed, as if having just tasted something wonderful.

Her jaw slackened, lips parted in surprise. "Y'all can't be serious." She looked each one in the eye. "Can you?"

No reply, or show of support came from anyone.

She tried to run.

Hammond tripped her.

She went down hard, face-first onto the ground. A groan came out as air rushed from her lungs.

Hammond straddled her and yanked her over onto her back.

Eyes shut tight, filled with debris, she spit grass and dirt. She opened her mouth to scream, but no sound had a chance. That oak club struck the side of her head.

Chapter 14

School, Orphanage, Prison

Annie woke. Low hanging clouds and a waist-high blanket of fog greeted parting eyelids. Fog covered the forest floor as if held down by an unseen force and not allowed to rise higher than a few feet. The musty odor of damp oak trees perfumed the air. She drew in deep earthy goodness and then sat up, looking around. Jake slept, as did Calamity and Eva.

Barney Tackitt was gone. He'd left a couple of hours before dawn under cover of darkness. He may have slunk away unnoticed by the others, but Annie's acute hearing roused her from a sound sleep. Without moving anything but her eyes, she had watched him leave. She did not try to stop him, or let him know she was aware of his departure. His unshakable negative attitude puzzled and dismayed her. He thwarted every effort to make his life easier and less dangerous. He was a lonely man; she understood that, but why were arrogance and pride so entrenched that it prevented showing a friendly side? Why did he work so hard to keep it hidden away? She also realized that a pattern of behavior had emerged. He would never be far away. He craved companionship but refused to address it, or do anything about it, aside from shadow her every move. Somehow, someday, she would take the time to dig deep inside his belligerent soul and coax out that other side he refused to reveal. What was stopping him from accepting change? She was now fully compelled to figure it out and fix Barney, someday, but for now, she could only respect his odd behavior. She liked the guy. She would tell him differently, but in her heart, she trusted him. Still, a tiny voice farther back in her head warned her not to put too much faith in him, or anyone else. After all, it was a genetic weakness as deeply ingrained as the superior qualities that made her who, and what, she was. She mentally added Barney to a long list of things to do.

Annie rose and rolled up the two tarpaulin scraps she used as ground cover bedding and blanket. As she did, she breathed in the pleasant aroma of the woods and listened to the chirps, songs and chatters of awakening wildlife—small things for sure, but they provided joy and contentment to begin the day. It remained one truth that could be trusted unconditionally in this dangerous world. She needed it to begin the day, this one especially. It was time to continue the journey to address yet another situation of people seeking to gain greedy advantage over the helpless and less fortunate.

According to what Calamity had told her, Barclay's Outpost lay approximately a day's walk north of where she now stood. That meant they had reached the halfway point. Therein lay partial reasoning for designating this particular spot as a resting place for the night. Strategically, it was not near enough for a longer-term campsite for Jake and Calamity. Annie figured a couple of miles out from the final destination would be better and still safe. Some distance out was necessary. Calamity could be recognized as a former resident of the school and home for children and put in harm's way. The operation to liberate the children would be complicated, maybe compromised altogether. Plus, a couple of miles would be close enough for quick access. The time would come soon enough when that would be necessary.

Annie dropped down onto one knee next to Jake. He snored softly. "Jake?"

No response. He continued to sleep.

She kissed him on the cheek and then said louder, "Oh, dear one, it's time to get up."

He drew a sharp, sudden breath and snorted.

She smiled at the only father figure she had ever known and stroked his stubbly blond beard. Gray had begun to show in it, more so in the sideburns and over his ears.

Weighted eyes opened slowly, and he grinned, plainly realizing the embarrassing noise that escaped his throat. He connected in a lazy way with Annie's eyes and then rolled to the flat of his back and stretched. "Good morning." He yawned.

"Good morning to you too." She gave his cheek a gentle pat. "You'll have to shave those whiskers, ya know; can't have you looking like a beggar when the time comes to play a wealthy bidder."

"Don't worry. Glory made sure I had the razor packed in my things."

"You do know how to use it without taking a slice out of your face, right?"

"I've learned. Glory made sure of it."

"Good." She stood and looked to Calamity and Eva, sleeping side by side. "Get up you two. We need to be on the move shortly."

She reached inside one of the leather pouches dangling from a tree branch. A honeybee had found its way inside and feasted on the loaf of crusty bread saturated with cane syrup. Annie shooed it away. "Off ya go, little one. You have to work for yours." She tore off a chunk and ate. She pointed at Jake and then swept the finger toward the two girls. "Y'all grab something to eat. We'll need the strength. We have a lot of ground to cover before this day is over. Now, hurry it up and let's be on our way."

* * *

After seven hours of walking, stopping only for food, water and rest, they came upon a clearing that had been carved out sometime in the past. It appeared to have been a cleared pasture, or possibly a field for crops at some point in the past, but now, abandoned and un-worked, it had grown over with wild grasses, small trees and even smaller saplings.

"This is the place," Calamity announced. She pointed northeasterly. "Barclay's Outpost is about a half-hour's walk in that direction. That small flowing creek over there eventually bends back to the east and you'll have to cross it if you walk in a straight line. At that point, once you break through the thick undergrowth on the opposite bank you'll see the campus of Barclay's School and Home for Children. It's a collection of red brick buildings, all built about the same time. I think I heard that it was originally a school of some sort and then restored to its original condition by Weems with help from the community."

"It sounds like it could have been a nice place," Annie said.

Calamity nodded. "Compared to everything else I've seen, those buildings and that campus are a gem to look at, but its beating heart is black. Weems and that school could've been wonderful, but they've ruined it. Greed and corruption rule everything they do."

Annie shook her head and frowned. "It's hard to figure people sometime." She untied the binding straps securing supplies to the horse's back and began removing bundles. "This is as good a place as any for a campsite. The creek will provide fresh water and there's plenty of game to hunt." She pointed to a line of trees about fifty paces away. "Plus, you have good cover from the trail beyond those trees."

The main trail, mostly level and obstruction-free, had made for an easy walk, even for Jake. Throughout the course of the day, they had met a few people along the way. Like them, they all had places to go and things to do, so encounters had been quick and cordial but of no consequence. Calamity made a point of turning away or obscuring her face, just in case they met someone who might recognize her.

It was mid-afternoon. Annie prepared to take Eva and head for the school and orphanage, hoping to be escorted into the so-called safe haven for children before dark.

Annie allowed the bow to slide from her shoulder and handed it to Calamity. "Use it all you wish, but please take care of it. Jake spent a couple of days making it for me. It's more than a weapon. The sentimental value is priceless."

"It's just a bow, not that big of a deal," he said.

She took one giant step to Jake and wrapped him up in a hug. "Oh yes it is. That bow is a symbol of the strength and love we share. Long after its usefulness has ended, I'll still have it. That's how much it means to me."

"I'll handle it with respect," Calamity said.

Annie gave her the quiver of arrows and the knife with the gnarled mesquite wood handle that Ethan had made for her. All Annie carried now was a leather pouch hanging from a long leather thong around her neck, dangling at her side. It contained the slingshot and a number of the perfectly round glass marbles Lizzy Longbow had given her. Eva carried the same thing. It offered the deceptive appearance of vulnerability, just the way Annie wanted it. "Jake, once Eva and I are on the inside and have settled into a routine, I'll find out about graduation day and the auction. Once I have enough information, I'll get back here and let you know what we should do next, and when."

"It should be coming up very soon," Calamity said, "judging by when they staged it last year."

"Don't worry about anything here," Jake said. "Cal and I will set up camp and wait."

Calamity approached Annie, stoic face unwavering. She did not stop until she stood in Annie's personal space. "You are a special person, Annie Henderson. Good luck and stay well. Remember, you can trust me. If you need me, use me."

Annie became emotional, and tears glossed her eyes. She pulled Calamity into an embrace. "Oh, Cal, you don't know how much hearing that means to me." She pushed away from her new friend and spun around before her more emotional side could spill out. "Come on, Eva, let's be on our way before I turn into a quivering lump of sobbing mush."

As she and six-year-old Eva McAdams walked away, Annie looked back a final time and smiled at them both. One she loved, the other she was coming to love. Both would be waiting for her return.

As Calamity had said, the campus near the limits of the town known as Barclay's Outpost was in sight once they walked to and crossed the bend in the creek and then navigated dense undergrowth on the opposite creek bank. It was not at all what Annie anticipated. The image formed had been something like the compound at Stalwart or her home of Myrna's Glory, an isolated group of buildings set in a more or less rural setting. What she saw was a beautiful school on landscaped grounds set within an urban area of straight, house-lined streets. She had never seen anything quite so orderly and inviting at a glance. Just the sight exuded cozy comfort, community stability and lent a feeling of peace. How odd, considering the reason they had come all this way. The school appeared to be a focal point for a planned community that had the solid look of good design and organization. No wonder Calamity had told her that getting the children out would not be easy. The entire community she spoke of surrounded it. It was not homes scattered at some distance throughout the countryside. They were all near the campus, and any call for help from the school could be answered in seconds by the townspeople.

Still, the plan Annie had come up with was a good one, even in this setting. It did not entail physical aggression. Getting into an altercation remained the choice of last resort.

"Is that the place?" Eva asked.

"That's it."

"What now?"

"Well, we need to look tired, hungry and lost."

Eva rolled her eyes and dragged her toes for melodramatic effect. "The tired and hungry part will be easy, because I am."

"Me, too. Let's put on our sad and desperate faces, head straight for the school and see what happens."

When they reached the outer row of small homes, focus sharpened on people and details of their daily activities. Some worked in yards, some tended gardens. Others wielded hammers and saws, building things. Had it not been for all the homes constructed from milled clapboard lumber and painted various colors, it would have strongly resembled an average day around the more rustic compound of Myrna's Glory.

Annie approached a man and woman working together setting fence posts in the ground. "Excuse me," she called out. "What is this place?"

Startled, the man straightened and turned to face her, allowing the carefully placed fence post in the open hole to lean off plumb. The woman, plainly distrustful, stepped in behind him. He studied Annie's face and then eyed her top to bottom. "This is Barclay's Outpost. Who are you and where do you come from?"

"My name is Annie Henderson and this is my friend Eva McAdams. Our parents were killed and consumed by cannibals in Old Dallas. We barely escaped with our lives. Now, we are wandering and lost." She forced her face into an expression of hopelessness. "Sir, Eva and I are very hungry. We'll starve to death soon without help." Her lower lip quivered as she feigned fighting back tears.

The woman came around the man and stepped lively toward Annie. "Oh, hon, you stumbled upon the perfect place for someone in your predicament." She pointed to the campus, a mere couple hundred paces away. "That is both home and school for children without parents. They will provide you a place to live, food, clothing and… well, just about everything you'll need."

Annie hugged her young companion and announced, "Eva, we've been saved."

Eva frowned, shooting Annie an accusing stare.

The man pulled a tattered straw hat off his head and mopped sweat from his face with a scrap of cloth. "Come on, kids, Martha and I will introduce you to headmaster Weems, Barclay Weems, the namesake of this community."

The couple took the lead, and Annie and Eva followed. The youngster tugged on Annie's finger to get her attention and then slowed her pace to put some distance between them and the older couple. She pulled the taller girl into a sideways tilt and put her lips to Annie's ear. "Your acting is awful. Even I couldn't believe what you said… and I'm just a little kid."

Annie shrugged and whispered back, "I'm not accustomed to lying. It's not easy. This may turn out to be more difficult than I thought."

They picked up the pace and caught up to the older couple that had stopped at the school's entrance. Annie looked up ten steps to large oak double doors fronting the three-story red brick building. The steps were between two impressive concrete lions that lay in repose facing out, as if listless on this sunny day, yet remaining in place to guard the entrance to this stately structure. Annie had seen crumbling buildings that may have been this nice two centuries ago in Old Dallas, but this was the first time to see such a place in pristine condition. As her eyes drifted from the concrete lions up the front of the building, she put on a show of amazement—mostly contrived, although it was truly impressive. "Gee whiz, this is beautiful."

"It's more than a pretty building. It holds hope and the promise of a good life for children who otherwise would have neither." The woman put her arm around Annie's waist. "Are you and your friend ready for a better life?"

Annie hesitated and looked into the eyes of the woman but could not detect insincerity, only kindness. "Yes, we are." Her committed goals for the shambles of a world they inhabited raced through her mind. Those goals made her reply truer than this woman could ever have imagined. The mostly artificial awestruck expression segued into one of adult seriousness. "I want better lives for us all, not just for Eva and me." Her eyes went back to the building they stood before, but this time she saw it for what it potentially was— a sweat shop that worked children for personal profit and deceitful gain for its administrators. Her heart and determination hardened. No amount of paint, landscaping and craftsmanship would deter her.

Annie wondered if anyone outside the school was aware of what went on inside, but then she thought: *If people are invited to a graduation reception that is a front for an illicit auction of teenage boys and girls, there has to be a network set up to get the information out.* Her face tightened with a chilling thought: *That network might be brokers dealing specifically in human trafficking from a much wider area than just here at the orphanage. This woman may not be aware of any of this, but there have to be people out there, possibly many of them, that do.*

"You look scared, dear," the older lady said. "Are you all right?" She placed what was clearly meant to be a soothing hand on Annie's forearm.

Annie nodded. She relaxed and forced a quick smile. "Just nervous, that's all. Your name is Martha, right?"

"Yes, Martha Ramos and this is my husband, John."

"If you believe this is the right place for Eva and me then I trust you."

Martha smiled and sighed. "You can trust John and me. This is my personal guarantee to you."

Annie again searched the woman's eyes for even a hint of connivance, but she detected nothing of the sort. "Honest people with good intentions are hard to find. I'm so pleased we happened upon you and your husband."

John Ramos knocked on the door. Shortly, a metallic clank rang out as a locking bolt on the door was released from the inside. One side of the double doors opened with an echoing squawk from a dry hinge. Before them stood a well-groomed man about Annie's height, six-foot, with oiled dark hair combed straight back close to his head, not a hair out of place. He was dressed as if about to attend some formal function in fine velvety pants and matching coat in a dark maroon color over a frilly white shirt. Annie thought the style peculiar for an average day in an orphanage, or any of the places she had encountered in her life. "Wow! Now that's something I don't see every day," she blurted.

Eva snapped a look up at Annie, the youngster clearly taken aback by the abrupt and crude honesty.

"Those are the fanciest clothes I think I've ever seen," Annie quickly added.

John and Martha chuckled and the man in the doorway smiled and said, "Thank you, but they're not my clothes, just a uniform that Mister Weems insists I wear. I'm Rodney, Mister Weems's personal assistant."

"I'm Annie Henderson and this is my friend, Eva McAdams, but I call her my sister. Our parents are dead. We are very hungry and have lost all hope for making it on our own. Can you help us?"

She had difficulty taking the man seriously because of his clothes, but it was no laughing situation. The last time she had seen such gaudiness on this scale was Fiam Lee Tam at the Stalwart compound last year, and as it turned out, she had to kill him to prevent being murdered by him. She was already developing a bad taste in her mouth about this place.

After a visual sweep up and down her and Eva, Rodney said, "Follow me. I'll see if Mister Weems can see you. I'm sure there is something we can do," he smiled cordially enough and added, "Because it's what we do."

Annie and Eva followed Rodney down a long hallway, John and Martha Ramos trailing behind. As they walked, Annie watched Rodney. He had spoken with a distinctly effeminate voice and his gait appeared equal to the voice. *The clothes may not be his but they do seem to complement his apparent personal preference.* The walls of the hallway were paneled in dark and richly colored woods and the hardwood floorboards glistened with a highly reflective coating of some sort. Everything smelled of waxes and oils.

They approached two young people on stairs, standing a few steps up near a landing. The girl held a bucket in one hand and a rag in the other, while the boy polished the banister and supporting balusters—both were ten, or eleven years old, perhaps. Neither smiled. Their expressions were vacant, clearly disinterested in the sudden appearance of strangers—Annie's first clue that the personality of this place did not live up to its elegant facade. In fact, Rodney's expression seemed distant and flat, as if maybe he didn't care for his job any more than those two kids on the stairs enjoyed the polishing chore. It would be worth exploring, but not now—another time perhaps.

As they walked by, Annie looked up to the working children on the stairs. "Hi," she said cheerfully.

No response, just empty-eyed gazes followed her as she walked by.

Annie saw right away that these children suffered from more than enduring a tedious chore, something systemic and troubling. That was clear enough upon their sad young faces.

Rodney stopped at a door different in style and more elaborate than the others that lined the hallway. He knocked, and from the other side, a muffled "Yes?" penetrated the dense wooden door.

Rodney opened it a crack and looked around its edge. "Mister Weems, we have two new potential residents. Do you have time?"

What sounded like a perturbed voice began, "Rodney, how many times must I tell you…"

"And Mister and Missus Ramos are with them," Rodney quickly interrupted.

A brief pause was followed by, "Oh, of course, show them in."

When Rodney fully opened the door, Annie had her first look at Barclay Weems. The man stood behind a huge ornately carved and garish desk. He was dressed as spectacularly as his assistant—hair neatly trimmed and combed, face slickly shaven, and his fingernails appeared to have been manicured and polished to a high gloss. He wore a black suit of clothes without a wrinkle anywhere, and there was an aura of arrogance about the man. It virtually oozed from his pores.

"Mister Weems," Rodney said, "I'd like you to meet Annie Henderson and her young charge, Eva McAdams. Of course, you know John and Martha."

Weems rushed around the large desk and took Mister Ramos' hand. "John, it's so nice to see you again." While still holding the hand, he reached for Martha's hand with the other and gripped it delicately. "And you, too, Martha. I want to thank you both for the wonderful charitable donations that you make to our home for children throughout the year. And that side of beef you gave us last month"—he kissed his fingertips— "was absolutely exquisite. The children loved it, and we love you for the gesture."

Annie listened. *His acting is no better than mine.* She wondered if the children got any of that meat beyond fat scraps and bone broth, or whatever Weems and the school board did not want. His over-the-top gushing performance was clearly for John and Martha Ramos' benefit. She took this moment to examine the man and his surroundings. So far, the dire story that Calamity had told her about the place seemed to warrant investigation. She committed to learning more.

"Rodney," Weems said, "take our new friends to the kitchen and see if any of that stew and bread is left from the midday meal. Let's get our newest residents fed." Weems gave Rodney a quick sideways nod of the head, a clear indication for him to take Annie and Eva away. "I'll visit with my dear friends, John and Martha, a while longer."

"If you don't mind, I'd like to follow the kids to the kitchen," said Martha. "As long as we've lived in Barclay's Outpost, I've never seen this home for children beyond these offices. May I?"

Weems appeared shocked by the request. Hesitatingly he said, "Uh, well, I don't suppose that would be a problem." He then added more forcefully, "Sure, why not? John and I will wait here while you have a look."

Rodney opened the door to the hallway and ushered Annie, Eva and Martha out of Weems's office.

"Rodney, might I have a quick word first?" Weems asked.

As he approached his assistant, he addressed the others. "Wait here for a moment."

Weems pulled Rodney to a distant wall in his office and whispered into his ear.

Rodney responded without a change of expression and a scant head nod.

Weems backed away. "Thank you, Rodney. That will be all." Weems rejoined John Ramos as Rodney stepped back into the hall and closed the door.

Annie watched with extreme interest. Even with advanced hearing, she could not quite make out what all Weems had whispered, but the words and tone of what she did hear was one of a warning. It seemed obvious this surprise inspection by Martha had to be prepared for. The gist of the whispered words had been something about not going beyond the kitchen and dining hall. They had only been inside the building for a matter of minutes and already, negative evidence mounted that Annie mentally catalogued. It seemed there might be enough to act on sooner than anticipated.

As they walked down the long corridor, Annie observed everything within purview, absorbing details. She did not know what information might come in handy as the plan unfolded. Better to learn it as she went. One detail seemed odd. None of the doors in this long corridor were marked— no numbers, letters, signs, placards, or anything to indicate what might be on the other side of any of them—and there were many. The other glaring absence was the children themselves. Aside from the two youngsters polishing woodwork on the stairs, there were no other children to be seen anywhere. Why couldn't she hear young voices? There should be laughter, or shouting, or bickering, but the place might as well have been vacant. All she heard was the echoing clop of their heels on the hardwood floor as they walked.

They turned down an adjacent hall and walked only a few more steps before coming to another unmarked and unremarkable door. "Wait here," Rodney said.

He opened the door and stepped inside. He did it in such a way as to prevent an unobstructed view of the interior and closed it securely behind him.

After a moment, Annie heard many shuffling feet and murmurs coming from inside, that Martha might not have been able to hear.

After another minute or so, the door opened, this time wide. Rodney gestured them in.

Annie saw only one long table with twelve chairs. At the far end of the dining area was a half-wall and a spacious, fully equipped kitchen beyond it—stoves, ovens, a wood-fired hot water machine, pots and pans hanging from hooks suspended from the ceiling and a long preparation table beneath them. Even from where they stood, Annie saw dirty dishes piled next to wash tubs filled with steaming water. Work had been in progress that Rodney had stopped before allowing them access to this area. No one remained.

"Very nice," Martha said. "But it was unnecessary to have your staff cease working just because of visitors." She approached the long dining table and walked its length, letting a finger glide over its surface. "This is a wonderful dining hall for the kids, but it would seem there aren't enough chairs for all the children to eat at one time."

Annie folded her arms across her chest and thought: *There's a reason for that, sweet Martha. This room has to be for the dining pleasure of Weems and his cronies. I wonder where the children eat. Where are the children?*

Chapter 15

Home Away From Home

It was late, after midnight by Annie's reckoning. She lolled her head to the side and saw that Eva breathed deep and even, asleep. Annie sighed. A twinge of jealousy wrinkled her brow at the sight of the younger girl sleeping peacefully. It somehow seemed unfair. How could the youngster drift off to sleep so easily? It was as if the task ahead was nothing more than a simple chore that her mother might have her do before resuming a rowdy game of tag with friends.

Just the passing thought of Lana put Ethan back on Annie's mind. She still loved him. Images flooded her mind, one layering upon the other. She shook her head. *I can't allow myself to bog down, must keep a clear head. I have other, more important things to consider. Besides, I'll just end up crying again.* The emotional wound of losing him to Lana was still raw.

She focused on Eva and smiled. It was easier to reconcile the end of her relationship with Ethan when she remembered that this cherished youngster lying next to her would be the beneficiary of Lana's and Ethan's love.

"Humph," Annie snorted softly. She suddenly realized that Eva had placed total faith in her to be guide and protector and felt no fear nor shred of hesitation while they remained close. That is why the girl seemed so at ease in this strange new environment. "Eva Louise, you little stinker," she breathed. She pushed errant strands of hair from the girl's face and then stroked her head. Of course, it might be a different story altogether if they should become separated. In a place like this so-called children's home, it was possible. That potential danger had to remain at the forefront of every thought.

At seventeen, Annie was young enough to enjoy childish romps with Eva and others the youngster's age, but at the moment, her head was in an adult frame. She remained committed to finding out the true nature of this home and school for children. Should Calamity Bloom's assessment be justified, she would do whatever it took to get the children out and away to the safer and more loving environment of Myrna's Glory.

Cal, as her new friend preferred being called, had told her that she and the twins were escapees from cannibalism in Old Dallas. That known, it was reasonable to assume most of the children in this place were orphaned the same way. The nearest boundary of Old Dallas was northeast of Barclay's Outpost, only a few miles farther up the same road they had traveled to get here.

Annie continued stroking Eva's hair. A few adoring moments later, her eyes drifted from the child as darker thoughts encroached. In the dim moonlight coming through the window, she scanned the bedroom with analytical eyes. Something was not at all right. This room had been elegantly appointed with deep, rich, wood-toned walls, deeply carved wooden tables and chairs, and a bed so soft it billowed around her body. It should be closely akin to squalor if

Calamity Bloom's definition of Barclay Weems's home for children was to be believed. She thought about that. After contemplating possible scenarios, she settled on the notion that since Martha Ramos had introduced them to Headmaster Weems yesterday, toured a portion of the facility, and then accompanied them to this room, it must be a ruse for the nice lady's benefit. Without Missus Ramos's presence, she and Eva may never have even seen this room, much less spend the night in it. She and her husband must be well known and respected members of the surrounding town of Barclay's Outpost. They also provided donations of food and materials, apparently on a regular basis. No wonder Barclay Weems would want to put on a show for staunch supporters such as John and Martha Ramos. If the truth yet to be revealed proved this line of reasoning, such a revelation would bring this place down in a day. Still, if no one believed it to be the truth, how much better off would she be to share it with people who lived this close yet were ignorant of the true nature of this home for children?

Okay, she thought, *even if the worst-case scenario is accurate, it answers nothing about where all the children are.* The need to know burned inside her and drove away desire to sleep. She glanced again to Eva. The girl slept—no movement, not even a twitch.

Annie eased her legs off the bed and sat up. She slipped on her pig hide boots and then rose. After a final glance to Eva, she glided silently to the door, opened it, then closing and latching it behind her. She stepped into the long deserted corridor lined with identical doors on both sides, extending for quite some distance in both directions. Curiosity to know what lay behind all these unmarked doors piqued.

She tried the nearest doorknob. It was locked.

She tried another, also locked.

She tried a third. It turned and with a click the door opened with the gentlest push. "Aha," she breathed, and then craned her head around the edge of the door for a look. Her eyes met disappointment. The room was totally barren; just a highly polished space with nothing in it.

She sighed, venting disappointment, and then backed out, pulling the door shut.

Annie continued working down the hall, trying knobs of doors on both sides. She discovered three more unlocked with the same result as the first, empty unfurnished rooms, used for nothing, not even storage. It seemed as though the bedroom where she left Eva sleeping may not have been the only ruse. This whole place was beginning to feel like an elaborate hoax.

Disappointment segued into frustration as an aggressive streak bubbled inside her. She became less worried about noise as she tried yet another door. It was unlocked. It looked the same as the rest, but it opened outward into the corridor. *Okay, this is different.* She again became aware of the importance of stealth.

Uncertain, she held the knob for a moment before gently pulling it fully open. Stairs began just inside, descending into darkness. She leaned back and looked one way then the other in the hallway. The only illumination was moonlight through three windows spaced at wide intervals on the opposite side of the corridor, but that was enough for Annie's enhanced vision. There was no indication whatsoever that this door should be anything different than the others, but it was. She neither saw, nor heard indication of people about. That, and a desire to learn, was all she needed to become fully committed to discovering what lay at the bottom of these stairs.

She stepped inside and pulled the door shut behind her. It was dark, so dark that even genetically superior vision proved useless. She held the banister and felt her way downward. After many steps, she came to what seemed to be a landing. She slid one foot forward, then the other—no more steps. She felt closeness straight ahead. She approached something.

She extended an exploratory hand deeper into the black, groping the air, thinking a wall could be in front of her. She discovered that the closeness was not only straight ahead, but right and left as well.

She took another half step forward. Her searching palm came to rest on what felt like a door. She swept the hand down to where a knob should be. She found it, turned it and pushed. A hinge squawked. She cringed and stood motionless with clenched teeth, waiting for telltale sounds of having been discovered.

After a moment, hearing nothing, she fully opened the door.

She noticed a dim orange glow of light coming from beneath another door about twenty-five paces straight ahead. It was not much light, but enough that she could see that this room was not like anything upstairs. A mix of noxious odors assaulted her. As she began walking toward the light, those smells could better be differentiated. She detected the odors of solvents, oils, waxes, burnt metals and things more disgusting, like unwashed bodies and even the faint smell of decaying flesh.

As she crossed the room, she walked between rows of small tables that appeared to be individual workspaces. Each table held unfinished pieces of sewn cloth and small wooden pieces, like candle stands and kitchen utensils, while others had scraps of sheet metal and fashioning tools atop them. The farther she walked, the more the unpleasant odors intensified. Finally, she came upon a series of tables holding animal hides, mostly cow, in various stages of the curing and tanning process. Green hides stunk. She slapped away a fly that buzzed her face when she came closer for a better look at the skins. She grimaced and then moved on.

She came to stand before the door that had guided her trek across the room. The glow of light beneath it shined across her boots. Light meant human presence. There could be no greater need for caution than now.

In extreme slow motion, she pushed a crude lever that served as a door latch. This door was rugged, more like something in a barn. A locking bar scratched across its receiver as she slowly released its hold. She felt the door lose resistance and begin to open.

She pushed it only a fraction of an inch at a time. After several long seconds, she had opened the door wide enough to see around its edge. The first thing she noticed was that the door had been designed to only open from the outside. There was no way to open it from the inside. Then, she saw what she came to see.

An oil lamp burned with a steady flame next to the door, illuminating three rows of cots, ten in each row. Twenty-seven of them were occupied. Judging by sizes of occupants, age ranges were from very young, four, or five perhaps, up to teens her age.

She stepped inside. The large room was unventilated and musty, and another odor made her wonder just how often these kids were allowed to bathe.

A small body beneath a tattered blanket stirred to her left.

Annie froze, but too late.

A young girl's head appeared from beneath the cover and looked at her. With balled fists, the youngster rubbed sleep from her eyes. "You're new here, aren't you? Is Calamity with you?"

Annie quickly put a finger to her lips. "Shh. Let's not wake anyone else, okay?" she whispered.

The girl nodded and sat up.

Annie lowered her body close to the child. She sat on her heels on the dusty, buckling, wood plank floor and put her lips to the girl's ear. "Calamity is my friend. Why did you ask if she were with me? Did you expect to see her?"

"Uh-huh. When she left, she promised she'd come back and take me out of here." Tears welled in her eyes, and her lip quivered. "I don't like it here."

Annie's eyes began moistening too. "Hush, sweet girl." Annie pulled the youngster into an embrace, offering her shoulder. "Shh. There's no more reason for tears. Calamity kept her promise. She asked me to come here to get you out."

The youngster pulled her head away from Annie's shoulder and looked up at her. "Will I see Pammy and Peter soon too? I miss them so much. I'm so alone without them."

The child was about the same age as the twins. Annie dropped her face so that she could be nose to nose with the girl. She offered the biggest smile possible. "Oh, yes. You'll be running, romping, laughing and screaming to your heart's content very soon. I promise. What's your name?"

"Lucy."

"Tell me, Lucy, who is the person in here that you trust most?"

Lucy rubbed her reddened eyes and flipped a finger toward cots one row over. "Him."

Slightly amused by the oversimplified response, Annie flashed a half-grin. "So, it's a guy, huh? Is he one of those lumps under a blanket over there?"

Lucy offered an affirmative nod. "Yeah, him." She pointed again, this time with a stiffened arm to a cot three away.

"What's his name?"

"Nicky. He's been here a long time."

"How old is Nicky?"

"Seventeen. He'll be graduating and leaving soon." The child's face began to pull down with fresh tears. "When he's gone, I don't know what I'll do." She covered her face with her hands.

Annie saw fresh scratches on the backs of Lucy's hands, some deep with crusted blood on them. She also saw scars. She pulled one hand away from the girl's face and pressed it between her own. She felt calluses and blisters on the palm, all the signs of hard labor. "Don't worry. Your time here is almost over." She kissed the mangled young hand, rose to her feet, and placed a finger to her lips. "Lie back down. I need to chat with your friend, Nicky."

"Okay." Lucy wilted over onto her side and pulled the dirty threadbare blanket back up to cover her shoulders, never taking her eyes from Annie.

All of the other children remained asleep. Annie came up on the tips of her toes and walked to the cot Lucy had pointed out. She again sank down to sit on her heels next to a boy who softly snored. She placed a light hand on his shoulder. "Nicky," she whispered. From a quick examination of his face, she marveled at how much he looked like a younger version of Ethan Turlock.

He roused, licked his lips, and his eyelids parted. Suddenly those sleepy eyes popped large. He drew a quick breath.

Annie placed a swift hand over his mouth. "Shh, don't say anything yet. Let me explain who I am and why I'm here before you speak."

His eyes darted around her face. He then nodded once.

"My name is Annie Henderson, a friend of Calamity Bloom's." As soon as Calamity's named cleared her lips, she felt tension leave his body. She removed her hand from his mouth. "Although I'm still developing a plan, I'm here to get you and the other children out of here. Okay?"

"How? You look as though you might be a little older than me, but not by much. What makes you think you can get it done, unless you brought an army with you? Did you?"

Although Annie heard all the questions, one comment put a sparkle in her eye. A grin stretched her mouth. "You think I look older than seventeen?"

"Well... yeah."

She patted his shoulder. "I like you already."

"Why?"

"Because I'm seventeen too."

"Then you'd better have brought an army with you, or you'll accomplish nothing except getting locked up with us."

"I *am* the army... sort of."

"Huh?"

"Never mind, I'll explain that comment later. Right now, I need to know how big the staff is here and if there's any one of them that you trust."

"There're twelve regulars that I see all the time... all men. One of them has been gone for three days and will probably be back tomorrow. Every year, just before the graduation party, he leaves and stays gone for exactly three days."

"That makes sense."

"Why?"

"Someone has to get the word out that an auction is coming up."

"An auction? What do you mean by that?"

"Never mind. Are you scheduled to graduate?"

He grinned. "Yeah. I can't wait to get out of here. I'll be one of six at that party. I don't know what my future holds, but I sure hope I get a good job. I've sworn to come back and get my younger friends out of here."

"You'll be one of *seven* at that party. I'll be there too, I'm sure. Weems is not going to miss an opportunity to add to his wealth just because I'm a new arrival. I'm sure he'll put me on the block just like the six of you."

"You keep talking like we're to be sold."

"You are."

"What?"

"The graduation and reception are just a cover for wealthy visitors to check out the latest crop. You and the others will be sold into slavery. It's not a real graduation and there are no paying jobs to be had."

"Seriously?"

"Seriously. Sorry, but you had to know the truth."

"In that case, I sure hope you know what you're getting yourself into."

"Yeah, me too. Now, is there anyone on the staff that you trust?"

"No, but if I were going to trust anyone it would be Rodney, Weems's personal assistant."

"Why?"

"Rodney was raised here. He was among the first to graduate from this place. Weems kept him here. Rodney knows what life is like here, but like so many others that came at a very young age, he has no idea what life is like on the outside. He accepts this as normal. I know better. I didn't come in until I was fourteen. I've seen Rodney step in and stop cruel criticism of the kids by board members. I've even seen him aggressively stop one of the members from whipping a small boy. He might be one that you can trust, but I can't guarantee it."

"Good to know." Annie nodded and thought for a moment. "One other question… I tried many of the doors upstairs and a few were unlocked. Those that I did look into were empty, not a stick of furniture. Do you know what's in those other rooms that were locked?"

"Nothing. They're mostly all the same. They were meant as rooms for the kids but it was easier for them to sell off all the furniture and keep us locked up down here. A few were left furnished, but that's just for show when visitors come to check out the facility." His head bobbled, embarrassed. "I suppose just knowing that should have clued me in to everything else."

"Don't worry about it. You trusted them and they are betraying that trust. Faith that people are truthful and doing the right thing is not a fault." She smiled and patted him on the knee. She tilted her head as a thought struck her. She placed a finger to her lips. "Ya know, Weems and his cronies are not only brazen, they've become brazenly lazy as well. They're ripe for a takedown. Complacency could work to our advantage. I think they arrogantly believe this set up can go on forever and may not be guarding their dirty little secret very well. Still, it'll hinge on the town coming to understand the truth about this place." She offered a reassuring smile. "Just rest and tell no one of our visit." She stood. "Thanks, Nicky. I think I have the basis for a plan to get all of you out of here."

"But what about—"

"Shh. I'll answer all your questions in time. For now, rest easy. I'm here to help all of you, but tell no one I was down here."

"Okay."

"Tell Lucy not to speak of it either."

As Nicky's head lowered back onto the pillow, he nodded.

Annie let out a contented sigh. "I think I can sleep now too. See ya tomorrow."

She blew smiling little Lucy a kiss on her way out the door.

Chapter 16

No Tasting Victory Today

"Lana, do you hear a child crying?" Ethan asked.

"I think I do." She got up from a rocking chair in the front room of the cabin she and Ethan now shared and hurried to a window. She pushed aside a roughly woven burlap curtain and looked into the early evening darkness. "It's too dark to be certain, but I think it's one of the new kids that came in with the group from Old Dallas. Lizzy… Lizzy Longbow, I think. She and Eva became fast friends."

Ethan jerked open the door and stepped into the night. He caught sight of the preteen girl. She sobbed, wandering through the open area surrounded by cabins. "What's the matter? Where's your mother?" he shouted.

Lizzy stopped.

Even in the dim light, Ethan saw that the girl was panicked. He trotted toward her and did not slow until she became clearly visible.

When he came into view, her searching eyes settled on him. She wailed, ran to him, and then into his open arms, her body slamming his. "I don't know where she is. I can't find her!" She pressed a tear-stained face into his chest.

Other cabin doors opened. People began coming out, responding to the commotion. Glory Jackson, Jake Henderson's live-in companion, ran to Ethan's side and dropped to her knees. She peeled the girl's arms away from Ethan, forcing the youngster to face her. "Calm down, child." Glory pressed Lizzy's cheeks between her palms. "Look at me, Lizzy." She gave the girl's fear-widened and darting eyes a moment to stop and focus.

Lizzy's eyes finally connected.

"That's better. Now, tell me what you know," Glory said.

"I was playing and Mama told me to be back at our campfire before dark. I did as she said, but when I got back she was gone. I waited, but she didn't come back." Fresh tears streamed. Her voice squeezed into a higher range. "She didn't come back!" Lizzy's breathing began sawing faster, on the verge of total loss of control.

Glory pulled the girl into a motherly embrace. "Shh. It'll be okay. We'll find her." Glory looked up to Lana, now standing next to Ethan. "Would you take Lizzy inside your cabin until we can locate her mother?"

"Sure." Lana put a hand on the girl's arm.

Lizzy was hesitant to come away from Glory's embrace.

"It'll be okay, sweetheart. I'll be along shortly and the three of us can wait together."

Lana's gentle coaxing and Glory's calm words worked. Lana led the youngster back toward her cabin. Then she stopped and looked back to Ethan.

"Glory's right," Ethan said. "You two keep her inside until we find her mother."

Lana turned to continue toward her cabin, but hesitantly so. "Honestly, Lana, this is how you can help. Take care of her," he urged. "I'll join you in a few minutes."

Suddenly, from out of the dark, Bo and Yowl stopped Lana before she got to her cabin. "Did I hear that right? Is Elizabeth Longbow missing?"

Lana was clearly taken aback and now more than a little ill at ease with the situation. She had become uncomfortable by the abrupt appearance of the giant wolf that stood four feet tall at the shoulders and the terseness of the even larger and very hairy Bo Juster. Her answer to his question came as a rapid, nervous nod. She then snapped another look back to Ethan, searching for reassurance.

"Please, Mister Juster, find my mother," Lizzy said, her voice strained to a squeak.

"Yes, it would seem she's missing," Ethan said as he approached to stand with the two women and the girl. "People just don't wander off into the woods alone after dark. It's not safe. There are as many violent and untrustworthy people as there are predator animals in this crazy world. Every missing person report has to be taken seriously and acted upon quickly."

Even before Ethan finished talking, and without responding, Bo walked around the four of them, heading in the direction of Elizabeth's campfire, explosive anger about to erupt.

"Wait a minute," Ethan said, "let's get a search group together. Don't go it alone. You don't know what'll be waiting for you if you do."

"Oh, I think I do," Bo growled as he continued walking away.

"Hey," Ethan added. "It's no safer out there for you alone than it is for Elizabeth."

"You be listenin' to Ethan, ya hear?" Dame Fortune stepped from dark shadows into his path, cutting him off. "Use dat big ol' brain o' yours and think about what ya be doin'."

"You're the one who told me something like this might happen," he shot back. "Why would you prevent me from handling it?"

"I'm not doin' dat a'tall. I be tellin' ya, fool, to think it through first. Yes, you need to be savin' dat sweet Elizabeth girl, but I see plain as anythin' through dese damned ol' blind eyes dat you jes be gettin' yaself killed, marchin' off all angry and such. Is dat whatcha be wantin'?"

"But Elizabeth might be in serious trouble."

"No 'might be' about it. She be needin' you bad."

"Then tell me how to handle it, if you can see into the future."

"Dat's jes the thing; I can't see because your head be a jumbled mess right now. I warned ya 'bout gettin' yaself killed 'cuz I saw it in my mind, but now da picture has changed and keeps on changin'. I can't tell ya how." Dame's voice deepened, becoming ominous in tone. "But, you be hearin' dis and be hearin' it well... you can still be gettin' yaself killed and everyone with you if ya don't get dat anger under control." The sound of her voice matched her naturally shocking appearance of milky blind eyes set in a face dark as the night and that explosion of white tightly curled hair on her head.

The warning was enough to chill even Bo, but only for a moment. He shook it off and turned to march away. "I don't have time for this. You just—"

Dame lifted her cedar staff and held it horizontally in front of her, as if blocking an attack. "Shut your mouth and face me!" she thundered.

Bo stopped. Slowly, he turned toward the old lady.

"Every time ya be openin' dat big hairy mouth o' yours, I see your future change. You keep movin' on like ya are and you *will* be gettin' Elizabeth killed! But, first, dey'll take your hide for a winter coat and slice you into bits!"

Bo took a breath, then huffed it away. "Okay, okay I get it." He let his head wilt forward; although, his face still virtually glowed with anger.

Henry, the self-avowed protector of Myrna's Glory, came trotting up from the other side of the compound, five-foot-long barbed hunting spear in hand. "What's the ruckus?"

"'Bout time you be showin' up, bigun." Dame pointed in the general direction of Bo. "Dis one be needin' a calmer hand goin' with him. I swear. Dat big damn wolf o' his probably thinks more before he acts dan him."

"One of the Old Dallas women has disappeared," Ethan added. "Her daughter can't find her."

"It's Elizabeth Longbow, the woman that was with me when we arrived here," Bo said.

"Is she in trouble?"

"No doubt," Bo snapped.

"Eh!" Dame stabbed the air with a gnarled disciplinary finger. "You be watchin' dat anger, boy."

"What kind of trouble?" Henry asked.

"Not sure yet, but I am certain she's being held by some of those people from Old Dallas and knowing their background, that bothers me." Bo looked to Dame.

She nodded. "He damn sure be right 'bout dat and good reason to be bothered."

Henry renewed his grip on the spear in his hand.

"Then let's go find her," Ethan said as he made a move to take the lead and head into the darkness.

Henry grabbed him by the shoulder and forced him to stop. "This is not a job for you, Ethan. You're too valuable to Myrna's Glory to be puttin' yourself in harm's way."

"But I want to help."

"You just keep designing machines and advancing our cause. Let us take care of enforcement."

Dame lifted her cedar staff high into the air and announced in raised voice, "Now, dat's a plan. You boys go bring our girl home." She turned the staff toward Bo. "And you be keepin' a cool head on dem big hairy shoulders, or you be changin' good ol' Henry's future in a bad way, right along with yours."

Ethan watched them walk away and considered following them anyhow. *I'm not helpless,* he thought, *and I sure don't want to get a reputation as a coward.*

Dame swiped her cedar staff toward Ethan. "You be gettin' such thoughts right outa dat damn head o' yours. If we be losin' you, Myrna's Glory be in big trouble, youngun. Not only dat, if'n somethin' bad happened, dat sweet Lana and little Eva be left alone a second time in jes a few days. Don't ya ever be forgettin' dat."

* * *

Bo, Henry and Yowl trotted in the direction of Elizabeth's campfire. When they arrived, the fire had all but died out; only glowing embers remained. They looked beyond it to the many other campfires of the Old Dallas refugees scattered about. Only a few continued to burn, a strong indication that the dying fires were no longer maintained, and it was far too early in the evening for that. It was a strong clue. "I count eleven fires unattended," Bo said.

"Yeah, eleven," Henry replied. Shifting eyes indicated he was thinking the situation over, and then he asked, "How are we going to conduct a search without light? We won't be able to see the trail. Even if we could, a torch would alert them before we're ready to be seen."

"Not a problem," Bo said. He dropped onto a knee in front of Yowl and petted the animal's muscular jaws. "Yowl, find Elizabeth."

The big wolf pranced its front paws. Bo had known Yowl long enough to trust the wolf's ability to understand. His friend would know exactly what to do. Yowl lifted his nose into the air and began moving away.

Bo sprang to his feet. "Now," he said, "don't lose sight of Yowl. He'll find her."

The trail wound through the woods. Myrna's Glory disappeared beyond the low growing oak and cedar trees behind them as the three moved deeper into the woods. They made their way into an area lower than the surrounding terrain. Undergrowth became denser. Yowl frequently stopped and sat on his haunches, waiting for the two big men to catch up.

As they moved through a dense patch of brush beneath a cluster of oaks, the glow of a fire appeared some distance ahead. The undergrowth thinned to reveal a small grassy meadow surrounded by dense cedars and oaks. Bo noticed first and grabbed Henry by the arm. "Wait," he hissed. He put a finger to his lips and then pointed toward the dull light.

"I see it," Henry whispered.

Yowl's demeanor changed, head slung low and moving slowly, stopping altogether on occasion to sniff the air.

The two men remained behind the wolf, moving only at the speed the canine dictated.

As they moved closer, the glow brightened until they saw flames licking skyward. Voices became audible.

They continued forward, but now inching along.

Finally, they reached a point where visibility improved, unencumbered by the flora. Bo now understood why Dame Fortune had insisted he not go it alone. Although Elizabeth had indicated that she believed only four men and their wives were involved, they witnessed thirteen men and nine women still feeding a fire with limbs and brush. If it had been just four, he could have taken care of that many alone. He had been quite certain of that, but not thirteen. Even the presence of Yowl might not be enough to fend off that many men armed with clubs, knives and axes fashioned from scrap metal. The light from the fire at this range was substantial. The count was accurate.

Bo craned his head above the brush they crouched behind. "I don't see Elizabeth?"

Henry nodded toward clustered trees. "Look there, at the edge of the clearing." He pointed to an area near a large chinaberry tree surrounded by saplings and taller grass.

Within new-growth trees, Elizabeth lay with hands tied behind her and bound to both ankles. She was gagged but spasmodic jerks of her body indicated she was crying. Standing next to her was a man wielding a crude but large makeshift machete-like knife and hacking small limbs from a long stout cedar pole. Other men, nearer the fire, worked on a crude support system for the pole to be suspended above the fire.

Bo grabbed Henry's arm. "If we don't do something right now, Elizabeth will be killed, field dressed like a wild pig, skewered with that pole and then cooked."

Henry pulled Bo's hands from his arm. "Hold on. Let's think about this for a moment."

The man preparing the skewering pole tossed it aside and stepped over to Elizabeth. Holding that knife in one hand, he roughly grabbed the top of her dress and ripped it away with the other.

There was no time to waste thinking.

With no further discussion, the two big men burst in unison from the shadows behind the concealing brush into the light of the fire. Yowl responded to their lead and leaped over the tangle of vines and sumac bushes to stand between them. "Get away from her!" Bo shouted.

The man standing over Elizabeth holding a crude knife sprang to attention and whirled around.

Henry advanced, firmly clutching his razor sharp spear held far in front of his body. His imposing gestures indicated that he had no intention of allowing the man to harm Elizabeth. "Make even the slightest threatening move with that knife at her or us, mister, and it will be the last move you ever make," he warned.

As Henry, Bo and Yowl walked toward him, the twelve other men and some of the women moved to surround the rescuers.

Henry and Yowl stopped. Bo did not.

"Come any closer and I'll run you through with this knife," the man shouted at Bo.

Bo kept walking, getting nearer, moving faster with each step. "Try it."

The man started walking, and then running toward Bo.

Bo roared like the lion he appeared to be.

The man raised the big knife to a thrusting position.

Bo carried no weapons. It did not matter. He grabbed the man's arm above his knife hand and twisted the entire arm from the shoulder socket with a grinding pop.

The man screamed in agony and stumbled away, his arm dangling at a grotesque angle toward his back.

"Damn," Henry said, frozen in place by Bo's burst of dangerous aggression.

The others hurried to the man's aid, clearly bent on attacking Bo en masse.

Yowl leaped into the space between the cannibals and Bo. Hair came up on his neck as the wolf's muscles tensed. Slobber strung from bared teeth. He crouched, preparing to counter-attack, but did not. He growled, holding his ground, as if even he knew there should be a better way.

Bo was angry, almost blindly, and more apt to run roaring into them than Yowl. "How could you fools do this to that sweet woman? She has done nothing to you, any of you!" He moved around the standing wolf, walking straight toward the cluster of fighting men. They were prepared and waiting for a melee to begin.

"Wait," Henry shouted. He ran to block Bo's advance. He put a hand against the big man's chest and stopped him. Bo's eyes remained fixed on the armed group.

Henry faced them. The cluster of men and women had been brought to a standstill by Yowl's protective stance. Still, they were ready for a fight. "I suggest all of you drop your weapons, or much blood will be spilled and I promise you, it won't be ours."

"Who are you to be tellin' us what to do and how to live?" an irate voice shouted from within the tightly bunched group of people.

"Show yourself," Henry ordered.

From between two men, Alister Beane hobbled into the light of the roaring fire. He had to use a cedar limb as a crutch due to the swollen and cleaved foot that Annie had given him to save her own life.

"When we accepted you and your group into Myrna's Glory, it was made quite clear that your old way of life would not be tolerated. That has not changed and we will not yield on that point, under any circumstances," Henry said, as he looked back to check on Elizabeth. "It's a sad day when a law has to be written just to keep people from eating one another."

"Elizabeth was your friend, your neighbor. Her husband, Ragland, gave his life against the Brickyard gang to insure your safety, for God's sake. What in the name of all that's holy would make you turn on your own like that?" Bo asked, but did not wait for an answer. He kicked up a cloud of dust. "Eh! You're hopeless, all of you!"

Bo turned his back on them to face Elizabeth. He allowed Henry to handle the crowd and walked back to her, kneeling to untie her arms and feet. He pulled her ripped dress up to cover her exposed breasts and untied the strip of cloth covering her mouth. As he removed the wadded gag that had been forced into her mouth, he whispered, "I'm so sorry I let this happen to you. I hope you can find it in your heart to forgive me."

Elizabeth cried and threw her arms around his huge hairy neck. "It wasn't your fault. It was mine." She fought for a good breath. "I was foolish."

Bo embraced her. "I'll never let you out of my sight again."

She squeezed him tighter.

Henry's attention remained fixed on the group. "Were the rules not made clear enough for you?" he demanded.

"What if we don't choose to live by your rules?" Beane asked with equal force.

"We will do whatever it takes to enforce the laws of Myrna's Glory, many of which haven't even been written yet. But if we are to be a civilized society, there will be rules based on compassion and good sense. How you lived in Old Dallas and what you planned for Elizabeth Longbow tonight fails on both counts. If you choose a lawless path then you only have two choices… die, or take your people and leave," Henry said in a matter-of-fact way. "The eating of humans is a repulsive practice that must end, not just with you and not just tonight, but everywhere forevermore."

Beane looked around those with him but did not wait for a response before offering a reply for them all. "We don't see it that way."

"See it any way you like, but if you continue this lifestyle, you'll do it far away from Myrna's Glory. If so much as a hair is disturbed on any of our residents again, I will take it upon myself to eliminate you all. Understood?"

"The hairy one is right," one woman said. "We did turn on our own. What's the matter with us? We've never done anything like this before. In Old Dallas it was us against the Brickyard Gang and that seemed right, but this… this is just wrong."

People around Beane began moving away from him, beginning with the woman. Another woman said, "I agree. I didn't walk all the way from Old Dallas to be turned out to fend for ourselves just because we refuse to adapt." She marched the few paces to a man that must have been her husband and pulled him farther away from Beane. He was hesitant at first but followed her. Other women did the same and led their husbands away.

Afterward, the only ones to remain standing together were the four men and three women that Elizabeth originally feared might be trouble. Ace Hammond's wife attempted to pull him away from Beane. He refused and stepped in to stand nearer to Beane. His wife became angry. "Ace, if you insist on being hard-headed about this, I'll not be following you off to God knows where. I plan on making a life here, even if it means following their rules. The choice should be clear to you."

"She's right," Henry said.

"The hell she is!" Ace fired back. "I've lived my entire life this way and see no reason to change now."

"Then you and your little band of idiots will be banished to follow that repugnant practice far from Myrna's Glory to survive on your own, if you can," Henry said.

"Oh, we can survive all right," Hammond said, "and flourish."

Alister Beane smirked. "There you have it."

Ace Hammond stood on one side of Beane while two men stood on the other.

"If that's the way it's going to be, then my hope is that you eat one another," Henry said.

Bo finally stepped away from Elizabeth and joined Henry. "I don't think you'll live a week out there, if eating people is your goal. You'll hunt a short time and then be hunted yourselves. The lot of you will be killed and forgotten. Frankly, if you choose that path, I wouldn't mind at all being among the group that eliminates you from the face of the planet." He stepped forward and stopped in front of Beane, taking an aggressive stance. He leaned forward and glared at the man. "You have a decision to make and I'll not allow you to walk away without declaring it. What'll it be? Live peaceably with us at Myrna's Glory, or take your chances in the wild like brutish carnivorous animals?"

Chapter 17

Rodney's Revenge

"No, Rodney, we won't wait until next year," Barclay Weems said.

"But, Mister Weems, she's just arrived."

The headmaster's face tightened. "You're right about one thing," he said in a thinly controlled tone, "...this is the first time we've taken in a new student of her age so close to graduation day. But, your opinion is unsolicited and unwelcome. Rodney, I'm losing patience with you continually pointing out the way things are, and should be, around here." His voice ratcheted to a higher octave. "This is not simply a school to learn a trade but also an orphanage that has a strict policy against housing adults. The Henderson girl walked through our front door already an adult. You know the rules. Seventeen marks adulthood here."

Rodney, Barclay Weems's personal assistant, knew the planned treatment of Annie Henderson was not right, given false hope only to be turned out so soon. He had no control. All he did have was an opinion and so far was getting nowhere with it. The whole thing must have been orchestrated to appease Martha Ramos, since she was the one to bring the girls in. Even without worldly experience beyond the walls of this school and orphanage, he was coming to believe there was something very wrong about this place. An innate sense of fairness and decent treatment of the kids was all he had, but it was enough. If only there were someone other than Weems to share concerns with that had authority to make changes. Unfortunately, he was talking to the top decision maker right now. The board members were little more than enforcers of Barclay Weems's wishes.

Rodney was becoming less reluctant to express his opinions, but he always did so in a reserved manner, fearing the unknown—the world outside these walls. Still, this was important. He pressed on. "Sir, *both* those girls need our help. I understand the importance of policy but why can't we give the older one at least time enough to learn a trade before we turn her back into the world?"

Weems clenched his jaws. His face reddened. He turned his back to Rodney and walked away, stopping at a large window overlooking the town of Barclay's Outpost. He stared out for a time. After a few seconds, he spun back around and exploded. "Don't ever talk to me in such a forward manner again!"

"But, Sir…"

"No 'buts'! If you continue questioning my judgment, I'll instruct the board to escort you out the front door and then you'll never be allowed to return! Understand?"

Rodney's head drooped. "Yes, sir."

"Now, get out of my office! Go tell the older girl that she will be assigned a mentor at the graduation party tomorrow evening, just like the other seventeen-year-olds."

Head downturned, Rodney nodded deeper that he understood what was expected of him. He stepped backward toward the office door as a gesture of respect before turning to exit the room, but respect for Weems had begun dimming long ago. Now, all demonstrations of respect were habit only. He hesitated. "What shall I tell her about the younger girl with her?"

"Tell her the truth. The young one will live here until her seventeenth year. This will be her home and she will learn a trade like the other children."

"Yes, sir." Rodney left and closed the door. He walked the long corridor toward Annie and Eva's bedroom. He glanced down at the clothing he was forced to wear, a suit of maroon velvet with a frilly white shirt and black tie. It was not something he had ever truly considered before now. Such extravagance while the children slaved and hungered disgusted him. The poor kids had to wear clothing little better than rags that they were forced to stitch together themselves.

With every step down the corridor, anger escalated, but it was at himself for lack of courage. He desired positive change but was powerless and he hated that. He wanted to help these kids to a good life but along the way, he'd convinced himself that there might not be a better way of life, here or anywhere else. This notion helped him cope. The kids were simply a source of profit, used up, and then tossed aside at the age of seventeen. It was a near-perfect setup, concealed under the broad heading of "school" and "orphanage". Over the years, he learned the imposed age limit for a resident was strategic. It happened to be the age kids began questioning why they had to work so hard, eat so poorly and dress shabbily, and then be locked in smelly sleeping quarters every night. Rodney's only memories were of this place. He'd arrived quite young and knew no other way. He now believed that was the only reason Weems became his mentor. He was ignorant and compliant. But Weems was mistaken, believing him too ignorant to glean truth as he aged in this environment.

He stopped at one of the few windows in the long corridor, an easterly view. The sun had not yet made its daily appearance, but the horizon was a vivid display of pink, orange, blue and their variations. The sun would be breaching the horizon in minutes. He longed for that kind of beauty in his life. He sighed and moved on, stopping at the bedroom door. It was identical to all the others along this lengthy hallway. He knocked and waited, struggling with how to tell the girls they would be separated forever tomorrow evening. It pained him that this had to be his duty—delivering a message that would alter both their lives in a cruel and abrupt way.

The Henderson girl opened the door. She was fully dressed but her eyes appeared heavy from sleep. She was equally as tall and beautiful. Long silky honey-blond hair, slightly disheveled, framed a flawless tanned complexion that sparkled with youth and almost matched the color of her hair. He sensed an aura of tough maturity. He wondered: *Will she become violent, sad, or accepting when I give her the bad news?*

Whichever way it went, one thing was undeniably true; she was an extraordinary young woman in beauty and stature. At that instant, he developed a flash opinion that the "voluntary" donation to this place might turn into a bidding war for this girl tomorrow night. For reasons he was beginning to believe were immoral, the "donations" were always higher for the girls. He envisioned a record high for this one. He suspected why, but never questioned this point aloud. Graduating boys were never worth as much. There had to be a reason for that. He feared it was not a decent one.

Annie smiled. "Good morning, Rodney."

He started to speak but did not, standing with his mouth open.

Her smile seemed so full of hope that his heart began to break. Even something as simple as a reply to her cheery greeting gagged him. He felt like crying, unwilling to tell her what he must.

Annie's smile dulled. "Is something wrong?"

He drew a breath, seeking an extra second to summon courage, but still the words would not come.

Annie took his hand. "Please come in and sit down. You don't look well. Color seems to be draining from your face."

"I—I can't do this... not anymore. I'm fed up with what I'm made to do and say." He sat in the chair Annie guided him to, and then reluctantly lifted his eyes to meet hers. "I'm so sorry."

"Sorry for what? I don't understand." She dragged a cane bottom, ladder-back chair across the glossy hardwood floor from across the room and sat facing him, near enough to place her hands on his knees. Rodney saw it as a heartfelt consoling thing. Her compassion touched him.

The scooting chair woke Eva. She sat up, yawned and rubbed her eyes. "What's going on?"

Annie Henderson kept her focus on him and did not look back to address the young girl. "I think Rodney and I are about to have a serious conversation about something," she said.

He was suddenly conflicted. *If I tell her everything I know and what I suspect, I will open a door I'll never be able to close. It would end my time here, maybe worse. Should I tell her anything... everything?*

* * *

Annie did not have to be intuitive to realize Rodney struggled, apparently on the verge of sharing something intensely personal—fear or concern, possibly both, easily readable. She must be careful not to upset him. He appeared skittish, like a hungry deer ready to bolt at the first flinch.

Treading lightly to develop a bond and build confidence seemed the way to go. This might be the perfect occasion to make an ally of him, if possible.

Nicky, the boy she had met last night in the basement, did say that Rodney might be someone she could trust. With time growing tight to make her plan and follow-through, this was a risk worth taking. She must find out what troubled him and if it might be to her advantage. She smiled again. "Rodney, what's your last name?"

For the first time, a smile creased his lip. "I don't know what my birth name is, first or last. The name Rodney was given to me when I came here as a very young child." His smile broadened. "I adopted Bloom just last year as a last name."

A veil of surprise dropped over her, freezing a corresponding expression on her face.

"What's the matter? Don't you like it?" he asked.

"On the contrary, I think Rodney Bloom is a wonderful name. Is there significance to it?"

"There was a girl here for a short while, a Native American girl that called herself Calamity. I admired her courage and tenacity so much that I chose her name as my own." He seemed to lose the moment to a thought, and then added, "If I had even the tiniest bit of that courage..." He sighed.

"I bet if Calamity Bloom knew that, she'd be touched by the gesture."

He stared at a point over her head. "Someday, I hope that I have a chance to share that decision with her personally. I wanted to get to know her better but, at the time, was scared of getting too close. Now I regret not diving in and getting to know her." He reconnected with Annie. "I sure hope she's okay."

"She sounds like someone I'd like to know."

"You'd love her."

She grinned. "I bet I would. Oh, and I'm pretty sure she's just fine."

"How would you know that?"

"I'm intuitive about such things."

"Oh?"

How old are you?" she asked.

"Not sure exactly… twenty, maybe twenty-one."

"And Calamity Bloom?"

"Seventeen, possibly eighteen by now. She was to have graduated last year but broke away with two younger children and left. It upset Mister Weems terribly. She did it so easily, especially having two very young children to contend with. By the way, I've never shared my choice of a last name with him, considering his feelings toward her."

She patted his knee. "Ya know what, Rodney? I have a feeling you'll be seeing Calamity again real soon. Now, tell me what's on your mind that has you so troubled."

"You're kind to offer me hope." He closed his eyes. "Now, I must dash your hopes and tell you what I came here to say." He squeezed his eyes shut even tighter. "Although you and your young companion have only just arrived, you will be part of the graduation party tomorrow night and assigned a mentor. Your friend will be kept here and raised to the age of seventeen to learn a trade. You will be separated and not allowed to see her again," he said without pause and slowly opened one eye—then both.

She was not at all surprised; she was thankful. She wondered if she should appear shocked and maintain the ruse a while longer, at least until she could determine if she could make an ally of him. This was what she wanted, to be part of the graduation party. It dovetailed nicely into a still developing plan, giving a confidence boost to move forward.

"You don't seem surprised or upset," he said.

If Rodney was a risk worth taking, then now was the time to take it. "Do you know what a leap of faith is?"

"I think so, yes."

"I'm going to make that leap right now," she said. "First of all, these people cannot keep me separated from Eva. If they try, they'll regret it."

He glanced toward the door. "Don't say such things. If a member of the school board hears you, a dizzy stick will be used on you."

"A 'dizzy stick'? What the heck is that?"

"Every member of the board carries them. It's a pliable limb from a willow tree about two fingers wide. They wear them like swords clipped to their waists. To be whipped with one is brutally painful, even to the point of passing out; thus the name—dizzy stick. It's a method of discipline but far too cruel, I believe."

"You're right. It is. I promise you, Rodney, no one will even touch me with one of those things. Tell me about this so-called graduation party. Does the entire town turn out for it?"

"Oh no. It's only Weems, the eleven members of the school board, and invited wealthy guests from places far beyond Barclay's Outpost. The guests offer jobs that presumably match a student's learned trade. The teens are then escorted away to begin new lives in new jobs far away from here."

"Are you sure that's what happens to them?"

"I have doubts."

"Yeah, me too." She sprang from her chair and paced in front of him. "So, the townspeople are not even invited. Is that right?"

"That's right."

"Is the graduation announced locally?"

"No."

"Rodney," she said, looking down at him, "would you like to leave this place behind forever and make a better life elsewhere?"

"Of course I would. But that's not possible."

"Oh yes it is."

"How can you say that? You came here homeless and in need. How can you possibly make such a claim, if you can't even do it for yourself?"

"Here's that leap of faith I mentioned; I'm not homeless and will get the kids out of here, but not before I bring down Weems, his so-called school board, and then end that barbaric graduation party that's clearly nothing more than a slave auction."

"You're just a young girl. What do you think you can do about it?"

She flashed a broad grin. "Do I have some really cool surprises waiting for you!" She enjoyed the confused puppy-dog look on his face. "Today, we'll go through whatever the regular routine is around here. Tonight, I'm going to send out invitations to a party."

Chapter 18

Crazy Beyond Control

Daylight appeared on the eastern horizon, the spring morning cool and pleasant within the compound of Myrna's Glory. Dew beaded on every surface, giving the air a pleasant, woodsy smell.

"I didn't get much sleep last night," Elizabeth said as she snuggled in closer to Bo's back. They lay spooned on a makeshift mattress of soft grass covered with a blanket. Young Lizzy, Elizabeth's daughter, lay at her mother's back and Yowl, the monstrous black wolf, was curled and snoozing next to the child.

"I don't doubt that at all, after the night you had." Bo reached and clutched her hand resting on his shoulder. He kissed it. "I didn't fare much better. My head spun all night over how close Henry and I came to being too late. If it had been even seconds later…"

Elizabeth shuddered. "Shh!" She yanked her hand from his grasp, covered his mouth and snuggled closer. "Let's never discuss this again. It will drive you crazy if you can't put it behind you. I know it will me."

"You're right." He paused. "Still, I shouldn't have allowed Henry's benevolent nature to influence me. I should have killed those men. If someone doesn't do it for us, they'll soon be trouble again. I'm sure of it. There is no manner of good sense remaining in any of them. Those who can be reformed have already returned."

"Maybe."

Bo sat up and, with a partially burned stick, began stirring ashes in the dead campfire within the circle of rocks. A red glow appeared from the raked ashes. He crushed twigs and dropped the wadded stems onto the red-hot coal. After only a few seconds a tiny flame popped to life. He snatched up larger pieces within arm's reach and tossed them onto the infant fire. As he did, he glanced to the cabin still under construction only a few feet away.

Elizabeth sighed. She curled her arm beneath her head and continued to lie on her side, watching Bo grow the fire. "Let's think happier thoughts, like getting that cabin finished so the three of us will have a home, a real home."

Bo's busywork of stacking firewood into a pyramid over the small flame stopped. "That cabin is for you and Lizzy."

Her smile broadened. "Yes, it is. But, if you haven't noticed, it will be plenty large enough for you too. I'm sure there will even be a corner that ol' Yowl can call his own to curl up in."

Bo turned away from her. He had difficulty processing the emotion that coursed through him. He ceased working the fire and began absently tossing twigs onto it.

"What's the matter?"

"It wouldn't be fair if I didn't stop you right there and tell you something that might change your mind about that offer." He paused. "I have strong feelings for you. I... couldn't move in with you and just be friends."

"Yes you could."

His eyes quickly met hers. "No, I could not."

"Silly, we would be the best kind of friends." Her smile mellowed in a seductive way. "In fact, it would be a friendship like no other," she cooed.

His head tilted to a quizzical slant. He frowned, certain that he appeared as his friend Yowl did when the wolf could not quite grasp what he was told. "Uh…"

Elizabeth snickered. "Do I have to spell it out for you? I'm asking you to be Lizzy's father and my husband."

He turned his face away. He tried coughing away the growing lump in his throat. He swallowed hard as his body began to tingle. Something unfamiliar was going on inside him.

"Well?"

He faced her, revealing an emotion-filled expression. "The way I look, all this hair that's like fur…"—he slapped his chest with a level of disgust— "…it never occurred to me that I'd find love, unless it was with a very hairy woman." He smirked. "That didn't seem likely, and still doesn't. I would have been satisfied… no not just satisfied, overjoyed to just call you and Lizzy friends for the rest of our lives."

"And we will be, the best friends you can imagine."

Bo sprang to his feet, rubbing clearer vision into his watery eyes. "Today, I'm going to pitch in and help the construction crew get your… our… cabin finished so *we* can move in together. Since Jake Henderson left to help Annie with the rescue at Barclay's Outpost, construction projects around the compound have slowed." And then, with a beaming smile, he concluded, "I think I'll see if I can do something to speed up the process."

Young Lizzy pressed her nose into her mother's back and giggled.

* * *

Throbbing pain in his leg woke Alister Beane first. He sat up and massaged the swollen foot with a gash on top, swaddled in rags. The sun had just made its first appearance for the day. He rose from the grassy patch he had chosen for a bed. Last night, pain and exhaustion had driven him into a fast, dreamless sleep. He now looked around. The women were gone. "Wake up, Ace." He retrieved the cedar stick he used as a crutch.

Ace Hammond began coming around, licking his lips. He moaned and then yawned. Eyes remained closed.

"Come on, Hammond, get your butt up. We have a problem."

Hammond's eyes popped open. The other two men responded to the order as well.

Ace sat up, looking one way then the other. "Where's Tess?" His wife was no longer next to him.

"She left during the night and took the other two women with her." As if talking to a child, he added, "Apparently, you couldn't maintain adequate control of your woman."

"What the hell..." one of the other men said and then made a quick search of the immediate campsite. The fourth man joined him, but to no avail. The women, all three, were gone. "I'm not walking a step further away without my wife!" the man railed.

"Nor I," the fourth said.

"It's the fault of that big hairy mutt of a man," Hammond said.

"Yeah," Beane added, "and the big bald one they call Henry. I bet your wives are back at Myrna's Glory right now."

Ace Hammond and the other two men traded escalating insults about Henry and Bo. Each new idea about how to treat the two became increasingly gory and brutal. They didn't just want to murder them, but hack them to pieces while still alive.

Beane, standing unsteadily, leaned back against the tree and smirked with a wicked lip twist. *It looks as though I'll have my revenge against Annie Henderson and I may not even have to lift a finger, or engage her at all. Ace and the boys will just kill her friends for me.*

* * *

Barney Tackitt trotted through the woods, around trees, under low hanging limbs and crashing through short brush. He never thought he would voluntarily go to Myrna's Glory, but the conversation he'd overheard earlier changed his mind. At the moment, his dour opinion of living a more structured life there, as Annie suggested, was of no consequence. Four violent men were on their way to kill Bo Juster and some guy named Henry. *I've never seen four crazier men in my life. It was as if an animal bloodlust had taken control of them. I would not have walked into that camp for all the free food in the former state of Texas.*

A spark of humanity burned inside him. It sort of disgusted him. He tried ignoring it, but it did not work. He tried minding his own business and getting on with his day. That did not work either. He felt a burgeoning sense of obligation to warn Annie Henderson—for her sake, not Juster's or that other guy. He felt as though he owed it to her. He also harbored an odd, still developing sense of solidarity with that big monkey of a man, Bo Juster, but it was not something Barney would ever share with him. Maybe this jaunt through the woods to warn Annie Henderson was because he thought of her as a friend. He could not be sure. Maybe wandering alone in the woods for so long made it necessary to redefine what "friend" meant. But there would be plenty of time to contemplate these things later. Right now, he ran toward Myrna's Glory, feeling time pressure to warn Annie about what he heard the four angry men threatening to do. Maybe she would feel as though she owed him a big favor. Realizing her considerable talents, a favor owed might be valuable if he found himself in trouble.

He burst into the open between two large bushy cedar trees to see the loosely organized collection of cabins, barns and other structures. *This must be the place.* He ran on.

He approached a man loading cedar logs onto a horse-drawn wagon. The man held an ax and turned to face him, holding the tool in a defensive manner. "State your business," the man shouted.

Barney continued jogging toward him. "Is this Myrna's Glory?"

"It is."

"I need to speak with Annie Henderson right away."

"She's not here. Now, be on your way."

Barney came to an abrupt halt. "Damn." He did not expect her absence. "How about Juster? Is he around here?"

"The big hairy one?"

"Yeah, him."

The man used the ax to point out a particular cabin under construction. "He's over there, working on that one."

Barney took off, running around the man. "Thanks."

"Wait a minute! You can't just..."

Still running, Barney shouted over his shoulder, "Sorry, can't wait. I have important information for Juster."

As he approached the cabin under construction, he saw Bo manhandle a horizontal log of considerable girth without assistance into place atop others. He was forming an outside wall. The show of strength caused Barney to slow his approach. *I don't think I ever want to really anger this guy.* He stopped.

Bo noticed him. "Hey, Tackitt, I thought you told Annie that you didn't want to live by any set of rules."

"I did, and I still don't want to live here."

Bo began approaching him, almost as if stalking. "Why are you here, to mooch a free meal?"

Barney stroked his chin. "Well, something to eat would be nice, but no."

"Then stop making me guess! Why are you here?"

"To warn you of danger."

"Me?"

"Yep, you specifically."

"What danger would you know of that would interest me?"

"I'm assuming you had a confrontation last night with people in the woods."

Clearly surprised, Juster reared his head. "How would you know about that? Were you there?"

"Not last night, but I was this morning. I saw four men working themselves into a murderous rage. They talked about doing disgustingly gory things to you and a man called Henry. And, of course, those things would end with both of you dead."

The big hairy guy stood for a moment, and then finally said, "I suppose I should be thanking you for the warning."

Barney could not contain a growing smile. "It galls you, doesn't it?" He smiled even bigger.

Juster walked right past, purposely bumping him. "Yeah."

"I'll take that as a warm and *fuzzy* thank you."

"Warm and… oh, shut up."

Barney laughed.

Juster walked on a ways and then stopped. He turned and shouted to Elizabeth who tended a fire. "If you don't mind, share our food with Tackitt. I guess he's earned it."

"I'll take care of it," Elizabeth said. She lifted a cast iron pot and set it on the edge of the fire.

"You'd better be careful, Juster, we might become bosom buddies," Barney said.

Bo continued on, not looking back. "I don't think so. Now, if you'll excuse me, I have to go get Henry and we have to do something before it can be done to us."

Chapter 19

Planning To Crash a Party

Rodney at her side, Annie avoided suspicion and probable questioning by school board members, and there were many occasions throughout the day it would have been likely had he not been with her. As she had been told, each board member carried a "dizzy" stick hooked like a sword to the waist—several small whip-like willow limbs bound together, designed for the sole purpose of whipping children to maintain submissive behavior. It angered her more each time she saw one. The so-called board members were no more fair and equitable policy setters of a school than she was a normal teenager. They were guards, pure and simple— prison guards. Their only function was to keep the kids docile and working without complaint so that school coffers remained brimming.

Rodney guided Annie through what was deemed and seen as an orientation of the school and orphanage, officially known as Barclay's Home and School for Children. It turned out to be a leisurely day. As the two went about touring, young Eva became acquainted with the other kids. It was a softer than usual approach to assimilation for both Annie and Eva, sanctioned by Weems to keep from spooking Annie into taking Eva and running away before the auction, a day away.

Annie stayed at Rodney's side while Eva sat with Lucy for much of the day, watching her new friend fashion candle stands from strips of thin sheet metal. They were the same age, six.

When Rodney and Annie toured the room in the basement where the work tables were located, Annie saw that the expert craftsmanship Lucy displayed was far beyond what would be normal for her age. The same was true for the work of all the other kids. She watched them stitch cloth, tan animal skins and fashion beautiful knives and other utensils from scrap metal. She assumed application of the dizzy stick had something to do with the absurdly advanced craftsmanship she witnessed—learn fast, or get a lashing. Annie knew without having to look that the back sides of all these kids had to be crisscrossed with scars.

Nicky, the boy she had met last night, was warned by Rodney not to show familiarity with Annie, not yet. When she sauntered by his work station, he smiled. Aside from that, he did not display awareness of her identity.

This was no time for taking the chance that a board member might realize they already knew one another, and then wonder how. That would create the wrong kind of questions. Three of the board members, and their dizzy sticks, guarded the work room—a visual reminder to keep working.

There would be time for talking with Nicky and the other graduating teens at the party later, where it would appear more natural. The annual evening gathering must go on as usual. Neither Weems, nor any of the board, could be allowed to suspect a plan was about to be set in motion.

At the end of the day, Rodney and Annie sat alone at the table in the kitchen. The other staff had eaten and returned to work. The two dined on beef stew. Loaded with potatoes, carrots and other vegetables, it tasted wonderful. After loading a spoon from the steaming bowl for another big bite, she noticed Rodney examining the contents of his own bowl. He dipped stew from it and hoisted the spoon to eye level. He then leaned across the table and whispered, "You're very lucky, ya know."

Annie swallowed a bite and was going for another. She was famished. "How do you mean?" she mumbled around a mouthful while her eyes remained fixed on the bowl of meat and vegetables.

"The other kids don't eat this well. The stew they get is made from the scraps and leftovers of what you are now eating... you know, like potato and carrot peels, pea hulls, the fat from the meat and an assortment of other food waste."

Mouth agape and ready to receive another spoonful, Annie abruptly closed her mouth and dropped the spoon into the wooden bowl with a splash. "You certainly know how to ruin a girl's appetite."

"Sorry, just trying to be honest."

"I know... and thank you." She stood. "I will not take another bite until all of us can feast together." She stepped to a small westerly facing window. "The sun has set. It will be dark in a few more minutes. After what you just told me, I don't want to wait another second to put my plan into action."

Rodney hastily swallowed. "You haven't shared details. Can I help?"

"Yes."

"What can I do?"

"I need you to help me get out of the building and make excuses for my absence, if necessary. I should only be gone a couple of hours, maybe less. When I return, if you'd be so kind, keep my exit point open and accessible to allow me to get back into the building and then escort me to my bedroom to legitimize my absence from bed, should they discover me gone."

"I think I can handle that."

She stared at him.

"What?"

Her face softened. "I know you can handle it," she said and then smiled. She walked around the table to his side and wrapped him up in a hug, pinning his arms to his sides. Deep natural compassion, genetically enhanced like all her abilities and sometimes problematic, had just taken control.

He groaned. "Wow, you're strong."

"And you're wonderful."

"No, I'm not. I'm a coward."

Annie released him and stepped away. "Don't say that." She slapped him on the chest. "Have a little confidence in yourself."

"I can't make even the tiniest changes for the better around here."

"You could, if given a chance," Annie said, voice slowing and fading as the words left her mouth. She suddenly brightened. "You have just given me a wonderful idea."

"Care to share?"

She gave him another quick hug. "Later. Right now I have to get this plan underway. Let's go." She handed him a glowing lamp from the table and took his other hand, leading him out the door into the hallway. She looked both ways. "Tell me now, which is the best and quickest way out of this place unnoticed?"

Oil lamp held high, Rodney guided Annie down the corridor and stopped at a particular door. It had no special markings and appeared like all the others in this long hallway. He removed a key from around his neck and unlocked it. They entered and he closed the door behind them. Annie saw that it was a deep, narrow supply closet with floor to ceiling shelves on both sides and at the end, but the end shelves were affixed to a hinged panel. Rodney ran his hand beneath one of the shelves until a slide bolt was located. With a click, he unlatched it. It was a door that opened to the outside of the building. Only the staff knew about it. It led out onto a small stoop about six feet off the ground with no guardrail, clearly used infrequently. Since it was kept locked from the inside, the door was never intended as access to the storeroom from the outside.

Annie stepped through the door out onto the small porch. It was now fully dark, no moon, star light only. The only other source of light came from the many dim orange lights from windows within the neighborhood, a hundred or so yards away.

Annie leaped from the tall stoop to the ground. "I want you to know, you are definitely no coward, Rodney. What you're doing now is courageous. More importantly, you're not doing it for personal gain, but for the kids. You could've chosen to remain quiet and do nothing, the safer choice... for you."

"Thanks, but I still don't feel it. Be careful out there. There's no way of knowing who is loyal to Barclay Weems around town."

"I think I know someone we can trust. Don't worry about me. Back soon."

As Rodney stepped back inside and prepared to close the door behind him, he said, "I'll be waiting."

Annie's leisurely pace that defined her day vanished. Her movement had become crisp and deliberate. She began jogging, slowly at first, looking for prying eyes. Genetically enhanced vision made navigating the dark no problem. She accelerated and ran directly for John and Martha Ramos's house.

It only took a matter of seconds to traverse the open area that separated the school and orphanage from the remainder of the town of Barclay's Outpost. She did not stop until reaching the rear of the Ramos's home, out of sight to the remainder of the neighborhood. She finally did come to a stop, taking time for another scan of the area. In that moment, Martha Ramos stepped out the backdoor with a pot of food scraps, presumably to toss into a chicken pen at the rear of the yard.

"Psst, Martha…"

The middle-aged woman stifled a squeal, dropped the pot, and spun around. "Annie Henderson? Is that you?"

"Yes. Could you please not speak so loud?"

"Child, you about scared the shoes right off me."

"Sorry, but I thought it best to only get your attention, no one else. I think I can trust you, but I'm not at all sure about others around here. I saw how you looked around Barclay's Home for Children yesterday. I also saw the suspicion on your face. You had a problem with the secretiveness of it all, didn't you?"

"That's very perceptive. Yes, something didn't seem right at all and too much of it was not shown to me. I felt as though I was being steered away from certain areas."

"That's exactly what they were doing."

"So, you think they're hiding something?"

"Oh yes, they're hiding something all right, and they're doing it cleverly. Weems and his cronies hide dark lies beneath thin layers of many truths."

"What do you mean?"

"We need to talk. I really need your help and it must be done tomorrow."

"By all means, let's get inside the house and talk about it."

* * *

241

As Annie ran from Barclay's Outpost into the night, she was now confident Martha Ramos would be a valuable asset. The dear lady had given her assurance that what needed to be done would be before tomorrow evening—seek out all those trustworthy in the town of Barclay's Outpost and, more importantly, those who cared about the children.

Annie ran straight for where she and young Eva had left Jake Henderson and Calamity Bloom camped, in the woods about two miles out. Swift feet covered the distance in short order.

She slowed and carefully approached the site, so as not to startle either of them. Jake and Calamity knelt around a small campfire, carrying on a conversation. "Jake, it's me."

Jake sprang to his feet. "Annie! Is everything okay?"

"So far, yes."

He came to her and embraced her. "Oh, Annabelle, I always worry when you're away."

She kissed his cheek. "I love you too." She gave her adopted father another quick peck and then backed away.

Calamity rose and approached, placing a friendly hand upon her shoulder. As usual, the Native American girl's expression appeared stoic and unchanging, but Annie had come to know her new friend well enough to see past that facade to the affection beneath. "How is Eva?" Calamity asked.

"She found a new friend her own age. They're probably together right now. I'm sure she'll be fine until we can liberate her and all her new friends." Annie smiled. "According to Eva's new friend, she knows you well. Her name is Lucy."

"Sweet Lucy; how is she?"

"Okay, just exhausted from long hours of forced labor and ready to get out of that mess they call a school and home for children, as are all the rest of them. I told her that you and I were working together to get it done. The boy, Nicky, is the only other kid that is aware of what we're doing. I think he was on the verge of following your lead and escaping had I not shown up when I did. I urged him to be patient a while longer."

Calamity nodded approval. "Nicky is a good friend. He'll do whatever you ask."

"Cal, I have other news that I think may surprise you and I'm sure will please you."

"Oh?"

"Rodney has become a close ally…"

"That's not surprising. He complained to me often about how the home and school were run, that it was unfair and harsh in its treatment of the children."

"He has become instrumental in helping us, but that's not the surprising part."

"Then what?"

"He adopted the last name of Bloom because he didn't have one and he admired you so much."

Although her face remained serious, Annie saw Calamity's lower lip quiver, ever so slightly.

"I—I have no words to express my thoughts."

Annie pulled Calamity close and gave her a fast buddy pat on the shoulder. She then held her friend and looked into the girl's sparkling dark eyes. "Well, when you do find the words, share them with Rodney. He's almost as big a fan of you as I am."

Calamity's dark skin suddenly took on new radiance— almost like a smile, but not quite.

"I know you have to hurry and get back," Jake said, "so, what is it that you need us to do?"

Annie left Calamity thinking about the revelation and faced Jake. "The job I had planned for you may not be as necessary as I once thought. Still, it's probably a good idea to follow through. You can shave and dress up and then join the graduation party tomorrow night as a bidder. I'll still need you to be a witness and provide proof that these children are literally being purchased at a closed auction. You must make the high bid on me. After you've, ahem... won me"—an eyebrow shot up sarcastically—"you can then see how it is that Weems asks for payment."

"And me?" Calamity asked.

"You can come with me tonight and stay with my new friends John and Martha Ramos at their house, out of sight. You and Rodney will be in charge of the children tomorrow night."

Annie placed a finger to her lips and thought: *I sure hope this plan works. I have no desire to get into a war with an entire town.*

Chapter 20

Taking Care of Business

"I suppose you were right," Henry said. "It probably is safer for the people of Myrna's Glory if we're out here, in case Beane and his band of merry idiots try anything. They might go after someone other than you and me and hurt them."

Bo heard Henry's comment but it did not have an urgent tone, so it did not register as something needing a response. He continued staring into the fire.

"Hey, Juster..."

"Huh? Oh, sorry... I was lost in thought."

"About what?"

"That guy you met that came to us with the warning, Barney Tackitt," Henry said, "what is he to you... friend, acquaintance... or what?"

"That's what I'm trying to figure out. He tried to kill Annie and me over a few measly quail she and Eva shot for dinner not so long ago."

"Then why did he go to the trouble of warning you about the cannibals?"

"Exactly. Now you know why I'm a little confused by the man. I don't know what to think." Bo pulled a sarcastic half-grin. "Although, I still believe the man is not quite right in the head and would crush my skull with a club if given a chance."

"Sounds like an odd fellow."

"Yeah. Oh, well… let's get some rest. I'll think that through another time. We have four crazy killers to deal with tomorrow." Bo fell over onto his side next to the fire. Yowl came to him, followed his tail in a circle, and lay at Bo's back. The wolf nuzzled him affectionately.

For a time, Bo watched flames of the campfire twist and dance lazily skyward. Henry began to snore. Bo reached back and stroked Yowl. "Good night, ol' friend," he whispered within a yawn.

"Bo… Bo Juster," a voice called out.

Startled, Bo sat up. He looked around. What he saw was not right—not at all. It was daylight; full sunshine. He was in the same place as he was when he fell asleep, but there was no campfire, no Henry, no Yowl. Everything within view was overly vivid. The colors of the trees, the grass, the sky, and the clouds were all brilliant. "What the hell…"

"Don't you be cussin' in dis beautiful place."

The voice that had startled him seconds ago now rang of strong familiarity. "Dame Fortune? Is that you?"

"It be for a fact."

He looked in the direction the voice seemed to come from. On a knoll some distance away, a beautiful and quite young black woman stood. The voice did not fit her appearance. "You sound like Dame but you sure don't look like her." He leaned forward and squinted, attempting to distinguish detail. "Not from here anyhow."

In the span of an eye-blink, she came to stand over him. "Hey, don't move like that. You scared me. I could have hurt you before knowing what I was doing."

She laughed that familiar cackling laugh. "I be appreciatin' your concern, but you be a big ol' hairy fool if you think you could be doin' anythin' to me in dis damned ol' dream."

"Oh… right." He rose and faced her. "Hey, wait a minute. You told me not to be cussing. You just did."

Dame laced her fingers together down in front and rocked to and fro. She twisted her head as a shy young girl might and batted her eyelashes up at him. "I be special," she said with an angelic smile." Her smile dropped. "But don't you be doin' it."

She was indeed beautiful, not heavyset, but young and slender. She no longer had the unruly and tightly curled white hair, or the clouded and blind white eyes. Nor were her fingers gnarled. Yet, he recognized her as Dame Fortune. "I must be dreaming. Annie told me stories about her encounters with you like this."

"I be thinkin' all dat hair doesn't be stoppin' you from thinkin' clearly. You're a smart feller. You be dreamin', for sure, but dis is no fantasy. It be real as real can be."

"How long have I been asleep?"

"What damn difference do dat be makin'?" she snapped.

"None, I guess."

She calmed. "Now, you back to bein' a smart feller. What is important is dat dose dangerous men be sneakin' up on you real soon. I be divinin' a real bad outcome for you and ol' Henry if ya don't get ready. Even your ol' buddy Yowl won't be survivin'. I can see it as plain as dat big ol' hairy nose on your face."

"We're going to die?"

"Not if'n ya prepare, fool. Dat's why I be here." She turned and began moving away, but then hesitated. "One last thing, when da time come, you must be savin' Henry to be savin' yourself… savin' Henry to be saving yourself… savin' Henry to be savin' yourself…"

Bo sprang from a sound sleep and sat up, Dame's words echoing. The world around him had returned to normal—Henry lying next to him, Yowl at his back and the smoldering campfire a few feet away, red embers glowing. He figured he had been asleep an hour, maybe a little longer. He leaned over and shook Henry's shoulder.

Henry stirred. "Morning already?"

"No, but you need to wake up. It would seem we have a problem."

* * *

Alister Beane and his little group of unrepentant cannibals agreed that the best time to make a move on Bo Juster and the big bald one they called Henry would have to be at night under cover of darkness. Beane and his three cronies did not want to chance having to engage the entire population of Myrna's Glory. It must be a quiet operation—exceedingly quiet; move in, slit their throats and then get away quickly into the dark. If it did not go as planned, they risked not only tangling with others in the compound but also that infernal wolf of Juster's. Beane saw how vicious that animal could be when they battled the Brickyard Gang in Old Dallas. He did not want to be on the receiving end of that. Beane surmised the four of them could handle hairy and baldy if the wolf did not show up.

Deep into the night, Beane tired of waiting. It would take about an hour to get back to Myrna's Glory, and he figured by the time they walked there, everyone would be sound asleep. He lifted himself up on the makeshift cedar crutch. "Okay…" he said while dusting his hands, "…it's time." He scattered the dying embers of their campfire to extinguish it. "Hammond, get the other two and let's go."

Even before Ace Hammond alerted the other men, Beane began hobbling in the direction of Myrna's Glory. His foot, with an infected gash, was swollen. It ached, but a deep psychotic need for revenge overrode discomfort. He limped, but did so quickly, with purpose. His three partners rushed to catch up.

Without looking back to his followers, Beane said, "The time for talk is over. We know what needs to be done. Let's go do it."

After a short distance, darkness slowed his pace. They relied on instinct to pick their way along the trail. Although not wide, the heavily traveled footpath was virtually grass and weed free. It appeared in the dim light as a lighter colored strip along the ground. Otherwise, little was visible except the outline of trees blotting out stars in the night sky.

Beane glimpsed an orange glow. "I think I see a fire. I wonder who that might be?" he whispered. "Be ready."

He did not know who they might encounter. Nonetheless, he drew a long knife from the rope belt at his waist. He had spent most of the day whetting it to a fine edge with a stone to cut and kill cleanly. Ace Hammond wielded a sharpened shard of steel lashed to a stick as a makeshift ax. The other two men carried clubs.

Every few feet, he stopped to study the path ahead and then pick a clean, quiet approach for the next short distance. The going proved slow, but it was necessary to remain undetected until they could identify the campers. They might have useable things to steal, or maybe, just provide meat to feast on after they had disposed of their targets.

Finally, the site came into full view. Beane was surprised by the sight. It was that ape of a man, Juster, and his bald sidekick in a monk's robe, Henry. They knelt at a campfire roasting meat on sticks, appearing oblivious. He had not anticipated seeing them outside the compound. *Now, what business would they have out in the woods like that?* He wondered.

A smile stretched across Beane's face. Those two had unwittingly provided him easy access. He and his men could kill them and be gone. But what about the wolf?

He moved a little closer. He did not see the wolf but had to make certain. The canine's senses exceeded that of a human and would alert the two before he and his men could carry out their mission. He walked as near as he dared, and then stopped. He scanned the area.

Minutes passed.

Still, he and his men did not move, or speak, giving ample time for the wolf to reveal himself. If the animal were around, it made sense that it would be lying near the fire, but Beane could not be sure enough to make a move—not yet. After considerable time, there was still no sign of the beast anywhere.

Beane smirked and turned back to Hammond. He cupped a hand against his mouth to shield his voice and whispered, "I think luck is on our side, boys. That damn wolf isn't with them."

Remaining quiet, the four picked up the pace and slipped into the orange circle of firelight.

Juster and Henry were on their knees sitting on their heels, both facing the same direction, away from Beane and his men. They still seemed unaware; both holding bits of meat skewered on sticks and suspended over the small fire.

Beane realized that if he rushed to surprise the two, he might be awkward and noisy. He handed his razor-sharp long knife to Hammond and urged him to move in for the kill. The other two men holding clubs headed straight for Henry.

Without looking back, Juster said, "Come on over, boys. You're right on time."

Hammond and the two club-wielding men slowed and then stopped short.

Beane's smirk vanished. "What... but how...?" He caught movement from the corner of his eye.

The monstrous black wolf stepped in behind Beane. His head was slung low, neck hair bristling, golden eyes reflecting firelight in such a way as to appear demonic.

Beane's look of surprise metamorphosed to hatred. *Damn the foot and damn the pain!* He shrieked and lifted the crutch high over his head as he ran directly toward Bo. "Kill them both! Do it now! Do it quickly!"

Beane moved as if the foot were no longer a problem. He ran past Hammond with the intent of clubbing Juster to a bloody death.

* * *

This guy is an animal that gives other animals a bad name, Bo thought.

He snatched up his spear with a fire-hardened sharp tip and blocked Beane's first attempt. He had no choice but to remain in defensive mode, stopping the shrieking man's relentless efforts to kill him, blocking repeated attempts in rapid succession.

Henry engaged the other two men. With both hands, he clutched his five-foot hunting spear with a metal point and multiple barbs up the shaft. The two attackers stalked him like circling coyotes, splitting his attention in opposite directions.

Bo swung his spear rapidly upward as Beane's crutch was coming down for another swing. With a loud crack, Beane's makeshift weapon went flying off to the side. Bo lined up his spear with Beane's body, about to run him through, when suddenly a searing pain exploded in his back to the right of his spine.

He slapped his back to feel a long knife embedded in his flesh.

And then, as if the words were spoken aloud, he again heard Dame's admonishment, *"Save Henry to be savin' yourself."*

Bo glanced to see Henry about to have his skull crushed by one of his attackers while distracted by the other.

He ignored debilitating pain and Beane. He sent his spear flying.

It went all the way through Henry's attacker just as the big bald man dispatched the other one with a lethal swipe of his hunting spear.

Bo spun to face the one who stabbed him. He moved aggressively on Ace Hammond, fully intending to rip the man's arms from his shoulders even though his own right arm had already begun to go numb. He weakened fast and stumbled to his knees, yet kept moving forward. He roared, a mixture of pain and determination.

Hammond turned to run away. He clearly saw that whatever the plan had been was falling apart. With ax in hand, Hammond ran into the woods.

Yowl joined the fray and took off after Hammond.

Bo stopped and felt the long knife yanked from his back. He roared in pain and fell onto his side.

Beane had already begun a downward thrust with the knife toward Bo's upper body.

Henry's hunting spear sailed in and stuck him in the back, penetrating entirely through his body, appearing below his ribs in front.

Bo saw the reality in Beane's eyes—utter shock that he had been bested.

Beane dropped the knife and looked down to the bloody exposed point of the spear protruding from his abdomen. He dropped to his knees, face frozen in fear, and then fell over onto Bo.

Bo shoved him off with a disgusted grunt.

All expression on Beane's face melted away as life left his body.

Bo took a breath. "So, that's what Dame meant when she said 'Save Henry to save yourself'," he mumbled. He looked up to the big bald man. "How about it, you okay?"

"Better than you, I'd say."

Suddenly, Ace Hammond screamed from some distance away out of sight.

"Should we just let ol' Yowl have his way with the last one?" Henry asked.

Bo became dizzy. He fluttered lucidity into his eyes. "Yowl won't kill him, if he managed to get the ax out of the man's hand." He had to take a couple of deep breaths to finish the thought. "I'm sure he's already sensed that there is no longer a danger here." He grimaced. "I don't think... I can... remain conscious."

From out of the brush, Yowl dragged Hammond by the forearm, the ax no longer in that hand. Hammond wallowed on the ground as the wolf dragged him along. The man had no choice against the powerful jaws and muscular body of the wolf.

Bo winced but struggled against pain to roll his upper body far enough to see. "Good job, Yowl."

"I'll take the shirt from one of these guys and make a bandage for you," Henry said. "We need to get that bleeding stopped."

"Thanks."

Yowl held Hammond firmly clenched.

"Get this animal away from me before he eats me!" Hammond yelled.

"Shut up, you man-eating coward!" Henry shouted. "That animal is more civilized than you ever thought of being. I don't think he'll eat you, but could you blame him if he did? You and these other idiots would have surely eaten us if this had gone another way."

Bo swallowed hard. "It would seem to be in our best interests if he did eat the guy."

"Don't worry, your friend Yowl can watch him on the way back while I tend to you," Henry said as he ripped a shirt from one of the bodies into long strips.

"Humph. It would seem we have a decision to make. Taking a prisoner never crossed my mind. Do we take him back to Myrna's Glory, or just kill him here?"

Chapter 21

Let the Bidding Begin

Jake Henderson let the old horse he rode have his head, allowing the braided leather rein to drape to the side of the animal's neck. He made no directional demands. His mount knew best how to stay on a trail in the dark. The nag walked at an easy pace toward Barclay's Outpost and the home for children, about two miles from his campsite. The night air felt exceptionally cool on his freshly shaven face. He stroked it, marveling at its smoothness. He shaved so seldom; it was always a novel experience when he did. He tugged on the buttoned up collar with the black cloth tied in a bow around his neck. It was constrictive. Jake did not like it at all. *If the life of the rich and powerful calls for dressing this way, it's not for me. I have new respect for poverty, if comfort comes with it.*

The slow pace in the dark gave Jake time to think. His mind went back to when he first met the ten-year-old girl he later named Annabelle, now known by everyone as Annie. Even after seven years, twinges of remorse dogged him that he did not attempt to save Annie's mother from being murdered by that mad man, Hiram Baker. He could have at least tried, but selfishly failed, stopping short of warning the woman of an imminent attack and then walked away, leaving Annie to sob over her bleeding mother's body. At the time, he'd hoped to forget the brutal slaying and pretend it never happened. If it had not been for Annie's tenacity, he likely would have left her to die alone. The thought of what might have happened brought on a shuddering chill.

A year later, it was Annie who saved him from the very same psychopath. She prevented his death by killing the man that murdered her mother. The poor girl had been forced into a situation to kill Baker before her eleventh birthday.

He shuddered. *Never again, Annabelle… never again. I swear it. Whatever you need, whenever you need it, I'll be there.*

Jake forced his mind away from such a negative time. He struggled to put that ugly episode behind him and focus on the job at hand, committed to doing his part as flawlessly as possible.

After half an hour, the horse picked its way over the rocky bottom of a small creek and into a thicket. Jake ducked low, lying flat over the horse's neck to avoid thorny limbs that snagged his clothing. The inconvenience was brief. He left the thicket behind to see lights glowing from high windows in a three-story building. The structure sat on an easy rise above many other glowing lights he assumed were nearby houses.

That must be Barclay's Home for Children.

He rode on and dismounted minutes later at what was obviously the front door to the home and orphanage. There were a number of saddled horses and a couple of horse-drawn wagons tied to hitching posts. He was certainly not the first to arrive. Instead, it appeared as though he might be the last guest to show up.

He examined his surroundings. The rows of glowing orange lights down the gentle hill that he had assumed to be houses were indeed that, blocks of houses just a few hundred feet down the slope. As he tied his horse to the metal ring on a post, he turned his attention to the large building before him. Massive oak double doors bookended by burning oil porch lamps lit his slow and calculating ascension up the steps.

Apprehension sent a quick chill up his spine. It was the unknown, wondering what he might encounter on the other side of the intimidating front door. He breathed in courage and began walking up the steps between two concrete lions. He used the brass doorknocker centered on one of the doors. He heard it echo back from inside. Hollowness from within did nothing to ease his hesitance.

In his travels he had seen many similar buildings, but never one in such grand condition; most had been in various stages of decay. When the world economies collapsed and global currency values plummeted to zero virtually overnight, it took many years for the general population to figure out that true value lay in knowledge and bartering of goods and services. Shiny metals and stones, or paper money meant nothing when pangs of hunger hi,t or any of the other basics of survival were needed. If it had no practical application, it meant nothing. Hoarders of money died away. The new power base became commodities and the intelligence to produce them, or steal them. In the meantime, the whole world fell into decline. Now, with the help of people like the Order of Theocratic Minds, there was renewed hope for a brighter future.

The door suddenly clanked and opened on groaning hinges.

Jake startled from his thoughts.

A tall young man, impeccably groomed in a burgundy velvet suit with a frilly white shirt, stood before him. He wore one of those silly black cloths tied in a bow around his neck too. His face was smooth and hair neatly trimmed, oiled and combed straight back. "Yes? May I help you?"

"I… uh… am here for the graduation party."

"Name?"

"Jake Henderson."

The young man began to smile. His formal demeanor vanished. "Hi, Mister Henderson"—he extended a friendly hand…" my name is Rodney. It might be wise that you not use your real name. Annie has already identified herself as having the last name of Henderson."

"Oh, so you're the one Annie told me about."

Rodney put his finger to his lips and glanced over his shoulder down the hall behind him. "Yes, sir, I am," he said in quieter tone. "Please keep your voice down. We mustn't let Weems or any of the Board know that we have a connection… not yet."

"Sorry," Jake whispered. "Scheming like this is new to me."

"I understand. I'm feeling my way through it too. Annie's the mastermind. Follow me."

Yeah, she always is, he thought.

Rodney led Jake upstairs, ending at the top in the center of a large space. Jake turned a full three-sixty, taking it all in and awed by what he saw. It was a library, encompassing the entire third floor. He pushed out his lower lip and nodded. "Impressive."

"Yeah. Too bad it never gets used," Rodney whispered.

"You're joking, right?"

Rodney's face was grim. He offered only a negative headshake.

There were already a large number of people present, mostly men, but there were a few women. Jake counted sixteen, all dressed for a party. They were scattered about in small cliques, carrying on subdued conversations while drinking some type of punch from a large crystal bowl set on a long table with many plates of finger foods. He noticed they seemed to take turns looking to a group of younger people around a table in the far corner. There were four sitting, one boy and three girls. Another girl stood behind a nearby podium where a massive book of some type lay. It was Annie. His apprehension went away. He had a game to play and committed to playing it well, for her.

"I have to announce you," Rodney said. "Who shall I say you are and where from?"

Jake had not thought about that. He could not say he was from Myrna's Glory, in case someone had already become aware of its growing reputation as home to the monk-like sect known as the Order of Theocratic Minds, sworn to restore technology and give it back to the people. There were many people of wealth that wanted to control the restoration of technology for selfish gain. Some here could be among them.

So, he said the first thing that came to mind. "Just say I'm from the area far to the south known as the Hill Country. And let's say my name is Orville Peabody. Orville sounds like something parents would name a defenseless infant, just ridiculous enough to be real."

Rodney clapped his hands once loudly. "Ladies and gentlemen, I'd like to introduce Mister Orville Peabody, hailing from the known southern extremities of the former state of Texas called the Hill Country."

There was a smattering of politeness and a few applauded and then all went back to their quiet conversations. From the center of a circle of five people, Barclay Weems appeared and approached.

"Ah, welcome Mister Peabody. You are new to this gathering, are you not?"

"I am."

"How is it that you know of our graduation party?"

Jake stared directly at Annie. "In my travels, I have heard that your school turns out exceptional teenage talent." His gaze remained firmly fixed on Annie.

Weems followed Jake's stare. "I see you may already have a notion of the type of… talent…you're after."

The sound of Weems' voice disgusted Jake. He stared at the fancy man with the manicured nails and narrowly trimmed moustache and beard. He thought briefly about punching this arrogant bastard in the nose, just to muss his perfect hair and watch him bleed. The sexual innuendo about his sweet Annabelle repulsed him. He struggled to control the impulse. Still, he began verbally stalking the man. "That girl, the tall girl with the long blond hair, just what is her… *talent*, would you say?"

Weems's smile transformed into something lascivious. He lightly stroked the back of his own hand, as if he relished the feel of the white, effeminate skin. "She is a new student but, as you can see, a fine healthy specimen. I'm sure a bright girl like that could be trained to any manner of task." He smirked and lowered his voice. "I'm sure that the limit of *your* imagination would be her *only* limitation."

Jake could no longer take the thinly veiled implications and had to turn his back to the man to control an overwhelming impulse to break his pretty face. "How do you suggest I become her mentor?"

"The process is simple. We ask that each mentor merely donate to the Barclay Home and School for Children, so that we might continue our good work into the future."

"So it would seem, from what I'm hearing, I purchase her."

Weems's smirk dropped. "Oh, no, that's not it at all. But, having said that, it would be unfair if you were not made aware that the size of the donation does matter." He gestured toward the guests. "As you can see, others may have their eyes on that girl too. So, it's a gauge for us to use as a means of determining the level of interest, so that we, in good conscience, can match the right intern with the right mentor. It's quite fair, I assure you."

Still with his back to Weems, to not give away the squeamish look of revulsion on his face, Jake nodded. "I assure you, Mister Weems, I am a man of considerable means. A donation to Barclay's Home for Children of almost any size would be no problem. You have my personal guarantee there will be no larger *donation* than what I'm about to offer." All the while he spoke, his eyes remained locked on Annie.

* * *

Nicky, the teen Annie had already met two nights ago in the basement dormitory, rose from his seat at the table and stepped over to Annie. Aside from Jake, Rodney and her, he was the only other one in the room aware of what was about to happen. "That guy Weems is talking to, is that your father?"

"I sure think of him as my father. Yes, that's Jake." Her eyes went from him to the three girls still sitting at the table. "How are they doing?"

"Like lambs to a slaughter, they're oblivious to the reality of this function. They still think they'll be placed in a pleasant situation to apply their tradecraft and be compensated."

Annie sighed. "Until I can bring this to a conclusion, it's best they keep on thinking that. It won't be much longer."

She directed Nicky's attention to the big book on the podium in front of her. "This is the first time I've ever actually seen a dictionary. When Glory, Jake's companion, was teaching me to read, she spoke of them but I have never seen one before. The full extent of my vocabulary is from her. From this one book, it becomes possible to know the meanings of thousands of words."

"Is that what that is?" Nicky asked. "I've never seen one before either. This is the first time I've ever been in this room."

"What?"

"None of the kids have ever been up here. It stays locked and off limits all year until the night of this gathering."

"How did the kids learn to read?"

"They didn't. None of them know how." He gestured to the three girls at the table. "They're phenomenally talented at their assigned crafts, but they can't write their own names, or even recognize them when written by someone else. I can read a little, but it's only because I was older when I came and had learned a few things before I got here."

Annie clenched her jaws. "That is *so* wrong." She stepped the few feet to the bookshelves behind her and ran her fingertips over the front of the books. They came away coated in dust. That was all it took for mortification to hit a new high.

Abruptly, from across the expansive room, Jake said in commanding tone, "Annie, it is done. You have just been awarded to me."

The room went quiet.

"Mister Peabody, that is not how we handle things here," Weems rattled. "Your outburst is a breach of decorum. The proceedings here should be handled with quiet sophistication." His head tilted. "How did you know her name?"

"Thank goodness, Jake," Annie said. "If I had to maintain this ruse a moment longer, I think I might vomit."

"Me too, Annabelle… me too."

"You mustn't speak in such a forward tone, young lady!" Weems shouted.

"Oh, shut up," Annie fired back. She looked back down to the big book and ran a finger down one side of the page it was opened to. "Do you know what the word "supercilious" means, Mister Weems?"

"What does that have to do with anything?"

Ignoring his question, she said, "According to this marvelous book called a dictionary, it means 'full of contempt and arrogance'."

"So?"

"*So*, it describes you perfectly… you arrogant, arrogant man. And, it has everything to do with what's going on here." She swept both arms in a broad circle. "No child in this place ever sees any of this until they are sold and taken away on their seventeenth birthday, and you have the gall to call this a home and *school* for children?"

"You'll not be talking to me that way and blaspheming this magnificent institution!"

"The era of quiet complacency has ended. It's time now for truth."

Two of the Board members appeared at the top of the stairs at the center of the room, each with dizzy sticks in hand. They marched toward Annie.

All the guests backed away, bunching in a far corner of the room. There was no talk, just slack-jawed gawkers.

Nicky ushered the three teenage girls at the table a safe distance away.

"Tend to the Henderson girl," Weems told them. "She's in need of firm discipline."

"Ha! I'm sure looking forward to seeing that," Jake said.

"Hold on, Annie, I'm coming," Nicky said.

Annie pumped an open palm his direction. "No, no. Stay over there with your friends. I've got this." She then mumbled, "In fact, I'm looking forward to it."

The first enforcer to arrive swung the stick at Annie's legs.

She jumped.

The stick whooshed beneath her feet.

The second man swung from the opposite direction.

That one she simply leaned away from.

It caught nothing but air as it swished by, a fraction of an inch from her breasts.

The two swung their sticks at the same time.

She grabbed the ends of both and yanked them from the grasps of the two men. And then, with blurring speed, she smacked the butts of both men three times apiece with blistering force before they could react and move out of reach.

The searing sting brought tears to their eyes. They were quickly rubbing points of impact, grimacing. The burly men could not stop their rolling tears.

"Tell me now," Annie said, "are ya feelin' a little dizzy? Hurts, doesn't it?"

Six of the other Board members had now reached the top of the stairs. Oddly, they seemed in no hurry.

"Go after her!" Weems yelled to the new arrivals. "This is intolerable. I will not stand for such impertinence!"

Jake watched with arms folded across his chest, grinning.

The first one to clear the top of the stairs looked to Weems and made no effort to go after Annie.

"That's an order!" Weems shouted. "Get the little tramp and do it now!"

The other five Board members joined the first one and backed away from the stairs, having no intention of approaching Annie after seeing what she did.

"What are you men doing?" Weems shouted even louder. "I'm ordering you to take that girl out of here!" His anger hit a fevered pitch.

Suddenly, John and Martha Ramos appeared at the top of the stairs, leading a tightly packed crowd of townspeople. As a group, they approached Weems who had suddenly gone speechless.

And then, Annie saw a beautiful sight... Calamity Bloom with little Eva Louise coming up the stairs, leading all the other children. Eva split away from the group and ran to join her.

"Hi, Punkin," Annie said, as she pulled the girl close to her side and stroked her hair. "Everything okay?"

"It is now," the youngster said.

Rodney's face lit up when he spotted Calamity. He hurried over to join her.

"Where are you going, Rodney?" Weems thundered. "You belong at my side."

"No, sir, I don't. I really, really do not." He now stood in front of Calamity, gazing affectionately into her eyes. "I belong right here." He took off the fancy burgundy coat and stripped the black tie from his neck.

"Thank goodness," Jake said, rolling his eyes. "It's about time." He pulled the black bowtie from around his own neck and tossed it to the floor. "I've had enough of that thing."

"Barclay Weems," Martha Ramos said in a loud voice, "disturbing things about this institution have been brought to our attention and we, the people of this town, have decided that substantial changes need to be made to preserve the true intent of this place."

Weems's arrogance seemed to have no bounds and bubbled right back up. "You can't do that. This is my school and my town."

"Correction: *Was* your school and *was* your town," John Ramos said. "You took a wonderful thing like this home for children and warped its objective for personal profit." He gestured to Annie. "If it had not been for this girl, you might have gotten away with these private little slave auctions a while longer. And, it answers the question we've had all along: If the kids were learning tradecrafts, why did no one in town ever see any of the wares they produced? Clearly they were traded for goods and services beyond this community to keep its true income concealed... income that was never intended to benefit the children."

One of the three girls standing with Nicky gasped and then asked, "Is that true, Nicky?"

He nodded. "Afraid so."

One of the male guests looked to the others and announced, "Well, it would appear our business here has just come to an unsatisfactory conclusion." He began walking toward the stairs. The other guests fell into line behind him.

Weems attempted to approach them. "Wait, please, we can still make this work," he pleaded. He stood at the top of the stairs and watched the last one disappear on their way to the exit.

He spun around to face the Ramos's and the people backing the couple. "You..." he seethed, "...all of you. You did this to me."

"We're not finished *doing* it," Martha said. "It has already been agreed upon that you and your cronies will be banished from this town. All of you must leave and never return."

"You can't banish me from the place that bears my name."

Five burly men flanked Barclay Weems and shoved him toward the stairs. "Get your hands off me," he shouted. He began down the stairs with no further prompt.

The enforcers, flagrantly labeled the School Board, followed of their own accord, two of them rubbing what had to have been bloody blisters on their buttocks.

"Weems was right about one thing," John Ramos said, "we can't banish him from a town that bears *his* name."

"How about calling it New Day?" Annie asked. "Because, when the sun comes up tomorrow that's exactly what it will be for all of you, and will represent a new beginning for the town and for the children." She looked toward the children and smiled in a loving way. "I have a strong feeling that these children can and will become the pillars of New Day well into the future."

John Ramos turned to the townspeople. "New Day?"

The peopled murmured and then all nodded approval.

"New Day... I like that," Martha said. "It has a fresh ring to it. Okay then, New Day it is, and this will become the New Day Home and School for Children."

"I have one final suggestion," Annie said. "I don't believe you'll find a better, or more qualified individual to run this facility than Rodney."

Calamity threaded her arm around Rodney's. "I agree with all my heart," she said.

Annie could not believe it. Calamity smiled as she looked adoringly at Rodney. She actually smiled.

"I would be honored," he said, head downturned and humble. He then looked up and addressed the gathering. "But I won't do it unless it is a shared responsibility with this girl, Calamity Bloom." Young Lucy ran and stood between them, grabbing both their hands.

Annie showed her pleasure by clapping and squealing like a little girl. "Yes, yes, perfect."

"Absolutely perfect," Martha Ramos said.

Suddenly, Annie's demeanor as a battle-hardened soldier vanished. Once again, she was just a young girl, desiring nothing more than being among people her own age and having a good time. "Well, here we are with lots of food and punch and this wonderful place to enjoy it in. It looks to me like there should be a party after all." She spread her arms wide and grinned. "Tell me now; what do y'all think?"

A loud cheer was answer enough.

Chapter 22

Friend in Trouble

"I'm going back to New Day real soon, ya know," Annie told Jake as they ambled along the trail toward Myrna's Glory. The gentle clop, clop, clop of the old horse's hooves set a relaxed pace.

"Can I go? Can I go?" Eva said, dancing around Annie at the idea of seeing her new friend, Lucy, again so soon.

"We'll see what your mama has to say about it when the time comes, Punkin, so hold that thought."

"Oh, boy!"

Jake glanced toward Annie. "I sort of had the notion that you might go back. Calamity Bloom turned into a great friend, didn't she?"

"She did. The girl has heart, but there's more to it than that. Although we didn't discuss it last night at the party, I told her I'd be back soon and that we would talk about going north into Indian Territory together in the former state of Oklahoma. She told me it was something she wanted to do, to connect with family she has never met, but that was before she agreed to help Rodney get the New Day Home and School for Children running smoothly."

Jake smiled. "That's as good a reason as any to go back for a visit."

"Yeah, I'd like to spend time with all those books too." She abruptly stopped walking. "Hey, I could read up on history and instead of listening to all your stories, I could debate you."

Jake snickered. "Yeah, right."

Annie resumed walking. She thought back to Calamity's sudden appearance in her life and the positive difference it made when the budding romantic relationship between Ethan Turlock and Eva's mother, Lana, was revealed. To have a confidant, someone her own age to talk to, was making it easier to get through the transformative pain of Ethan moving from boyfriend to simply friend. This was an area of her life where genetic enhancement could not be of any help. The heartache was real and it lingered, but Cal's friendship helped lessen the pain. It occurred to Annie that Cal might need her friendship just as much, someone to talk to about personal things. Everyone needs a special someone, a pal, a friend in his or her lives who listens and understands. Dame Fortune did great at filling the void; so did Eva, Jake, Glory and all other wonderful people of Myrna's Glory, but it was not the same.

Jake, Eva and she walked on quietly.

"Great party last night... I don't think I've ever seen happier kids in my life," Jake said after a time.

"Yeah, and what about all those wonderful books? I can't get them out of my mind. There is so much to be learned. Well, at least the way the world was a couple of hundred years ago."

"I'm sure much of that knowledge is applicable for today's world."

"I wanna learn, too. Maybe I can stay with Lucy, Pammy and Peter and we can all learn to read together," Eva said.

Annie stopped walking again. "Hey, that gives me an idea. How about we suggest that everyone at Myrna's Glory spends time, let's say a couple of months, or more, at the New Day Home and School for Children? They could learn to read if they can't and then immerse themselves in books and learning. The tuition price could be a food donation to the children and helping with maintenance and other odd jobs for the duration of their stay."

"Rodney and Calamity would likely welcome that idea. It's an excellent way to re-establish a system of education that has not existed for several generations. Plus, it would take the burden off the children so they could spend time learning and, frankly, just be kids."

"In a couple of weeks, when I take Pammy and Peter back, I'll talk to Calamity and Rodney about setting up an education exchange or co-op. Even the people of New Day should want to take advantage of that. The word will spread fast and give New Day a positive reputation as an educational hub. And, of course, I'll have the conversation with Cal about a trip north together. One way or another, I want to spend time with her and really get to know her. Time not spent plotting, or planning some mission, simply time to enjoy her company. It would be a vacation, time to do girly things."

"Your head is always spinning out ideas."

"I'm sorry. I know I've been babbling. Every thought seems to be falling right out of my mouth." She flashed a shy smile.

Jake drifted over and pulled her into a sideways embrace. "In only three days you've corrected misuse of a school and orphanage, re-directed an entire town and, now, have an idea for a school to benefit more than just the residents."

"You forgot to mention that it was all done without having to hurt anyone."

"There're two former board members who might disagree with that."

"I don't think a couple of blistered butts should count."
He laughed. "Neither do I."

A veil of seriousness dropped over Annie's face. "We have to remember, though, that Barclay Weems and his band are certainly no fans of ours." She scanned the woods. "They're out there somewhere, roaming the countryside with no survival skills and probably getting pretty hungry by now. They might become desperate enough to do something stupid."

"I don't think that the word 'might' belongs in that statement. It's only a matter of time till we see them again. The next time, Weems will be armed with more than arrogance, firm talk and demands. He'll be after revenge. Of course he must survive the life of a forager until that time."

"That, or as a thief."

* * *

We're almost there," Henry said.

Bo's head spun. He shuffled along, dragging his feet. An exposed root snagged his toe, and he stumbled, but regained balance before going down. He saw Myrna's Glory, now struggling for one good breath. "Yeah, it's close... I hope... close enough." He veered left, about to lose balance.

Henry grabbed his arm and pulled it over his shoulder. "Come on, Bo, just one foot in front of the other a little while longer."

Bo had lost a dangerous amount of blood from the stab wound in his back. The wadded rag that Henry had bound it with was saturated. The wound radiated heat, as if infection had set in, but how could that be? It was too soon. He grimaced and then groaned. "I wonder what Beane had been using that knife for. I've been cut and stabbed before, but it never burned like a lit torch had been shoved into the wound. The pain is unbearable."

"Who knows?" Henry said. "Maybe he cut up something your body is not tolerating and then Hammond injected it into your back on the tip of the knife."

Eyes swimming and loose lipped, Bo nodded. "Sensitivity to certain plants has always been a weakness." He continued stumbling along with Henry's help.

Yowl whimpered, instinctively aware of the danger his friend battled. He walked behind Bo, nudging the man's hairy calf with his snout, urging him toward the safety of Myrna's Glory in his own way.

As they neared the compound, Dame Fortune stood alongside Elizabeth Longbow, daughter Lizzy, and Corky McCann, the man Annie rescued from Stalwart the previous year. The blind seer shouted, "Listen to me, Henry, Bo be in a bad way, worse dan ya know. We must be workin' fast to be changin' what I see comin', and it be comin' soon if ya don't be hurryin'."

Elizabeth and Corky ran to meet them. "Let me help," Corky told Henry, as he poked his head under Bo's other arm, providing additional support.

Elizabeth walked backwards in front of Bo. "Don't you be passing out. Stay with us."

Bo began losing control of his legs. He now stepped only occasionally. The rest of the time Henry and Corky dragged him, toes plowing the ground.

Elizabeth slapped Bo on both hair-covered cheeks. "You hear me? Stay conscious," she said, voice strained with worry.

The sting of her palms against his face caused him to try harder. His eyelids fluttered as he attempted reinvigorating. Still, the world in front of him spun and moved away. "I'm sorry," he muttered and then added, "I love you, Elizabeth."

"Dame knew your condition and had all of us gather some things," Elizabeth said. "We're ready to help, but we have to get you into Glory's cabin and off your feet."

Dame fell in behind and smacked the heels of Henry and Corky with her cedar walking staff. "Keep dem big ol' feet movin', you two, we must be hurryin'. Dis is no time to be amblin' along."

Just as Henry and Corky helped Bo up onto the plank porch of Glory Jackson's cabin, the big man lost the battle with consciousness. When he fainted, even the substantial combined strengths of the two men helping him could not support his weight and the big guy went down.

* * *

Ooh-wee! I did not like da sound of dat, Dame Fortune thought.

Glory Jackson opened the door. "Drag him in here and let's get him on the bed."

Dame heard the sound of hands grabbing Bo and pulling him inside the cabin to the side of the bed.

"Okay," Henry said breathing hard, "On the count of three…"

Corky counted. At three, multiple groans and then a squeaky bed frame indicated Bo had been successfully lifted onto it.

Yowl came through the open front door. Dame heard the click of his claws on the wood plank floor, as the wolf went to a far corner of the room. He circled, paced and whimpered.

"It be a damn good thing dat big ol' Bo not be conscious for dis. Roll him onto his side. Glory, get a sharp knife and be takin' away dat hair from around da cut. Corky, you be gettin' dat iron rod from da fire if it be glowin' red. Let's be gettin' dat bleedin' stopped so I can begin healin' da inside."

Dame backed away to allow them room to work. The tap, tap, tap of her cedar staff guided her to a short three-legged stool near the door. She sat and listened as they carried out her wishes. She closed her eyes and leaned her head back against the wall. *I'm comin' to ya big man... I'm comin'...*

As Dame's mind melded with Bo's, the first thing she saw was a dark cloud hanging low. There was no color in this, the landscape of Bo Juster's mind, only a storm over shades of gray—the limbo of a man on the verge of death, a mental world of negligible clarity. Lightning flashes danced in feathery fingers through the storm cloud. Bo was lost inside his own head. Death... the storm... stalked.

Come on, Bo, be revealin' yourself. "I know you be in dat dark mess somewhere," she shouted at the fringes of the storm. "I can't be goin' in dere. It's not allowed. Ya gotta be comin' to me."

Dame moved in as close as she dared to the realm of the dead. "You must be fightin' da urge to stay in dere! It only be feelin' safe. Have da courage, boy, have da courage to be comin' out!"

A wrinkle appeared on the boiling gray cloud. Bo appeared from within it, as the colorless mass receded behind the big man. "Dat's it. You be comin' on out of dere now. Come on over here and stay wit' ya ol' friend, Dame."

Suddenly, a lightning bolt flashed from within the boiling black and gray mass of the storm, drilling Bo in the back. He convulsed and went to his knees roaring. He looked down and saw his body becoming translucent. "What's happening?"

"Your friends be stoppin' life from leakin' out of dat wound by fire. Da shock of it be almost bringin' you around, but don't you be wakin' up, not yet. Stay here wit' me."

"You mean I have the power to do that? I can will myself to remain here, unconscious?"

275

"All dis be your mind. You can do anythin' on dis side dat your mind can be conjurin'. Now, come on over here next to ol' Dame. You must be farther away from dat storm cloud. It'll suck you in if ya let it, ya hear?"

In a blink, Bo was standing before the young, beautiful and sighted version of Dame. She spun in a circle, the brilliant white dress she wore bloomed like a big flower, and she sat upon the colorless ground. "Lie here next to ol' Dame. Put dat big beautiful hairy head o' yours in dis lap o' mine."

Bo made a move to comply. He stopped and looked back to the turbulent but silent gray and black storm cloud. "It was so comfortable and warm in there. It felt right."

"When da time comes, it will be right. But, dis does not need to be da time."

Still looking to the storm, he nodded and then sank to his knees and on down to lie on his side. He surrendered to Dame's will. His eyes locked onto hers, and he placed his head on her lap. "I feel an odd sense of peace. Are you doing that?"

She stroked the hair on his head. "I jes be helpin' you to sleep." She continued gently stroking his head. "You be lettin' your mind and body help us heal you. You be needin' rest, real rest, not gettin' lost in your head and playin' a dangerous game of hide and seek wit' death." She kissed his cheek and whispered, "Now, bigun, sleep… sleep… sleep." She hummed a lullaby.

As quickly as Dame entered Bo's mind, she left. Her consciousness rejoined her body in the real world. She drew a breath and heard Glory whispering. "Glory, whatcha be seein' now?"

"We cauterized the wound and thought the shock and pain of it was about to make him regain consciousness, but it didn't. He gasped and breathed heavily for a few seconds and then, miraculously, his breathing evened out. I applied the coal tar poultice and bound it tight with a bandage. Now it would appear he's actually asleep, not just unconscious."

"Dere be a poison inside him. All dat blood he lost only be makin' it work faster and be more potent dan it would be on a healthy feller. Let's leave him be. Rest will do more to heal him dan anythin' we could be doin'. Let's be takin' turns watchin' him. By da time da sun be settin' dis evenin' we be knowin' if dis humble man be havin' a future or not. Ol' Dame be seein' nuthin' but darkness ahead, but it don't be havin' to stay dat way. If ya be havin' faith in a god, might do some good to be sendin' up a prayer right about now."

Elizabeth cried.

Chapter 23

Vigil

Annie opened her eyes and felt as though she had never been asleep. She sat up and saw what she had come to expect at these times—a brilliantly lit day and extraordinarily vivid colors, but no sun to be seen. "I must be dreaming. This is your doing, isn't it, Dame?"

"It be for a fact, child."

"Why have you come into my dream?"

"Our friend, Bo, be hurt bad. I be knowin' you, Jake and Eva still be a day away but you best be hurryin'. Ol' Dame be afraid for him. He be weak… real weak… and wantin' to yield to da storm."

Annie knew what Dame meant by the 'storm.' Last year, when injuries resulting from her battle with Fiam Lee Tam at the Stalwart compound caused excessive blood loss and unconsciousness for an extended period, she witnessed that storm within a dream state. It was never close enough to be of concern, but visible for a time on the horizon of her mind. She remembered it well.

Before she could respond to the alter ego, the beautiful young black woman Dame Fortune chose to appear as began abruptly flying backwards, as if sucked away, until only a speck was visible at a great distance. And, then, even that vanished.

"Dame! Wait! What happened?" Annie listened. She received no answer. Dame had left her mind. *Where did she go? I've never seen that before.*

Annie felt panic welling. Maybe the old lady was too weak to maintain a mind connection. Why? Caring for Bo? Now agitated, Annie sprang to her feet. "I have to wake up." She slapped her cheeks, but felt nothing. "Come on, wake up!" and then louder yet, "Wake up!"

Finally, she did.

When her eyes popped open she saw the world as it should be. It was early morning and dark under a moonless but star-filled sky. A soft, mild breeze brushed over her. Oddly, she was already on her feet, like in the dream. Anxiety that swarmed her during the dream state carried over. She figured if they left now they could be back at Myrna's Glory by late afternoon, maybe before sunset. "Jake, Eva, wake up."

The urgency startled them both. They woke at the same time. "What's wrong?" Jake asked.

"It's Bo, he's been injured and is in grave danger of dying."

"Dame Fortune?" He asked while getting to his feet.

"She came to me in a dream."

As she answered, Jake was already gathering his belongings. He ceased questioning those dream visits by Dame long ago. "Then let's get going."

"Ride the horse. We'll be moving fast and I'm afraid you won't be able to keep up with Eva and me on foot."

Jake stopped strapping camping equipment to the horse's back and began removing it. "Then we can do without all this stuff." He kept only a cloth bag of food and tied it to his waist. He led the horse to stand near a fallen tree and stepped up and over onto the animal's bare back. "Let's go."

Annie and young Eva began jogging, setting the pace. The horse trotted to remain close. For an hour, their speed remained unaltered. Dawn broke in the east. A ribbon of light swelled on the horizon, adding a blaze of colors. Annie stopped running but continued in a fast walk as they approached a small creek. "Let's stop and rest a moment." Her breathing was only slightly heavier than normal, but Eva was winded.

Jake pulled a small round loaf of crusty bread and strips of dried meat from the cloth bag tied to his waist. "You girls eat. If you plan on maintaining this pace you both have to keep your energy. I don't care how genetically blessed you are."

Annie took the loaf and meat portions. She ripped a chunk of bread for her and one for Eva. She took a big bite of bread and then meat, mauling them between her teeth, chasing it with water from the creek. Ravenous from the exertion, she ate fast, gulping every bite. She then said around another mouthful, "You need your strength too."

"I have the horse. I'll be fine." He led the animal to the creek and allowed it to drink and then munch on a patch of grass while the girls ate and drank their fill.

Shortly, they were on the trail again and re-established the grueling pace.

After three hours of alternating between a jog and a fast walk, exhaustion began taking a toll. Although remaining on the move, speed slowed significantly.

"Annie," Eva whined, "I can't go on. I need to rest."

Sympathy for the youngster came fast and without comment. Annie stopped and helped Eva up onto the horse behind Jake. Annie's muscles burned from overuse—her breathing labored. Eva's shorter legs magnified the same problem. "It's not much farther." Every breath Annie took was deep. Even genetically enhanced physical endurance had limitations.

"I'm not sure this horse can make it at this sustained speed," Jake said as he patted its sweaty neck. "He's not a colt anymore."

Never the one to be cruel, Annie stepped in front of the old horse and placed her forehead against its perspiration soaked face. As she stroked its jaws she asked, "Can you hang on for a little longer?"

The horse slobbered in rivulets, fatigued. Flaring and pulsating nostrils told the story of an animal suffering from oxygen deprivation, bordering on fatal exhaustion. "I'm so sorry that I have to do this, but we have to press on."

"Annabelle, why don't you go on alone," Jake said. "Eva and I will stay behind and allow the horse to rest and graze awhile. Don't worry about us. We'll be fine."

Annie thought about it and then nodded. "I'm getting muddle-headed. I should have considered that."

Jake dropped from the horse to the ground. "That worries me. I've never seen you so exhausted that you couldn't think clearly."

"I'll be okay. Y'all rest and follow when you can." She pulled away from him and began walking away. "I'll see you both back at Myrna's Glory about sunset." Unsteadily at first, she began to jog.

Even though exhaustion drove her toward the breaking point, she maintained the pace and was back at Myrna's Glory by early afternoon. On the outskirts she stopped, bent at the waist, dropping hands on knees. *Must rest. Can't go another step. Have to catch my breath.*

Forcing deep and even breathing, her mind cleared. She lifted her head and saw where she needed to be. People had gathered outside Glory and Jake's cabin. She did not need to guess where Bo was, and that provided all the encouragement necessary to begin moving again.

From a distance, she heard someone tell people inside the cabin in a raised voice, "Annie's home."

Annie wanted to complete the journey as it began—fast, but her body would not cooperate. Her agile legs had become leaden. She shuffled along, kicking up small dust clouds behind dragging toes, but she kept eyes fixed on her destination—the cabin, determined to keep moving regardless of speed or awkwardness of step.

Corky McCann came out of the cabin and trotted to meet her. He clutched her hand. "Come on, girl, let me help. Put your arm over my shoulder."

"How's Bo?" She asked between heaving breaths.

"Not good. Blood loss and some kind of poison are working together against him. Dame told us about the storm that represents death. It's tugging at him and, apparently, the pull is powerful. Dame says he's willing to let it take him. Dame is the only thing preventing him from crossing that line and not coming out. She's losing energy fast, entering his mind at regular intervals to coax him away from the storm."

Annie nodded. *So that's why Dame disappeared from my dream so abruptly this morning. She can't keep up the physical demands of mind-to-mind connections.*

Corky continued. "Each time she comes back, her expression tells us how grave it truly is, although she speaks of hope. She can't keep up that level of concentration much longer without endangering her own life."

Corky helped Annie up onto the porch and through the door, into the cabin. Henry and Glory stood at the bedroom door and waved her over. Annie bounced a quick tired smile, the only greeting as she approached. The two parted, allowing her through, into the room where Bo lay. Elizabeth

Longbow sat next to him on the other side of the bed, holding his hand. Dame Fortune sat on a stool just inside the door. The old lady did not look or act well, head leaning back against the wall, lips parted, energy spent.

Annie dropped to her knees next to the old lady at eye level. She wrapped her arms around the old lady's neck. "Oh, Dame, I hurried as fast as I could."

With difficulty, Dame lifted her head. "I be knowin' dat ya did, child." Her voice was labored.

While still on her knees, Yowl came to Annie's side, whimpered and nudged her shoulder then licked her cheek.

Annie petted the back of the wolf's head. "You have been a great friend to Bo. He loves you. I see your affection is at least equal to his."

"I'm glad you're here," Elizabeth said, her eyes puffy and red.

Annie's gaze shifted from Yowl to the big hairy man on the bed a few feet away. Henry's borrowed robe was draped across Bo's midsection as he lay on his back. *We never did get that new suit of clothes made for you, did we?*

Requiring more effort than usual, Annie rose and trudged over to stand next to the bed. She leaned over and kissed his hair-covered cheek and then stroked his face, a face resembling that of a lion. His breathing was shallow, the rise and fall of his chest barely responding to the big man's need for oxygen. Even through thick hair, she felt heat of high fever rising to meet her hand. While continuing to rub his cheek and stare, she leaned in. "Shortly after we met, I told you that I was reserving the right to hold your hand at a later time of my choosing," she whispered into his ear. "That time is now." She scooped his big square hand into hers, sandwiching it between her palms. Elizabeth held the other.

Annie sank to her knees beside the bed. Tears flowed and dripped from her chin—she was too exhausted to care about restraining the display of emotion. She let her head wilt forward and rested it on the edge of the bed. Her head told her to maintain hope. Her heart had control. Sadness ruled.

* * *

She be so damn tired, Dame thought. *Dat make it too easy to be givin' up. Got to try one more time… 'bout all da strength I have left for.*

Still on the stool, she let her head tilt back against the wall and closed her milky white blind eyes. When she opened them, she was no longer blind nor old. The scene before her, in Bo Juster's mind, was as she left it.

He was on his feet, standing next to the black and gray mass of boiling clouds, pushing his hands into it, then retracting them and staring at his palms. He did this repeatedly. He looked up to lightning bolts that created an electrically charged crown, lauding superiority. The look on his face was one of longing. He knew Dame was behind him. "It's so beautiful," he said, as his eyes meandered all over the face of the cloud. "I want to go in there and stay." He again looked to his hands. "I can feel the love, even in my fingertips."

"Dat feelin' ya got be love for sure, but it be da love of Annie Henderson and dat sweet Elizabeth. Dey both be wantin' you back so damn bad."

Bo pulled his eyes away from the cloud. He looked at the beautiful young black woman that Dame appeared to him as. "Annie? Is she with you?"

"Dat she is, but not here in your mind. I barely be havin' da strength to come alone. She be at da side of your bed holding dat big hairy hand o' yours. Elizabeth got da other one. Dat's what ya be feelin'."

He resumed examining the silent roiling storm. "Dame, I'm tired…very, very tired."

"Den come on over here and put dat big ol' head in Dame's lap again."

Still facing the storm, he said, "It's not that kind of tired."

He took a step toward the churning opaqueness.

Before Dame could respond, a swirling vortex rushed in around her head.

Her thoughts jumbled.

She had no choice—her presence in Bo's mind had come to an end. Physical strength had abandoned her.

It felt as though a giant wind hit her head-on, lifting her up and blowing her back and away at tremendous velocity. Her body provided no more resistance than a leaf would in a hurricane.

Her mind shut down.

All went black.

* * *

Annie heard a hefty thud that shook the floor of the cabin.

She lifted her head off the bed at Bo's side and looked around.

The old blind seer had fallen off the stool onto her side on the floor. She had lost consciousness.

"Dame!" Annie sprang up and hurried over, dropping down next to the old woman. Sliding a hand gently beneath the unruly shock of white hair, she lifted Dame's head. "Are you okay?"

The old lady's eyes opened. She raised a heavy hand. It appeared to take all her strength to get it done. She pointed in the direction of the bed. "Stay wit' him. He be slippin... away..." She passed out.

Elizabeth shouted, "Bo!"

"What's the matter?" Annie asked, and then slid a rag beneath Dame's head and returned her to the floor. She rose and spun around.

"He stopped breathing!" Elizabeth collapsed over onto the big man's chest. "His heart... I can't hear his heart!" She wailed.

Annie was at a loss. She did not know what to do, standing paralyzed, unable to move, realizing the worst. *Of all my talents, is there nothing I can call on to change this?* She pounded her forehead with the heel of hand, searching for a fast idea. *What can I do? What can I do?* After several agonizing seconds, Annie became resigned to the brutal realization that there was nothing left that could be done.

Yowl, head and tail drooping low, walked out of the bedroom. The animal knew. He walked through the front door to the outside and did not stop until he stood on a knoll some distance away. Dropping hard onto his haunches, looking into the setting sun, he threw his snout skyward and let it out. It was a mournful howl. The last of his family was dead.

Chapter 24

A High Price Paid

Jake Henderson took the bend in the trail, clearing the final line of trees. He saw Myrna's Glory a few hundred yards away. The sun shone in a narrowing arc on the horizon, minutes away from sunset. He heard the howl of the giant black wolf. Thinking of no other reason for it, Jake feared the worst.

"Why is Yowl doing that?' asked young Eva.

"I'm afraid something bad has happened." He no longer felt it necessary to hurry. He sighed. "Come on, Eva... almost there." He clucked his tongue at the old horse and rattled the reins. The animal needed no more encouragement to follow. As they approached, he noticed no activity. All was still. The usual bustle was non-existent. It was quiet, far too quiet. His ears rang. His heart raced, preparing to hear bad news. A small circle of people stood in front of the cabin he shared with Glory Jackson.

Again, the wolf sounded off, a long and doleful howl.

The gathering of people parted and allowed them through. There was no talk, only sad faces.

Jake tied the horse's reins to the debarked cedar post supporting the porch awning at his cabin. Corky McCann's wife, Cynthia, approached. "It's that big hairy guy, Bo, he's... gone. It happened a few minutes ago. Elizabeth

287

Longbow is inconsolable. Annie's no better. She's absorbing all the blame for his death."

"How could she possibly…" He mumbled and then without finishing the statement walked past Cynthia on through the door, straight into the bedroom. Entering, he saw young Lizzy Longbow and her mother embracing. They cried. Dame Fortune lay on her side on the floor and seemed to have just awakened, or regained consciousness. Henry and Glory were helping her up. But, then, his eyes went to movement in the far corner of the room to what concerned him most. Annie sat on the floor with knees drawn up, face resting on top of stacked arms. He backed up to the wall and slid down to sit next to her. He sat quietly, staring at the floor between raised knees. Finally, he said, "There's nothing you could have done to change what happened, you know. It's not your fault."

Annie lifted her head, but her gaze remained fixed on the floor. "I talked him into this," she said in a whispery monotone. "Everything Bo did was the result of my suggestions… going to Old Dallas to face those cannibals and then staying here to keep an eye on them. Oh, Jake…" Her voice broke. She sobbed. "…if I hadn't—"

"Shh." He pulled her head onto his shoulder. "Bo was a strong man, capable of thinking for himself. Yes, you made suggestions, but he heard the wisdom in your words and chose to follow them."

"No! I can't accept that." She looked to Elizabeth Longbow and her daughter.

His eyes followed hers, understanding the refusal to deflect blame. Elizabeth had lost two loves in an absurdly short time; husband Ragland Longbow and now, Bo Juster. It was probably best that he not speak anymore and allow Annie to work through grief in her own time.

"I—I can't be in here right now." She sprang to her feet.

"Wait, Annabelle—"

"I can't breathe. I have to get out of here." Annie hurried for the door.

Jake did not attempt to stop her again. *There is no making this journey easier. She has to get there on her own. All I can do is be here for her.*

* * *

Annie stopped at the bedroom door and stooped to kiss the top of Dame Fortune's head. She had regained consciousness and had been helped back up onto the stool.

Dame patted her hand. "Go on 'bout ya bidness, child. I be fine. Just tired. Gotta rest. I be so damn sorry 'bout all dis."

"You did all you could," Annie mumbled. She continued on past Glory and Henry at the bedroom door and then outside onto the plank porch. As she walked by Lana McAdams and Ethan Turlock, he held his hand out to her, but her limp arm slid over his palm as she kept moving. Romantic feelings had spiraled to the bottom of her priorities. She would always love him, but at the moment, he did not matter—no one did, except Bo. All that romantic stuff suddenly seemed selfish and, now, unimportant as well. She hurried on by Cynthia McCann and her husband, Corky.

"Are you okay?" he asked.

She kept walking. "No, I'm not," she mumbled, head down, moving fast beyond the gathering crowd of compound residents.

Yowl sat on a treeless knoll some distance away, alone.

Annie walked the distance and stood next to the wolf. He needed consoling as much, maybe more, than any human. To him, Bo was family. It squeezed her aching heart to see the animal having to mourn alone. She sank to her knees facing the big black canine with golden eyes. "I vow to you that Bo will not have died in vain. With every breath in my body and every step I take, as long as I live, it will be with his memory in mind. I'll work to make this world better… for you…," her voice cracked, "…for us all." She sobbed.

Under a large oak tree not far away, she noticed a human figure. Once she cleared tears away, she saw that it was Barney Tackitt. He approached, but hesitatingly.

Yowl paid him no mind.

Tackitt came to stand next to Annie. "Your friend, the big hairy guy, did he…"

"Yes." She nodded fast.

"Is there anything I can do for you?"

She looked up at him with tear-filled eyes. "Yes," she said, reaching for his hand and clutching it. "You can help Yowl and I honor a fallen friend. Whether you realize it or not, he was your friend too."

"I think I knew that." Still holding her hand, Tackitt dropped onto his knees next to her.

The wolf, again, lifted his head and howled.

* * *

Jake stepped outside the cabin and paid particular attention to the sun going down. It happened to be emblematic and appropriate. He looked around the gathering of people—all motionless, gazing at the same thing; Annie, Yowl, and that strange guy he met on the trail—the thief. The view was rife with symbolism. It painted a picture of hearts and minds going out to Annie, but it also depicted something disconcerting—growing dependence on her.

Annie stood. So did Yowl. Barney Tackitt walked toward the woods, leaving Annie and the wolf to stand alone. Jake's daughter-by-circumstance and the wolf faced the setting sun, her hand resting on his neck. It appeared as if they saw something in the distance. Maybe they did. Maybe she was already planning her next move. Whatever the motivation, he saw compassion and strength in that picture.

Even through his sadness for the loss of a good man, Jake Henderson felt a smile crease his cheeks as he looked on with the rest of the group, because he realized that he, along with everyone else, was only an invited guest in Annie's world.